PRAISE FOR LYDIA ADAMSON'S ALICE NESTLETON MYSTERIES

"Refreshing. . . . Adamson's success is a tribute to her dynamic characters and her ability to leave readers wanting more." —*Booklist*

"Reading a Lydia Adamson cat mystery is like eating potato chips. You cannot stop." —Painted Rock Reviews

"[The] series is catnip for all mystery fans."
—Isabelle Holland, author of *Paperboy*

"Another gem for cat mystery fans." —*Library Journal*

"Cat lovers will no doubt exult . . . charming sketches of the species."
—*Kirkus Reviews*

"A fast-paced, quick, entertaining read." —The Mystery Reader

"Highly recommended." —I Love a Mystery

"Light and easy to read . . . perfect for a short airplane ride or for when you have a few spare hours." —*Romantic Times*

"Cleverly written, suspenseful . . . the perfect gift for the cat lover."
—*Lake Worth Herald* (FL)

OTHER BOOKS IN THE
ALICE NESTLETON MYSTERY SERIES

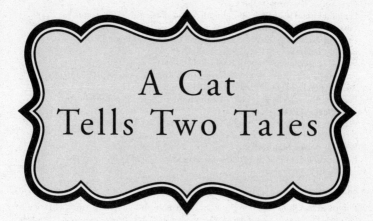

A Cat
Tells Two Tales

TWO
ALICE NESTLETON
MYSTERIES

LYDIA ADAMSON

AN OBSIDIAN MYSTERY

OBSIDIAN
Published by New American Library, a division of
Penguin Group (USA) Inc., 375 Hudson Street,
New York, New York 10014, USA
Penguin Group (Canada), 90 Eglinton Avenue East, Suite 700, Toronto,
Ontario M4P 2Y3, Canada (a division of Pearson Penguin Canada Inc.)
Penguin Books Ltd., 80 Strand, London WC2R 0RL, England
Penguin Ireland, 25 St. Stephen's Green, Dublin 2,
Ireland (a division of Penguin Books Ltd.)
Penguin Group (Australia), 250 Camberwell Road, Camberwell, Victoria 3124,
Australia (a division of Pearson Australia Group Pty. Ltd.)
Penguin Books India Pvt. Ltd., 11 Community Centre, Panchsheel Park,
New Delhi - 110 017, India
Penguin Group (NZ), 67 Apollo Drive, Rosedale, Auckland 0632,
New Zealand (a division of Pearson New Zealand Ltd.)
Penguin Books (South Africa) (Pty.) Ltd., 24 Sturdee Avenue,
Rosebank, Johannesburg 2196, South Africa

Penguin Books Ltd., Registered Offices:
80 Strand, London WC2R 0RL, England

Published by Obsidian, an imprint of New American Library, a division of Penguin
Group (USA) Inc. *A Cat in the Manger* and *A Cat of a Different Color* were previously
published in Signet editions.

First Obsidian Printing (Double Edition), October 2012
10 9 8 7 6 5 4 3 2 1

Set in Adobe Garamond
Designed by Spring Hoteling

Printed in the United States of America

Contents

A Cat in
the Manger

1

It was the day before Christmas and the day after my forty-first birthday. I was sitting on the floor of my apartment wearing jeans, a white fisherman's sweater, and Chinese boots.

I had just started my annual musing on the possibilities of peace on earth, goodwill to men, and all that, when the phone happily jangled. I picked it up swiftly. A deep voice identified itself as belonging to Mr. Harmon, from the humane society.

"Is this Alice Nestleton?" Mr. Harmon asked.

"Speaking," I replied, perplexed.

"Your cat has just been apprehended shoplifting in Saks Fifth," Mr. Harmon said in a gruff voice. "Now, what the hell are you going to do about it?"

Before I could respond to the startling charge, the voice changed and I realized it was Harry Starobin. Old Harry was making one of his jokes.

"Relax, Alice," he said. "Your cats wouldn't know how to

shoplift if they were plunked into an anchovy store. Is everything all set? We expect you."

"All set, Harry," I replied, and listened as he gave me my usual instructions on where to meet him. Then he hung up without another word, as usual. I replaced the receiver. I felt peculiar, as I always did after one of his rare phone calls. I felt like a child who had done something wicked. Why these feelings? Disgusted with myself, I changed gears quickly. After all, Christmas was almost here.

My Maine coon cat, Bushy, was asleep on the crocheted afghan draped across the maroon velvet sofa.

"Bushy, open your eyes," I said to him. "Here's your Christmas present."

One eye opened and closed. One paw twitched. Bushy was clearly not interested.

I opened the box and plopped his gift on the sofa beside him. "Merry Christmas, Bushy," I said, and gently yanked one of his beautiful ears to get his attention. Bushy opened his eyes, flicked his ear, and stared at the basketball. "It's not just any basketball, you silly cat. It's special. Look at the design."

I had found the ball at FAO Schwarz. There were raised, colorful, horrific designs embossed on it. The moment I saw it I knew Bushy would love it. It was a psychedelic sphere. It was a ball from outer space. It was a ball from another dimension. It would suit Bushy's whimsical nature perfectly. I could envision him whacking it across the room.

When Bushy didn't move, I pushed the ball along the sofa so that it rested against his nose. He sniffed it, yawned, and turned over so that his feet were straight up in the air like a dead bird's. Then he went back to sleep.

So much for that gift. Well, there was still Pancho.

I carried Pancho's gift into the kitchen. It was a small container of saffron rice. For some odd reason, Pancho had developed a passion for Indian food. But, then again, Pancho was a very odd cat.

I had adopted him at the ASPCA three years earlier, when he was about six months old. He was all gray. His eyes were yellow. His whiskers were rust. He was missing part of his tail and had a large, ugly scar on his right flank.

Pancho seemed to have one goal in life: to escape from his enemies. With this in mind, he spent his days and nights racing through the apartment. He loved cabinets and bookcases and window ledges. The higher the route, the better.

Opening the container, I placed it in the sink. "Merry Christmas, Pancho," I called out.

I heard nothing for a moment; then a *whoosh*, and a second later I saw a gray blur flinging itself from cabinet to cabinet. *Poof*—there he was in the sink, his face in the rice.

I proceeded to unwrap the small barbecued chicken I had bought for dinner. Carla Fried was to arrive at six. Her visit was the nicest Christmas gift I could have gotten. She was an old and dear friend, and I hadn't seen her in years. We had been roommates at college, studied acting together, moved to New York, and shared an apartment before I was married, and again for a brief time after I was divorced.

I was looking forward to her visit; I couldn't wait to talk

with Carla about theater. How I craved theatrical conversations since I had become more and more isolated! As to the reason for that isolation? Well, I had gotten the reputation of being "difficult" and "quirky" and "kooky."

This translates into the simple fact that I no longer cared for mainstream American theater. I craved to act in something new and different, something on the edge. I was searching for an avant-garde theater that didn't yet exist, and in doing so I was alienating a lot of my old friends. I ended up working in a lot of wild one-night-stand productions by bold experimenters. And because the avant-garde always attracts academics, I got some occasional work lecturing in university drama departments. Was it my avant-garde tendencies that had prevented me from "making it" as an actress? Who knows? My ex-husband used to say I'd never make it because I was too beautiful in a bizarre sense. I was every man's sexual fantasy, a Virginia Woolf character moving across a darkened wild moor wearing a see-through Laura Ashley dress. I was tall, golden-haired, painfully thin, and always available: half desirable woman, half taboo child. Or so he said.

I arranged the barbecued chicken on a paper plate and covered it with cellophane. Then I made a tomato-and-onion salad and set the table.

It was time to pack.

The cats and I were going to Old Brookville, Long Island, on Christmas Day. It was my annual three-day cat-sitting job for Harry and Jo Starobin.

Now, there are cat-sitting jobs and there are cat-sitting jobs. Most of them are just quick daily visits to cats in apartments whose owners are away on business or vacation. I collect the mail. I open the door. I feed the cat. I water the plants. I talk to the cat. And then I leave.

My annual cat-sitting assignment with the Starobins was different. At the Starobin estate, I slept in a small cottage with my cats, but spent most of the time catering to their eight Himalayan cats, who lived in the main house. The Starobins spent every Christmas in Virginia, leaving the moment I arrived on Christmas Day. It was lucrative, it was fun, it was a chance to get out of Manhattan. I had loved the Starobins from the first moment I met them—and I had met them under very painful circumstances.

A friend of mine who taught playwriting at the Stony Brook campus of the State University had killed himself. Or so the police told me. I didn't believe it because I had spoken to him about ten days before his death and he wasn't depressed at all. So I went out there, offering to clean out his apartment and office because he had no living relatives. What I discovered was not suicide. He had seduced a young male student. The student had murdered him and faked a suicide. When I found a series of letters from the student to my friend, I showed them to the police and he was questioned. He admitted the murder but claimed he was the victim of homosexual rape. A jury subsequently believed him and sentenced him to only eighteen months in prison on a minor manslaughter charge. My murdered friend had left two lovely cats. A professor at Stony Brook mentioned Harry and Jo Starobin as a couple who could find a home for the cats if anyone could. The professor was right. The Starobins found a home for the cats, and when they found out I was an actress whose main source of current income was cat-sitting, they hired me.

I pulled two matched Vuitton bags—gifts from an old admirer—out of the closet, carried them into the bedroom, and opened them on the bed. First towels, then shoes, then toilet articles, then cat food, then clothes, then some Glenn Gould cassettes, then the new biography of Eleonora Duse. I stopped. There was more to pack, but I was tired. I walked down the long hallway into the living room, lay down on the sofa next to Bushy and his psychedelic sphere, and fell asleep.

∽

The buzzer woke me a few minutes after six. I jumped up and ran to the wall to press the release for the main door, accidentally kicking Bushy's new toy to the far end of the room, where it rattled a lamp. I was so dopey from being suddenly awakened that I wondered for a moment how a basketball had gotten into the apartment; then I was confused as to why there was no Christmas tree, until I remembered that I had stopped buying them because the cats ate the needles. It had been a very deep sleep.

I opened the door and stepped outside to see if the visitor was, in fact, Carla. If it was anyone else—and anything was possible in my neighborhood—I'd slip back inside to safety.

I leaned over the staircase railing and saw a woman on the third-floor landing. "Is that you, Carla?"

"No," she responded, "it's the ghost of Christmas past."

I kept watching her as she climbed the final two flights. Yes, it was Carla, but she looked different.

Carla Fried had been a flamboyant young woman. Her views, her clothes, her behavior, were always on the wild side. But the woman approaching me now was wearing a sober business suit, complete with, of all things, a tie. An expensive, sheepskin coat was draped over her arm. I knew that she was the executive director of an acclaimed theatrical troupe in Montreal, but this was a bit much.

My critical distance dissolved, though, as she rushed up the remaining stairs. We embraced like adolescents, laughing, weeping, squeezing each other with the strength of seven years of separation.

I pulled her into the apartment, picked up Bushy, and shoved the large red-and-white long-haired bundle against her chest. She hugged him. Bushy looked perplexed.

"And that's Pancho," I said, pointing him out in his attack posture on top of the table, dangerously close to the barbecued chicken.

"It's been too long," Carla said as she sat on the sofa. She was a bit stout, and her long black hair was in a demure bun. She wore no makeup except for eye shadow.

"Do you still drink Heineken Dark?" I asked.

"Always."

I went into the kitchen and returned quickly with a bottle, remembering that Carla had always preferred to drink out of the bottle.

The moment I sat down beside her, we started babbling

about old friends, old events, old lovers; about men, theater, apartments, weather, politics, food; about Montreal and New York; about Camelot and Hades.

The outburst ended. Carla leaned back against the sofa and drank her beer. Her face was still beautiful, though I could see white in her black hair.

"Where are you staying, Carla?" I asked.

"At the Gramercy Park Hotel."

"Posh," I noted, and added, "You're welcome to stay here for a few days. I have to leave tomorrow morning."

"Why?"

"A cat-sitting job on Long Island."

"Yes, I heard."

"You heard?"

"I mean, when I was in Chicago last year, Jane told me you had to become a cat-sitter because your taste in theater had started to run to the lunatic fringe."

I laughed. "Cats and lunatics, Carla. I always loved them."

"It is very hard for me to imagine you onstage in a painted leotard while a naked woman plays the cello and a borderline psychotic makes violent speeches in blank verse to the audience."

"Times change, tastes change," I noted, gesturing at her new mode of dress. She acted hurt, then flung a pillow at me.

"I also hear, Alice, that you're beginning to dabble in crime."

"You mean shoplifting?"

"I mean Tyler."

Tyler was my gay friend who had been murdered at Stony Brook.

"It was very strange, Carla. The police called and told me that Tyler had killed himself—slit his wrists. I had spoken to him only ten days before his quote, 'suicide,' unquote and he was fine. Also, I knew that Tyler would never slit his wrists—he had an absolute horror of the sight of blood. Anyway, I went out there and found this very bizarre term paper by a student in one of his classes. Then I found a couple of letters. Then I put two and two together and went to the police. Anyway, it turned out that Tyler and the young man were lovers, and Tyler had paid the price for an affair gone bad."

"What a funny expression, Alice."

"What expression?"

"An affair gone bad."

"Well, that's what happened."

"Why did the police think it was suicide?"

"Well, Tyler's wrists had been slit open with a razor blade. The young man had drowned Tyler first in the bathtub and then immediately slit his wrists. It was ugly and ingenious. The police thought it was simply a familiar suicide with the usual progression: slit wrists, loss of blood, loss of consciousness, drowning."

"Grisly."

"It must have been."

"Tyler was a wonderful guy. Remember that essay he wrote on Pinter's *The Birthday Party*?"

"It was on *The Homecoming*," I corrected.

"Well, anyway, you ought to visit me in Montreal if you like grisly murders. They're the specialty of bilingual societies."

"I don't."

"Have you ever been up there?"

"No."

"It's really very nice."

"Carla, you mean it's very nice to you, don't you?"

She laughed and nodded her head. "Even nicer lately. Did you ever hear of Thomas Waring?"

"No."

"He's a lunatic Canadian millionaire who thinks he can buy culture—buy anything. So he gave me one million five."

"Gave you?"

"Right. Gave me. Just like that. He gave me one million, five hundred thousand dollars to put on three plays next year. That's half a million a production. Do you know what that means to us? I've been putting on productions for the past three years with peanut butter jars and milk cartons."

"What are you planning to do with it?"

"The first production is *Romeo and Juliet*—next fall. And guess who we got to direct."

"Grotkowski," I quipped.

Carla laughed and clapped her hands, remembering the ferocious arguments we used to have about the Polish director when he first expounded his theories in America.

"No," she said, "not Grotkowski, but close. Guess again."

"I give up."

"Portobello," she said.

"Giovanni Portobello?"

"None other."

"That's wonderful," I said. And it was. I had heard Portobello lecture at Hunter College. He was a tiny, misshapen man who spoke so quietly you could hardly hear him. But his ideas were exciting. He believed, for example, that Shakespeare was so familiar, had so entered the popular consciousness, that his plays were no longer theater; they were like sing-alongs. His idea for presenting Shakespeare was to maintain absolute historical integrity in the costumes and language—while at the same time changing radically one of the main characters; deforming that character, in a sense, with bizarre costume or accent, to present the audience with an intellectual jolt in the midst of an otherwise standard production. Thus, two of Lear's daughters would be dressed like Berlin whores in an otherwise impeccably Elizabethan production. And that was only the beginning; he took his theories much further.

"I'm glad you approve, Alice," she said.

"You never needed my approval before," I noted.

"True. But now I do. Because I want you in the play."

I didn't respond at first. It was something I had never expected. I felt strange, like a bug was crawling up my arm. "Are you hungry yet?" I asked.

She held up the bottle, indicating that she would prefer to finish her beer first.

I got up and walked to the far window. The street below was ice-crusted. The enormity of what had happened was beginning to become clear. My eyes flooded with tears. When I had been a young girl on a Minnesota dairy farm dreaming of the theater, all my dreams focused on one part: Juliet. There has never been and never will be another part like that. It is love and death and eros and repression all rolled up into one body. I didn't want Carla to see my tears, although she, of course, would understand them. How could one be an actress without being Juliet? Dialogue began to course through my head. What an astonishing gift Carla was offering to me.

Then I heard her say, "The Nurse is a wonderful part, Alice. And you can make it very special."

The disappointment was so sudden and savage that I had to hold on to the window frame. Not Juliet for me. The Nurse. Then shame at my arrogance and my delusion flooded through me. Had I become demented? How could a forty-one-year-old woman seriously believe that she was being offered the part of Juliet?

Turning toward Carla, I said in the brightest, cheeriest voice I could muster: "Let's eat now, Carla."

2

The Christmas-morning trip began poorly. Just as I was about to leave the apartment for the Long Island Rail Road, I realized that I could not handle two valises and two cat carriers. So I unpacked the valises and shoved the stuff into a large duffel bag I could carry slung over my shoulder, leaving each hand free to handle an imprisoned cat.

That duffel bag was an old friend. An aunt, one of those truly bizarre women one finds only in farm communities, had given it to me years ago when I had first enrolled in acting classes at the Guthrie Theater in Minneapolis. It had gotten so beat up over the years that I had started bringing it to the Laundromat once a year to get it bleached.

Penn Station was crowded with old women carrying shopping bags full of wrapped presents, clinging couples who seemed to have severe hangovers, foreign-speaking groups who sat on their luggage and proudly displayed Dunkin' Donuts paper bags, and hundreds of homeless people who had come in out of the nine-degree cold and were sprawled along the walls of the terminal in ironic celebration of the holiday.

I purchased my ticket, located the gate, and waited for the 8:22 to Hicksville. Bushy was beginning to act up in his carrier, as usual—scratching, meowing, complaining. He hated traveling. Pancho, on the other hand, was quiet, reflecting in his cage, staring straight ahead.

When the train pulled into the station and we were able to board, I chose one of the double seats at the end of the car so that I could place the two carriers facing each other. That quieted Bushy down somewhat—he could at least stare at Pancho when he was upset.

The train pulled out and I settled down in the warmth of the car.

Every time I went to the Starobins' I felt like a little girl going to collect a birthday present. The Starobins were a wonderful old couple. Harry was seventy-nine with an enormous shock of snow-white hair, a face so lined it looked like it had been ravaged by a garden rake, and a long, lean, often brittle body. He was a combative old man who loved cats and horses and butterflies and all sorts of strange creatures. He was a noted cat-show judge and he knew more about cats than any person I have ever met in my life. To watch him play with his flock of Himalayans was a rare, giddy treat. Whenever I thought about Harry Starobin for any length of time, I realized that deep down in my perfidious brain I longed for him as the good father/bad father I never had. It was disconcerting.

As for Jo Starobin, well, she was Harry's match. A tiny,

hyperactive woman with cropped white hair, she gleefully attacked and argued with Harry in public and made up with him publicly. They were the only senior-citizen couple I ever met who seemed to be enjoying sex as much as they did when they were young.

As for the Starobins' estate, it was as though someone had plunked a nineteenth-century Russian farm into very posh Old Brookville. Their buildings were crumbling; their paint peeling; their carpets thinning; their horses old or dead; their livestock nonexistent; their heat cut off; their phone off the hook. They obviously were very land rich and very cash poor, and it didn't seem to bother them in the least. It usually took them six months to pay me in full for the cat-sitting job—but then again, their fee was very generous. Everything about the Starobins was generous.

Then I fell asleep. When I awoke I thought about Carla's offer to play the Nurse in her Portobello production. I had told her I would think about it, and I intended to. Noticing that Bushy was becoming obnoxious in his cage, I drummed my fingers on top of the carrier to comfort him.

Finally, an impersonal, bored voice announced, "Hicksville." I gathered the duffel and the cat carriers, exited the train, and walked down the high platform steps, crossed the highway, and entered the parking lot where Harry Starobin always waited for me.

Harry was not there. I waited five, ten, twenty minutes, but there was no sign of Harry or his beat-up station wagon. I went over the instructions in my head to make sure I had done nothing wrong. Take the 8:22 to Hicksville on Christmas morning. Exit on the east side of the station. Go to the north supermarket parking lot across the highway from the station. That's exactly what I had done. Where was Harry?

At ten fifteen I hired a cab to take me to the Starobins'. It wasn't easy because I didn't have his address. I knew how to find the place once I passed a certain gas station and then passed an overhead traffic light, et cetera, et cetera. Because of this, the cabdriver had to go slowly and make numerous detours. By the time we finally arrived, the cabdriver was so angry that he dumped me and the cats on the road right next to the Starobin mailbox.

I looked around. Everything was the same. I walked over the rise and stood at the beginning of the gravel driveway which led to the main house. The old long-haired handyman whose name I always forgot was chipping ice with a shovel. He stared at me, then went back to work. He was an odd duck. The decrepit barn was still standing to the left of the house, accessible by its own path. An ancient carriage horse was being groomed in front, steam billowing out of his nostrils. The young woman brushing him waved at me. I waved back. That was the stable girl, Ginger, I remembered.

The cottage I stayed in was to the right of the main house, reached by a narrow path. I picked up Bushy and Pancho and started toward it. The path had been recently cleaned, but there were patches of ice that had to be negotiated carefully.

As I inched forward, I saw Harry's station wagon was in the garage next to the main house. So Harry was in. He must have just forgotten about my coming out. The thought infuriated me for a moment, but I mellowed quickly. After all, he was an old man, and when I reached his age I probably wouldn't be able to remember even my cats' names.

I reached the steps of the small frame cottage with a brick chimney and left the two carriers on the porch. The door was unlocked as usual, and when I pushed, it opened reluctantly. It was an old cottage, low-ceilinged and dank. As I walked in, I smiled. The Starobins had cleaned it up for me. The floor was freshly swept. The cot had obviously been newly made, and even the pillows were fluffed. I looked in at the small kitchen. They had put in a new overhead light fixture and someone had shined the chrome fixtures in the sink.

I walked back outside, brought the carriers in, and opened them. Bushy flew out and leapt onto the cot, rubbing himself against the newly fluffed pillow. Pancho walked out slowly, evaluating the new terrain for possible enemies and flight paths. I picked up the duffel bag and laid it on the cot next to Bushy, ready to unpack.

Then I turned to shut the door.

Harry Starobin was there! He was right there—staring at me!

I laughed out loud in joy. "Harry!" I shouted.

I was about to take him to task, both for sneaking up on me and for forgetting to pick me up at the station, when I realized that I was staring at a corpse. Feeling suddenly weak, I sat down quickly on the edge of the cot.

Harry was hanging on the back of the door, a rope fastening him by the neck to the clothes hook. His eyes were wide open. His face was bruised and distorted. Blood spotted his white hair.

I could not look at him anymore. I grabbed Bushy tightly and buried my face in his coat.

3

Only the Christmas tree in the main house had escaped destruction. With all its ornaments and limbs intact, it stood in front of the fireplace, surrounded by slashed cushions, broken lamps, ripped-up carpets. Jo Starobin sat in her rocking chair, her face as white as her hair.

A detective from Nassau County Homicide named Senay stood in front of the tree fingering an ornament. He was holding his crushed wool hat in one hand, along with a checker-lined raincoat. Wearing a blue flannel shirt with a red tie, he was a tall, heavyset, oddly unbalanced man.

The Himalayan cats were wandering in confusion around the wrecked living room, sniffing the broken items. From time to time one leapt up onto Jo for a moment and then leapt off. She ignored them. What beautiful cats they were—essentially Persians with Siamese coloring—a profusion of long-haired colors dancing across one's eyes. They were looking for Harry.

Jo started babbling bitterly to no one in particular: "Where was I? I'll tell you. I was playing cards in Smithtown. Playing cards while Harry was dying! I was playing cards and poor Harry was dying!"

She started to rock furiously.

I closed my eyes. I couldn't stand watching her despair. My stomach was still queasy from the night before. I still had the shakes. And I could not get the image of Harry Starobin hanging grotesquely on that door out of my mind.

Detective Senay left off fingering the ornament and began to pace, making sure he avoided the cats. "Mrs. Starobin," he said, "we are going to need an inventory of valuables."

"What did you say?" Jo barked, staring at him like he was a lunatic.

"An inventory. We have to know what they took."

"What who took?"

"The ones who did this, Mrs. Starobin. The ones who murdered your husband. They were looking for something— money, gold, antiques. We need an inventory of what you lost."

Jo laughed shrilly and rocked even more furiously. Then she mocked him savagely: "Money? Gold? Antiques? We have it buried beneath the floor. We have it buried under the fireplace bricks. We have it buried under the bathroom tiles."

Then she collapsed in tears, and when she recovered, she whispered to the detective, "We have no money. We have nothing but this place and our cats." She closed her eyes, stopped rocking, and dropped her head onto her chest.

Detective Senay looked at her, realized she was overcome,

and walked over to me, standing next to the sofa. He had already questioned me about the night before: why I was out there, how I had found the body. "We need that list," he said to me in a low voice.

"I can't give it to you."

"But you're her friend. Talk to her."

"I'm her cat-sitter. I come out here once a year. Besides, she said they have nothing of value. From what I know of the Starobins, she's telling the truth."

"Listen, those thieves beat that old man to death slowly. They were trying to get information from him. They were looking for something. He died from a crushed skull inflicted by a blunt instrument; then they hung him up. If we get a list, we'll get them."

He paused, then leaned over me in a solicitous manner and asked, "How you doing?"

"Fine."

"Rough scene. You were in shock last night," he noted. He switched his hat and coat to the other hand and sighed warily. "What else can you tell me about Harry?"

"He was a wonderful old man."

"Yeah, I heard that. I mean something important."

"Like his shoe size?" I asked nastily. Senay's mode of discourse on Harry was beginning to irritate me.

One of the Himalayans leapt up beside me, rubbing against my arm. I scratched her gently.

"I never liked cats," Senay said, then asked: "You make a living doing this?"

"Doing what?"

"Looking after cats."

"More or less," I replied. He arched his eyebrows in disbelief. I was about to tell him that I was an actress as well as a cat-sitter, but was interrupted by a blast of frigid air from the front door.

It was the stable girl, Ginger. She shut the door behind her and walked quickly toward Jo. She was obviously agitated.

"Mrs. Starobin, Veronica and her kittens are gone! Vanished!"

She caught her breath and pulled at her thick, long red hair. She was wearing several sweaters, making her normal huskiness even more pronounced.

"I thought maybe she had been frightened by all the police cars and ran into the woods. But I've been looking for hours. She's gone! Vanished! Her and all her kittens!"

Her tone was pathetic: frightened, guilty, seeking absolution for something that she clearly considered her fault.

Jo opened her eyes and stared at the stable girl. Then she suddenly leapt up out of the rocking chair and screamed, "Shut up!"

It was such an explosive, violent exclamation that the Himalayans scattered to all points of the room looking for places to hide.

"Who is Veronica, Mrs. Starobin?" Senay asked.

Jo sat back down, shaken. "The barn cat," she mumbled.

Then she exploded again at the girl: "Harry is dead and you come in here crying about the barn cat. For all I know, she's under the barn with her kittens or on top of the barn. Don't you know Harry is dead?"

The stable girl could not face the old woman's rage. She turned and ran from the house.

"I have to go upstairs," Jo mumbled after she had left. "I have to lie down. I have to think."

She left the chair, woozy at first, then walking more steadily. We heard her clump up the wooden staircase.

Detective Senay sat down in the rocker. He seemed to be relieved now that Jo had left. It was rapidly becoming dark outside. The cab would pick me up at six and take me to the train station. I wanted to avoid the cottage until the last minute, but I didn't relish sitting there with the policeman. It dawned on me that I disliked him. But why? I had also disliked the police officers I had met in Stony Brook when I was out there concerning my friend's alleged suicide. I resented the way they went about things, I decided. They chose a script and they played it out no matter what. This one's conviction that Harry's murder was primarily a robbery seemed to me peculiarly at variance with the Starobins' obvious poverty.

Detective Senay was now rocking just as Jo had. The shock of discovering Harry's body was beginning to wear off me—I realized I was becoming confrontational. "I find the whole thing difficult to understand," I said to him.

He looked at me quickly, stopped rocking, and then played silently with his hat.

"I mean about thieves breaking in to find gold coins or Tiffany lamps."

"Who said gold coins? Who said lamps?" Senay asked.

"Whatever."

"These kinds of break-in murders happen all the time.

This is a neighborhood of rich people. Break into any house in the area and the odds are you'll find something salable."

"They couldn't just have picked this house by chance," I said.

"Why not?"

"Because this is the one house for miles around that a thief wouldn't enter. It's run-down. It looks like a slum compared to all the houses around it." My comment irritated him.

"Look," he said, speaking to me very simply, as if I were some kind of idiot, "it could have been a random break-in or it could have been premeditated. We'll never know until we find them, and we'll never find them if we can't trace what they stole, and we can't trace that stuff if Mrs. Starobin doesn't give us that inventory list."

We sat together in silence until Jo came down again. I said good-bye to her, nodded to the detective, and started back to the cottage to collect the cats and the luggage. The cab would wait for me on the main road.

When I reached the door of the cottage, I heard the most peculiar sound. At first I thought it came from within—that the cats were carrying on. But it came from outside, from the rear of the cottage, in the clump of pin oaks. It sounded like a hurt, crazed animal.

What could it be? I didn't really want to find out. There was nothing about the cottage inside or out that I could approach without fear. Harry's corpse had guaranteed that. But I couldn't leave it either. The sound was too pathetic.

I started moving around the cottage carefully, quietly.

The wind was picking up, scattering dry twigs. The sounds stopped. I stopped. They started again.

When I turned the corner, I realized what I was hearing—someone weeping so hard that the whole body seemed to resonate. It was the stable girl, Ginger. Her hands were braced against the back of the cottage as if she were too weak to stand without support.

She heard me approaching, but she couldn't compose herself. I stopped two feet or so away. I had never seen anyone weep like that.

I didn't know what to do. But I had to do something. I placed my hand on her wrist and squeezed. "They'll find the kittens, Ginger," I said.

She screamed at me, gasping for breath: "Fuck the kittens. I hate the kittens," and then she just collapsed.

I knelt beside her, trying to cradle her body against me. But she was thrashing about.

"Harry," she started to whisper again and again with a desperate persistence: "Harry, Harry, oh God, Harry."

Then she grabbed me and held on. We huddled there on the ground in the dark cold. Finally, she started recovering her composure.

Her behavior perplexed me. Why had she sought out an isolated place to weep? Jo was weeping. Weeping was acceptable; almost demanded. A much-loved man had been murdered. Obviously Ginger didn't want someone to see her weeping. But who? And why?

I helped her up. She couldn't speak, but merely nodded

her thanks. It had to be Jo Starobin from whom she wanted to hide her horrendous grief. But why hide grief from Jo? Jo, above all, would understand.

Unless, of course, it was the grief of a lover.

As I walked Ginger to the front of the cottage, holding tightly to her arm, I realized with astonished certainty that this young girl and old Harry Starobin had been lovers.

4

At six in the morning, four days after Harry's murder, I heard from Jo Starobin again. Her call woke me from a deep sleep. As usual, at that time in the morning my apartment was freezing. As usual, Bushy was on the pillow next to me. Pancho was somewhere else, plotting his next escape attempt.

"Am I speaking to Alice Nestleton?"

That's what I heard when I picked up the phone. For some reason, in my sleepy state, it seemed to be one of the funniest things I had ever heard. Is this Alice Nestleton? Is this Joan of Arc? Is this Ti-Grace Atkinson?

My laughter irritated the caller.

"Maybe I have the wrong number. I'm looking for Alice Nestleton."

"This is she," I answered, which seemed even funnier.

"Alice, it's Jo. Jo Starobin."

I felt stupid and ashamed. "Jo, I'm sorry. I just got up."

"I'm sorry to call so early. I'm in Manhattan, at the Hotel Tudor."

"On Forty-second Street?"

"Yes. Can you meet me this morning? At nine o'clock?" Her voice was hurried, demanding, hopeful.

Did I have any appointments? I couldn't remember any. I said that I would meet her.

"At the Chemical Bank," she said, "on the corner of Fifty-first Street and Third Avenue."

And then she hung up abruptly. I listened dumbly to the dial tone. Then I replaced the receiver and pulled the blankets around me. I was glad she had called. In the days since the murder I had tried desperately to think of some gesture or some way to tell her that I understood her grief. But nothing had seemed authentic enough, so I had done nothing—not a card, not a flower, not a call; nothing. Now, at least, I could be of some assistance. Maybe she wanted a shoulder to cry on. Maybe she wanted to tell me about Harry.

The phone rang again as I was dressing. It was Carla Fried.

"Are you back in Montreal?" I asked.

"No," she laughed, "Atlanta. Something came up. You know how it is with us famous theater people."

I hoped she wasn't going to press me about the part. I had other things on my mind.

"Look, Alice, I just wanted to tell you how wonderful it was seeing you and talking to you. I could talk to you for five days straight."

"Like old times," I said.

"Like old *good* times," she corrected, and then said breathlessly, as if she was in a great hurry, "Look, Alice, I don't know my schedule. But if I pass through New York on my way back, let's get together again."

I agreed. She hung up. Given the horror of what had happened in Old Brookville, the idea of my old friend Carla Fried dashing across the country like a Hollywood version of a theatrical entrepreneur seemed somewhat frivolous.

❧

I left my apartment, which is on Twenty-sixth Street and Second Avenue, at eight o'clock and walked slowly uptown. It was one of those peculiar days between Christmas and New Year's Day when people seemed exhausted and confused. A black teenager's boom box blared some rap song that I foolishly thought for a moment was an updated version of a Christmas carol.

I arrived at the bank around eight forty-five. Jo was standing there like a lost child, wearing a pair of old-fashioned earmuffs.

"We're early. We'll wait," Jo said.

It had never dawned on me that Jo really wanted to go into the bank. I had thought it was just a place to meet. But she obviously was waiting for the bank to open. She looked terrible—exhausted, nervous, confused. She grabbed hold of my arm and held it.

When the bank doors opened, I followed Jo inside and down a flight of stairs to a large glass door obviously locked from the inside. Jo rang a buzzer. The door opened and an elderly man wearing a gray jacket with a white carnation ushered us into the safe-deposit-vault area. Jo signed a slip and handed him a key. He vanished into the vault area and returned quickly with a large steel box, which he carried toward the rear of the room, Jo and me following.

We entered a small carpeted room with three chairs and a long table. He set the box down on the table and left the room without a word, closing the door behind him.

We just sat there and stared at the box. I didn't understand what we were doing there.

Finally Jo said, "I was down here yesterday to pick up Harry's will. Do you know that it was the first time in fifteen years I had looked in the safe-deposit box?"

"I never had one," I replied.

"Oh, they're quite nice, quite functional," Jo replied, and I caught a hint of sarcasm. Or was it bitterness?

"Would you please open the box for me, Alice?" she asked.

I leaned over, disengaged the latch, and lifted the heavy steel top. I straightened up quickly. Inside was more money than I had ever seen in my life. The box was stuffed with packs of hundred-dollar bills held together by rubber bands.

"Do you see it? Do you see it?" she asked in a hysterical whisper.

I passed my hand over the top layer, gingerly touching the money.

"Three hundred and eighty-one thousand dollars, Alice. Three hundred and eighty-one thousand! Where did Harry get all this money? Why didn't he tell me? How did he get the money?"

I shook my head. I couldn't even fantasize an answer.

"Do you know what I think, Alice? I think this is why he was murdered. I think this is why." She slammed the top of the box shut.

"Have you told the police?" I asked.

"No," she replied abruptly. She paused, staring at me, and then said, "I was going to tell them. But I thought about it. And now I'm not. Look, Alice, Harry and I didn't have a dime. Everything was mortgaged. We owe everybody. And I think Harry wanted this money to pay off our debts and give us the farm free and clear. Harry would want me to use the money for that. Whatever he did to get the money, I know he did it for us, and the cats, and the carriage horses. This was his Christmas present to all of us, and if I tell the police, they're going to impound the money or do something like that or take half of it for taxes. Do you see what I mean, Alice? I'm not being a thief. I know what Harry would have wanted."

"He never said anything about this, Jo?" I asked skeptically.

"Never. Not a word. I swear, Alice. Never, never, never." Then she stood up, placed her palms on either side of her head, saying, "Do you think he robbed a bank? Poor Harry. Maybe he robbed a bank because he wanted a Christmas present for all of us. I said to him about a month ago, when we couldn't pay the heating-oil people, that I was so sick of it I wanted to die. He just kissed me on the forehead and said I shouldn't get upset."

She started to cry, then caught herself and clapped her hands together as if she was a teacher and I was a boisterous kindergarten pupil. "I want a cup of coffee, Alice. Can you take me for a cup of coffee?"

Five minutes later we were sipping coffee from containers in the Citicorp Atrium. On the walk over, Jo had kept chattering nervously: "Have you ever seen so much money?" "Did you see the way it was packed?" "All those rubber bands. All those hundred-dollar bills!"

As hundreds of children raced through the atrium, brought there to view the Scandinavian Christmas decorations, which hung from ceiling to floor, Jo sent me for another cup of coffee and for something sweet. I returned with a raisin Danish. She began picking off the raisins with a plastic spoon.

"Now, listen to me, Alice Nestleton," she said. "I called you for a reason, not just to stare at money or buy me coffee. I know a lot of people think I'm a little crazy."

"No one thinks that, Jo. Everyone I ever met out there loves you, Jo, just like they loved Harry," I replied, and I meant it.

"Well, I know why Harry was murdered now. It was for that money, right? But it doesn't mean a thing unless we know how he got the money. Because if we know how he got it, we'll know who wanted it. And I know how to find out who murdered poor Harry. He never threw anything away. He saved letters and bills and business cards and cat-show programs and scraps of paper. He saved everything and it's all there and all I have to do is go through it all. But I can't do that, Alice. I can't see too well. And I don't have patience. But you can come out for a few weeks, Alice—and your cats too—you can help me. I'm going to pay you two hundred dollars a day. And we can find out what Harry did and who murdered him. Can't we do that?"

I didn't know what to say. If the killers had been after Harry's cash, why hadn't they guessed it was in a bank vault? And why kill him? Only he could get the money out. They would want him alive to extricate the cash for them. No, it had to be something else.

Poor Jo! She looked so vulnerable sitting there, those ridiculous earmuffs all twisted up on the side of her head. I wondered what kind of old woman I would be if I ever reached her age.

"You don't have to tell me right now. Take your time, Alice. You can call me at the hotel."

❧

When I have to think—I mean really sit down and think—I like to sit in front of my mirror. It's a sort of reverse-narcissistic game I play that gets my brain working.

An hour after leaving Jo, I was staring at myself in the mirror. As usual, I found my appearance baffling. As usual, there was the confusion over which one of us was the audience.

Two plum offers had suddenly appeared. Should I play the Nurse in *Romeo and Juliet*? I no longer had any allegiance to classical theater. I was interested only in the far reaches of the envelope. I would rather be paid nothing to stand onstage stark naked reciting Baudelaire's reflections on whores while eating a tangerine. No, I decided the theatrical offer was not pressing. It could wait.

Jo's offer was more pressing. The money was certainly tempting. Yet the idea of spending a few weeks with Jo Starobin was unappealing. The woman's grief was so pervasive that those around her simply couldn't escape it.

I stared at my hair. There was a lot of gray in the golden flax these days. My eyebrows were getting paler. The face in the mirror was impassive. I had never understood how people could characterize me as beautiful. My face was too thin—wan, as they used to say. I chuckled. I squared my shoulders. It was my posture that they had always confused with beauty. When I had been younger and walked into a room, I always created a stir. Stage presence.

I saw a blur move across the upper-right-hand side of the mirror. Then it stopped. Pancho was on top of the bookcase, next to the volumes of the *Tulane Drama Review,* one of which contained a picture of me performing in a one-act play at the Long Wharf Theatre in New Haven.

Pancho's image was staring at me.

Without turning, I said, "Look as long as you want, Pancho."

He didn't answer. His half-tail was moving back and forth. His face was set.

"Oh, Pancho, why can't you ever relax? Why can't you ever play?"

No response. I longed at that moment to gather Pancho in my arms, but I remained seated. Pancho was a good teacher. His reserve, his peculiar sense of constant danger, made him a good teacher. Some people, some animals, could only be loved from a distance. Intimacy was impossible.

"Run, Pancho, run," I whispered to his image in the mirror. All he did was lift a foot and begin to groom it with his tongue. He would flee when he was ready.

I touched the mirror with my fingers, running them along the glass just as I had run my hands along the top of the money in the safe-deposit vault.

Jo's offer had been financially generous. Two hundred dollars a day for two weeks ran to twenty-eight hundred dollars tax-free. That was a lot of cat food. Plus, the offer came at a good time. The first few weeks of the new year were always depressing and empty of possibilities.

I smiled at myself in the mirror, a bit grimly. An old lover of mine had once told me that my smile was terrible; it was totally dishonest. I made a face. It was irritating but true that I often evaluated myself by what men I had known told me. Why did I believe them? I was too old for such nonsense.

A blur flashed across the mirror. Pancho was on the move.

I picked up a hairbrush and balanced it in my hand. It was a beautiful tortoiseshell brush with fine, stiff bristles.

It was perfect for a head of thick hair like that stable girl had, I realized. Ginger had that gorgeous thick red hair. I remembered her with a sudden flash of hatred. My reaction was so bizarre, I stood up and walked away from the mirror. I sat down on the bed.

Why wasn't I feeling compassion for that girl, like I felt for Jo?

Ginger's grief had been stupefying. She had wept like someone who had lost everything. No, I realized, I did not hate her. I was jealous of her.

Why? Because Harry and she had been lovers!

Agitated, I left the bed, walked into the hallway, and then back to the bedroom.

Why was I jealous? Harry had been a surrogate absent father—kindly, eccentric, wise, comforting, *safe*. Was that the way I had really felt? No, I wanted to be in that girl's place. I wanted to mourn Harry as a lover.

I walked quickly down the hallway and into the living room. I scooped Bushy off the sofa and hugged him. He accepted the attention stoically.

"Bushy!" I called his name. He looked past me. I whispered into his ear, "You knew all along I would accept Jo's offer, didn't you? You knew it all along."

I lay down on the sofa, still holding him. There was no reason not to go back out there. I had discovered Harry's corpse. Why shouldn't I discover his murderers? What else were fantasy lovers for?

5

I left the cottage and walked hastily toward the main house. It was a wet, cold morning. The trees were threatening— naked, precarious, hovering over the property. I had no qualms about leaving the cottage because Pancho and Bushy had settled in nicely; although Pancho seemed perplexed at the lack of space in which to flee. He would have to develop a circular flight.

"Is that you, Alice?" Jo cried out from the kitchen when I entered.

Then she appeared in a ludicrous outfit. She was wearing a huge leather apron with deep pockets—like a blacksmith would wear—and around her neck was an enormous and very frayed kitchen towel. "You arrived just in time. I was making eggs," she said.

Her ancient kitchen table with its splintered wooden legs was piled with utensils and condiments, as if she was embarking on a major feast rather than a modest breakfast for two.

She pointed to the clutter and said, "Harry always made the eggs. He used to say I didn't know how to fry them, scramble them, poach them, or even boil them. I never knew whether he was serious or not. Well, here I am, without Harry, and I'm going to make eggs. How would you like them, Alice?"

"Scrambled would be fine, Jo," I replied, sitting down at the table to watch her. It was zany, but that was one of the Starobins' most wonderful qualities: they always did things outlandishly.

Carefully, almost painfully, she broke five eggs in a saucer and then proceeded to whip them with a flourish, her black-smith's apron continually getting in the way. When the scrambling was finished, she collapsed suddenly into a chair.

Two of the long-haired Himalayan cats leapt onto her—one on her lap, one on her back. Two more leapt on the table, prowling, inspecting. One nuzzled my foot. In the space of seconds, they all changed places in a macabre, swift game of musical chairs. Then they all ran from the kitchen as if they had sensed the ghost of Harry Starobin in the eggs. It was very sad. The cats seemed lost.

"God, I'm tired," Jo said, and then she broke into tears, choked them back, and stood up. "It's doing all those stupid things around the barn. I find it very, very hard. I hadn't mucked out a stall in ten years."

"What about Ginger?"

"Oh," she said with an airy flip of her whisk, which she had not relinquished after scrambling the eggs, "she left two days ago."

"Left? Where did she go?"

"I don't know. How should I know? She quit."

This was totally unexpected. I had thought the girl would stay on, if only to assuage some of her guilt for being Harry's lover.

"Did she say why?"

Jo started to butter a pan, making a lot of clanking noises at the enormous black range. I could see that she had put much too much butter into the pan.

"She didn't say why," Jo replied, gazing thoughtfully into the melting butter, "but I know why. She was sad. Harry was like a father to her. And she was sad about the calico barn cat, about Veronica. That's stupid, though. Barn cats always vanish—sometimes for months. Especially when they have kittens. Veronica is probably living with some neighbor down the road now, quite happy, and one day she'll just meander back. I told her what Harry used to say—that cats can predict earthquakes and other natural disasters long before they happen. And they vanish. I told Ginger that maybe Veronica knew that Harry was going to be murdered so she ran away with her kittens. But Ginger wouldn't stay."

Jo poured the eggs into the sizzling butter and leaned over the pan, her tiny frame dwarfed by the gigantic apron.

I would have to tell her that Ginger was Harry's lover, I realized. Of course, I had no proof of it, only very circumstantial evidence—desperate weeping in seclusion. But Jo and I could go nowhere unless at the outset we were totally honest, unless even informed intuition was honored. What was the point of any other approach?

She finished the eggs triumphantly and shoveled them

onto the plates. Then she stepped back and shook her head.
She had been so engaged with the eggs that she had forgotten
everything else—bread, coffee, juice. Clumsily she covered
the eggs on the plates and proceeded to make the remains of
the meal. I should have helped, but I didn't. My mind was on
how to approach the matter of Ginger and Harry Starobin.

Finally we ate, amidst the clutter, the eggs cold, the coffee
weak, the bread stale.

When we were finished, Jo heaved a great sigh, as if she
could not handle such an assignment again for a long while.

"Jo," I said, moving my chair closer to her, "I want to tell
you something, but I don't really know how to go about it. I
don't want to . . ." I stopped, at a loss for words.

"Then just tell me. I'm too old for nonsense, Alice. Don't
you know that?"

I started to pile the plates, moving the condiments, gathering the dregs. "I think Ginger was having an affair with
Harry."

"You think?"

"Yes. I think so."

"What do you want me to say?"

"What you know."

"I knew nothing of that," she said quickly, and began to
clear the table.

"Jo, please, tell me what you know."

"Listen, Alice," she said, leaning against the sink, undoing
the leather apron, "Harry was a very strange and wonderful
man. He had many enthusiasms. Sudden enthusiasms. He
would suddenly take a fancy to a person or an animal or a

house—anything—and he would give that person or thing his total attention. He would do anything for people. A lot of people loved him. He loved a lot of people. But that Harry and the girl were sleeping together . . . well, no, I don't think so."

"Why not?"

"Because," she said, flaring angrily, "he would have told me."

"He didn't tell you about the money," I noted.

She had removed her apron and the towel, and began looking out the window, anything to avoid looking at me. Obviously she was trying to control her anger toward me.

"Do you want more coffee?" she asked stiffly. I shook my head. It was a very awkward moment. But I had done the right thing. I wasn't there to be a nursemaid.

"Look how gloomy it is out," she exclaimed, and shook her head as if the world was truly deranged.

"Maybe it'll clear up," I said tritely. "Maybe the afternoon will be better."

"I want to show you his files," she said abruptly. Relieved, I stood up. We walked together through the long kitchen and into an adjoining storeroom. Flanked by two small, filthy windows, a door at the far end led out into the yard.

The room was filled with cardboard cartons piled on top of one another. Between the cartons, in haphazard fashion, lay ropes, old boots, pots and pans, and piles of clothing that obviously hadn't been worn in years. Jo opened one carton and beckoned me to peer inside. It was filled with letters and correspondence of all kinds. On the side of the box was written in now-fading Magic Marker: "1984."

"Everything," she said, "he kept everything. It's all here. Harry never threw anything away—not his letters, not his bills . . ."

I saw that each carton had a year written on the side. There were also many large manila envelopes among the cartons, and these too had dates. But there was no order to them at all. They just lay randomly in that damp, cold room, which was illuminated only by a single overhead light bulb.

"I can bring it all out to the living room and you can work there when you are ready," Jo said tentatively. We both realized that we had embarked on a problematic task—it could all be worthless as a key to his death. And even if we found one or two or three pieces of paper mentioning the source of Harry's newfound wealth, how were we to recognize them when they passed through our hands?

"Look," Jo said, pulling a sheaf of photographs from a carton marked "1975." She flipped through them and held up one for me to see. "That's Harry and some friends of his in Vermont. Look at the porch of that hotel . . . so lovely . . . do you see the rocking chairs?"

She didn't wait for an answer. She pushed the photos back into the carton. She was trembling and trying not to cry.

"I'll start on it tomorrow, Jo," I said, wanting to get her out of this room that was causing her such pain.

She made a motion with her hand for me to stay put. Then she said, "What if Harry lied to me only once in his life? About the money. And he didn't tell me only in order to protect me from something terrible. What if the only lie Harry ever told me in his life killed him?"

There was nothing I could say to her. She was babbling. Husbands lie to wives, wives to husbands, children to parents, everyone to everyone.

Someone called out from the kitchen. It was the old long-haired handyman—his name was Amos. He was saying something we couldn't hear. Jo shrugged and walked back into the kitchen. I followed.

Amos looked as pale as a ghost. His hands were clasped behind his neck as if he were about to try some exotic calisthenics.

"What's the matter with you, Amos?" Jo asked, half-angry, half-solicitous.

"I just came from down the road," Amos said, his voice scratchy and broken, "and they told me what happened. They murdered Mona Aspen last night, just like Mr. Starobin. They murdered her and hung her on a door."

6

All the heaters in the cottage were on, but it was very cold. What a bizarre way to spend New Year's Eve, I thought. I sat in the rocker, two blankets around me, like an old whaling woman in New Bedford waiting for the fleet to return. Bushy was lying on his back in front of one of the heaters. Pancho was cautiously circling the room, still confused because there were no high cabinets.

The small traveling clock beside the cot read 11:25. When, in fact, was the last time I had a good New Year's Eve? It was a long time ago, when I had been in New York only about two years. I had gone to a party in the West Village, filled with young actors and actresses and designers and writers, all hungry, all dedicated, all expounding youthful theories. As I rocked, I pictured the apartment and the food and the drinks, but I couldn't remember a single name. Where were they all now?

A knock on the cottage door brought me out of my reverie. For a moment I was afraid. Then I heard Jo calling my name. She walked in carrying a bottle and several manila envelopes.

"I just couldn't be alone on New Year's Eve," she said, "and I found some old table wine."

I went into the small kitchen and brought back two glasses. The wine was terrible, but so what? Seeing Jo slump into the rocker, I sat on the cot.

"Last New Year's Eve, Harry and I consumed a whole bottle of pear brandy." She paused and rocked. "Well," she added, "maybe it was the year before." She laughed crazily, despairingly, and then: "But there won't be any pear brandy ever again . . . will there?"

Pancho began to circle the rocker. Jo put her glass on the rocker arm, then decided it was not secure and placed it on the floor. Pancho flew away.

"I thought," she said, tapping the manila envelopes she held on her lap, "that we should start looking through it all tonight."

She stood up, walked to the cot, placed the envelopes down on it, and returned to the rocker. I could see the writing on the top envelope: "1980–1981."

Her request startled me. It was New Year's Eve, almost midnight. She had brought in some wine, seeking company. It wasn't the right time to start digging through old letters.

I looked at her skeptically. She stared back at me—defiant, a bit frightened, a bit pleading.

Suddenly I realized why she had brought the envelopes to

me. If her neighbor—that woman Mona Aspen—had been murdered in the same manner as Harry, it might mean that the police were right. Perhaps a pack of homicidal house thieves was prowling the area, breaking into houses for valuables. Harry's murder might have been just a random event; he was in the wrong place at the wrong time. Jo didn't want to believe that.

I opened an envelope and shook a few items out onto the blanket. The first was a letter in a torn envelope. It was written to Harry from a woman in California who asked for advice in the raising of Russian blues. Her handwriting was very hard to read. I could see a mark on the upper-right-hand corner of the letter, signifying that Harry had answered it and noting the date when he had answered it.

The next item was a request from a man in Madison, New Jersey, who wrote that he had met Harry at a cat show in Philadelphia and now he needed an out-of-print book on eye disease in cats. Did Harry know where he could get hold of a copy? Again there was the telltale mark on the corner indicating that Harry had responded—but there was no way to tell what his response had been. I started to look at the next item—a note attached to a newspaper clipping—when I heard Jo say: "Please, I didn't mean you should start right now. I thought . . . I mean, we must drink the wine, at least until midnight." I put the clipping down.

Jo started to rock furiously in her chair. She closed her eyes and said, "Mona Aspen was a wonderful woman. Did you know that?"

"I didn't know her at all," I replied.

"I thought maybe you had been to see her horses and met her."

"Was she a breeder?"

"No. Mona's place is down the road. It's a layover barn. Trainers send their sick and broken-down racehorses to her. She nurses them back to health. Years ago there used to be many horse farms around here—layover barns, breeding barns, and all kinds of horses. Now, only Mona was left."

I looked at the clock. We had missed the moment. Happy New Year.

"Such a wonderful, kindly woman," Jo said, "and such a good friend to Harry and me."

"Her husband. Is her husband still alive?" I asked, remembering that the handyman had, during his disjointed conversation, once referred to her as Mrs. Aspen.

"I don't know. He lives in Connecticut, I think, or he did live there. They were divorced ages ago. Mona's nephew and his wife live on the farm with her."

"How old was Mona Aspen?" I asked.

"Oh, about five years younger than I. But much more vigorous. She still mucked out stalls."

"Did she keep valuables in the house?"

"No, I don't think so. Oh, wait—antiques, yes, a lot of old things like vases and writing desks and paintings and such. Mona was a great one for horse paintings. But I don't know if they were really worth anything."

She drifted off into a private reverie. I returned to the

items on the blanket for a moment, and then lay back—I didn't feel like going through them anymore at that time. I was tired and cold. The wine was playing tricks in my nose.

"I must get back to the house now," Jo said a bit grimly. But she didn't move off the rocker.

Then she said, "Will you come to the cemetery tomorrow for Mona's funeral? There will be only a short graveyard ceremony."

I nodded. She got up, smiled in a motherly, almost beatific fashion, and left with the empty wine bottle.

I started to undress, then noticed that I had hung my winter coat on the hook behind the door. Just as the killers had hung Harry there after they were through with him. The coat had to come down. If I woke during the night, as was my fashion, and saw it hanging in the darkness, there would be an ugly panic. I removed the coat from the hook and placed it on the back of the rocker.

∽◦

What a strange little cemetery it was! The headstones were ancient, chipped, obscured. The grounds lay behind a huge new shopping center just off the main east-west road. A strong, swirling wind whipped the overgrown weeds against the legs of the eight or ten mourners. A minister with a large muffler wrapped around his neck said the words over the open grave. Two men with shovels and one with a small earthmover stayed about twenty yards behind the mourners, waiting for the ceremony to conclude. One of them cupped a lit cigarette in his hand.

Jo held on to my arm tightly. She said in a desperate whisper so close to my ear I could feel her lips, "I'm glad I did what Harry asked. No funeral. No burial. I cremated him and spread the ashes on the gravel driveway from the road to the house. I could not have survived him being buried in this place."

The thought struck me as grotesque. I shivered, realizing that every time I walked to the main house I would be crunching Harry deeper into oblivion.

As the minister began the final prayer, Jo continued to hold tight to me. She was beginning to restrict the circulation in my arm, but I didn't have the heart to pull away.

"God, Alice," she said, her voice breaking, "what a good friend she was to us . . . to me and to Harry and to Ginger. What a wonderful and kind woman she was."

It was over. We threw some dirt on the grave and started back to the car. A couple came up and began to speak to Jo. Feeling out of place, I walked to the car to wait for her.

A large man was leaning against the fender. It was Detective Senay. Another plainclothes detective sat in an unmarked car near the cemetery entrance.

"Cat-sitting again?" Senay asked.

"Something like that."

"Did you get that list from Mrs. Starobin?"

"What list?" I asked.

"The inventory of valuables."

"No."

"You know, Mrs. Aspen's nephew is cooperating with us. I don't understand why Starobin's widow isn't."

"Maybe, Detective, it's because there were no valuables in the house."

"What were they looking for? Chicken soup?"

I was about to tell him that Jo didn't believe Harry was murdered by random breaking-and-entering thieves. But I didn't. "Were the killings the same?" I asked.

"Close. Mona Aspen was murdered by a blunt instrument. We'll get them. They'll have to sell what they took. We'll get them. And we'll get them quicker if Mrs. Starobin helps."

"Ask her yourself. I'm not really working for the Nassau County Police Department," I noted.

"I have asked her, and I'll keep asking her. By the way, who are you working for, Mrs. Nestleton?"

"I'm not married," I said.

"Too bad."

"Sez you."

"You know, I have a funny feeling about you," he said, taking off his hat and passing it from hand to hand.

"That's your problem, Detective."

He nodded, smiled, waved his hand, and walked toward the unmarked car.

Jo and I drove back to the house in silence. I made no mention of my brief strange conversation with Senay. As we approached the drive, Jo said: "Do you think that Mona's nephew will find in their deposit box what I found in my safe-deposit box?"

The logic of her question was so startling and so plausible that I almost laughed out loud in discomfort. Why not? I thought.

I didn't get a chance to answer. Jo laughed suddenly. Then she said, "How stupid of me! If Mona had that kind of cash she probably gave it to her nephew straight out to bail him out of his gambling debts. That young man was always in trouble, and poor Mona just kept cleaning up after him as best she could. He looks and talks like a gentleman, but believe me, he's not housebroken."

She laughed again, a quieter, almost wry laugh this time, then continued. "Harry used to say that we old Long Island families were like carefully piled stacks of kindling. Lovely on the outside but a world of maggots underneath."

She dropped me off where the path to the cottage began. As I walked toward the cottage I saw the caretaker, Amos, staring at me, leaning against a short ladder right outside the garage. He didn't wave. He made me uncomfortable. I didn't like him and I think the dislike was reciprocated.

I went into the cottage and fed the cats. They were sulking, unhappy. "Get used to it, my friends," I said. "Momma has to make a living." Then I relented and promised Pancho some saffron rice when we got back to Manhattan.

I spent the next two hours attempting to straighten up the cramped cottage. As I did, I felt increasingly as if I had missed something important. I made a cup of tea and sat down on the rocker. Bushy leapt onto my lap to get scratched.

I knew it was something that Jo had said.

As the day progressed, that "something" began to fester in

my head. I kept closing my eyes and reconstructing the conversations I had had during the past twenty-four hours. The clue was very close to consciousness but kept slipping away, like the name of an old friend or an old restaurant.

It finally caught up with me, as usual, after I had stopped worrying about it. I was doing the dishes in the tiny sink with one of the Brillo pads that Jo had so kindly left me.

On New Year's Eve Jo had told me what a good friend Mona Aspen had been to herself and Harry. But at the cemetery Jo had told me what a wonderful friend Mona Aspen had been to herself and Harry *and* Ginger.

It could mean, of course, absolutely nothing. But it could mean an awful lot. Two people had been brutally murdered, and a stable girl was friend to one, lover to the other. I had to find out where Ginger had gone.

7

We were sitting at the kitchen table. In front of us was a carton marked "1985." Beside the carton were piles of paper and two empty coffee cups and a plate with uneaten toast. We had been working for about an hour and had developed a procedure in our search. One of us would pick up a letter or note or bill, study it, then briefly recite the contents to the other. If not suspicious, we went on to the next one.

Jo was wearing Harry's old volunteer-fire-department jacket; it was always freezing in their house. "That detective stopped by early this morning when I was in the barn. It must have been seven o'clock. He keeps bothering me about that list." She paused in her recital and stared at one of her cats.

Then she continued. "I keep telling him that nothing was stolen that I know of. He doesn't believe me. I am beginning to dislike that man. He's devious. He also asked me if Mona and Harry were in business together. And then he asked about their relationship. I really did not like the way he used the word 'relationship,' as if they were in the Mafia."

I laughed. Harry in the Mafia was a funny image. But I wasn't really interested in Senay's inquiries. I was interested in Ginger.

"What did you mean yesterday, Jo, when you said that Mona Aspen and Ginger were good friends?"

"Well, they *were* good friends. Mona was the one who sent Ginger to us for a job."

"I'm confused, Jo. Was she living at Mona's?"

"That I don't remember. Maybe. But they were friends. Even when she was working for me, Ginger used to go over to Mona's to help her out in a pinch. If a horse was really sick, or when the blacksmith came."

"What is Ginger's last name?"

Jo sat back with a testy flourish of her hands. "I honestly don't remember. Why are you asking me all these questions about Ginger?"

I waited for a moment to let her calm down. "Where did she live when she was working for you?" I asked.

"I don't know. Not far from here. But a lot of the time she just slept in the barn."

"Jo," I said, very gently so it would not appear to be a demand, although I was surely willing to make it a demand if Jo became difficult, "I want to talk to Ginger."

The request startled her. "Well, I don't know where she is."

"Who would know?"

"Maybe Nick."

"Who's Nick?"

"Nicholas Hill, Mona's nephew. You saw him at the cemetery."

"Can we go there now?"

Jo exploded. "But here is where Harry is," she yelled, plunging her hand into the pile of aging letters, bills, and notes.

"Calm down, Jo. Listen to me. I have the very uncomfortable feeling that the one person on earth who knew Harry and Mona best was the stable girl. Do you understand?"

Jo shook her head, keeping her face averted from me. "What a cruel thing to say," she replied.

It was cruel. But I had no option. I was making a point.

Suddenly Jo's face lit up and she said, "Wait, I remember her last name. It was Mauch. Ginger Mauch." Then she said wearily, "Okay. Let's drive over to see Nick. I don't want to fight with you, Alice. We need each other."

It was a two-minute drive from the broken-down Starobin farm to the freshly painted, well-manicured complex of buildings over which Mona Aspen had once presided. I followed Jo across a fenced field to the stable area. Nicholas Hill was just inside one of the barns, laboriously cleaning a shovel. I could see the heads of the racehorses as we entered. They were peering out of their stalls without much concern. A few were grabbing chunks of hay from hay nets hung outside their stalls.

Nicholas was a middle-aged graying man, well-dressed even when working. He nodded to us, but kept on cleaning the shovel.

I remembered that Jo had said he was a heavy gambler. He

didn't look like a man who would take large bills out of his pocket and bet them on a horse. But then again, I didn't look like a woman who did cat-sitting. Nicholas banged the shovel on the ground to shake more dirt loose. His hands were large, lined, and powerful.

A slouch hat with a fishing feather tucked into it was precariously perched on his head. It was an odd hat for winter.

"We're trying to find Ginger," Jo said almost happily.

Nick let the shovel drop and stared at it reflectively. He seemed to think he was not doing a good job. Then he looked up, smiling at Jo, removed a glove, and blew on the hand. His actions were very measured, calm.

"I haven't seen her since about a week before she left your place," he finally replied.

"Do you know where she lives?" I butted in.

He smiled at Jo again as if they both understood it was a stupid question but one that could be expected from an outsider.

"I never knew," he replied, "although she did stay with us for a while some time ago. But so what? She was just another wounded thing my aunt picked up. That was Mona, wasn't it? Wounded birds. Wounded people. 'Get out of the car, Nicholas,' she used to say, 'and see if that smashed squirrel is still alive.' Of course, he had been dead for a week."

I could tell by his tone—alternately bitter and loving—that it would be a long time before he would get over the death of his aunt.

"Anyway," he continued, still looking at Jo, "when Ginger started to work for the Starobins, she got her own place. No, wait. It was before that. I remember she kept moving around from place to place, because she was always borrowing my pickup truck. Look, I never said more than ten words to that girl!"

What a strange thing for him to say. Why should he make such a comment? It was as if speaking to Ginger would implicate him in something. What was he afraid of? I didn't trust Mona's nephew one bit. A horse whinnied in a stall down the aisle, and then came two, three, four explosive sounds, like gunshots. Frightened, I stepped back, toward the entrance to the barn.

"Relax," Nicholas said, "that's only the new filly they shipped in from Philadelphia Park. Eye infection—nothing serious, but she's crazy as a loon. She just loves kicking walls."

A gust of wind blew down the center of the aisle, stinging our eyes and ears. Nick tried to pull his hat down on his head. "There's coffee in the house, Jo," he said.

As Jo shook her head, I asked, "Would you have any idea where Ginger is now?"

"Well, she used to be friendly with a guy named Bobby Lopez. He works in the Chevron station on Route 106. Do you know it?"

Jo nodded that she did, smiled at Nick, and we both started walking back toward the car.

We hadn't gone more than twenty feet when Nick called, "Jo!" We looked back. He was leaning on the shovel, his face now a bright red from the wind. "Jo, do you think we'll survive the winter?"

Jo stared at him dumbly for a moment, then walked

quickly back to him. I saw them embrace. I heard sobs. I turned away. I didn't want to intrude in their shared sorrow—but I felt a longing to be with them, to hold and be held. It was silly. What, really, had Mona and Harry been to me? Or I to them? And yet these two murdered people were beginning to envelop me in a peculiar way, as if there had always been another me—another Alice Nestleton longing to be part of them. The whole thing was perplexing.

Minutes later, we found Bobby Lopez sipping coffee in one of the repair bays of the Chevron station. At his feet was an enormous mongrel bitch with floppy ears who kept rolling over and over.

Bobby had a beautiful face with deep-set almond eyes. He didn't appear happy to see us at all. His hands and arms were stained with a bluish grease. But he answered our questions with dispatch. Yes, he said, he knew Ginger. No, he said, he hadn't seen her in weeks. Yes, he said, he knew where she lived.

When we asked where specifically, he balked for the first time. "Why do you want to know?" he asked suspiciously.

Jo was wonderful. She lied like a producer. She told Bobby Lopez that Ginger was still owed a week's wages and she wanted to deliver the money to her.

He smiled grimly at us and lit a cigarette. He prodded the dog playfully. He stared at Jo, then at me. He seemed to be evaluating us against some standard.

Finally he said, "She lives over the Tarpon Bar in Oyster Bay Village. It's right at the crossroads of the town. You can't miss it unless you want to."

His knowledge of her lodgings sort of dripped with the

idea that they were both very close—lovers, in fact. Jo asked, "Where did you meet her?" And her voice was so incredulous that the mechanic bristled. He understood what she meant. How could a nice girl like Ginger end up with a grease monkey? Jo was making her class prejudice explicit.

"At Aqueduct racetrack, lady. We both used to work for Charlie Coombs."

◦◦◦

Bobby Lopez was right. One couldn't miss the Tarpon Bar if one drove through the center of Oyster Bay Village. In a hallway next to the bar, we found Ginger Mauch's name on a mailbox.

A very rickety staircase took us up. The landings needed paint. The floors were covered with pocked linoleum. The doors of the apartments were warped.

Ginger Mauch lived on the third floor in the rear apartment. The door was wide open. A few pieces of furniture were scattered throughout the single large room. The closet was open and empty. The drawers of the dresser were open and empty.

Ginger had obviously moved out in haste.

In one corner of the large room, in front of the window, was a pile of posters, clothes, records, and other items she had obviously discarded as not important enough to take with her. I could see some unopened cans of soup in the pile.

"Poor Ginger," Jo said, sitting down wearily on a folding chair.

I was mystified. Why had she moved out in such a rush? Was she frightened? Of what? The more I tried to comprehend the stable girl and her behavior, the more elusive she became.

Jo stood up suddenly and walked toward the pile of discarded junk.

"Do you see anything, Jo?" I asked, because her move was purposeful.

Her foot had found something and was pulling it out from the pile, as if it was something dirty. It was a photograph of a laughing Harry standing in front of the barn, a calico cat draped around his neck like a muffler. He was smiling his wonderful smile.

"My God," Jo whispered, "I've been looking for this photograph for a year. It's the best photo Harry ever took. And that's Veronica, the barn cat, on him. Harry told me the picture had just vanished, but he was lying. He gave it to Ginger. Why would he do that? And now she just left it in a pile of garbage."

Her foot pushed the photo back into the pile. The corners were discolored.

I bent over to pick it up.

"Leave it. Please leave it," she said, sitting back down on the flimsy folding chair, the color drained from her face.

I left it alone, and instead looked about the room. My gaze settled on the denuded wire hangers in the closet. The more elusive Ginger became, the more I realized I had to find her.

"Do you know Charlie Coombs?" I asked Jo, remembering what Bobby Lopez had said.

"The trainer?"

"Is he a trainer? I'm talking about the name Bobby Lopez mentioned."

"Yes. Of course he's a trainer. I know him. He used to lay up horses at Mona's place. Just like his father did before him. A lot of trainers swore by Mona. She had a healing touch with sick horses, like Harry did with all animals. Old Man Coombs even used to call Mona when he had problems training a yearling . . ."

She paused, then added in a choked voice, "It seems like all the wonderful people are gone."

I walked over to Jo and took her hand, squeezing it. "Come with me back to Manhattan, Jo, for a day or two. We'll go to the Aqueduct. Charlie Coombs may know where Ginger is. If she worked for him before, maybe she went back to him."

"I'm very tired, Alice," she said.

"But Harry and Mona are dead, Jo, and we won't find their killers in this pile of junk or in Harry's pile of junk in the storeroom."

Jo stared at me for a moment, then at our joined hands. "Okay, Alice. Why not? What else are old ladies for?"

8

I was sitting in my apartment watching Jo prowl. My apartment fascinated her. She kept walking from one end to the other, picking up things, putting them down. I didn't understand her acute interest, particularly after a long day. Was it conceivable that a wise old woman like Jo thought the life of an actress to be exciting and glamorous, reflected somehow in her furniture and bric-a-brac? There was not one glamorous item in my apartment.

Finally she sat down on the sofa and said, "Well, I hope all the cats survive. The last time I left them with Amos, I was afraid he was going to eat them." She stared down at Bushy as if contemplating Amos contemplating eating him.

It was nine o'clock in the evening. We were both very tired, and Jo had said we had to leave at five thirty the following morning because trainers exercise their horses really early. If we wanted to speak to Charlie Coombs, we had to catch him then.

"Do you want some tea, Jo, or something stronger?"

"Nothing, thank you," she said, looking around again with that wide-eyed curiosity. Then she smiled. "You know, Alice, I just never thought your apartment would look like this."

"Like what, Jo?"

"Well . . . so . . . so conservative."

"Did you think I led a wild life in the big city, Jo?"

"I didn't know what to think."

"Men are scarce, Jo, at least at this time."

"But you're a beautiful woman," she blurted. I didn't know how to respond. Maybe she wanted me to recount my brief fling with promiscuity. But that had happened a long time ago, after my marriage had broken up, and I remembered little about it. Furthermore, it was none of her business.

When I looked at her again, she was crying. I closed my eyes and opened them again only when she began to speak: "You want to hear something funny, Alice? I was a virgin when I married Harry. And I never slept with another man. Only Harry. So if I die tomorrow or the day after, I'll never really know if what Harry and I had was real love . . . or real passion. Do you know what I mean, Alice?"

"It's not too late," I quipped, and then was immediately chagrined at the stupidity of my remark.

She smiled at me. "Oh, I think it is. I think it is."

Bushy was now circling the sofa, wondering whether to jump up on the strange woman who had captured his favorite place. He looked alternately confused and angry. His tail switched. His ears did what passes for a Maine coon cat's dance.

I went to the hall closet and pulled out pillows, a quilt, and a woolen blanket older than me that had been on my grandmother's farm in Minnesota. It was a strange blue—like a frayed psychotic sky. I laid all the bedding on a chair next to the sofa, along with a clean towel for Jo. Then I went to sleep.

∞

When we pulled up at the racetrack entrance gate the next morning, we found it manned by uniformed guards who were very suspicious. For some reason, I had always thought the racetrack was open, like a mall. I soon found out otherwise, for they would not let us in. First of all, Jo couldn't get Charlie Coombs on the phone. He was somewhere on the racetrack but not available. Then, when she finally contacted him, we had to wait for passes to be made out. And then, after we were through the gate, we got hopelessly lost in the barn areas. "I haven't been here in twenty years," Jo kept telling me by way of explanation.

It was past six thirty when we reached Charlie Coombs's stalls. Suddenly we were surrounded by horses that had just come back from their morning workouts. They were steaming from sweat in the freezing morning air. Young men and women stripped their saddles and bridles, covered them with blankets, and then started to walk them in slow circles around the stable area, guiding them with rope halters.

I had never been that close to racehorses before, and was staggered by their power. I could sense that they were only a step away from flight. These majestic beasts were capable of bursts of awesome speed. And even in the darkness I could sense their individuality—an eye, a turn of the head, a sudden distinctive whinny. Of course they frightened me, but I longed to make some kind of contact with all that power.

Jo pulled me out of an almost trancelike state, and together we entered a small, cluttered office. Seated behind his desk, Charlie Coombs was talking on the phone when he saw us, and he gestured emphatically with his hand that we should sit and wait.

People came in and out of the office without saying a word, wearing riding helmets or stocking caps, bundled up against the cold, their movements quick, almost choppy, as they used the coffee machine occupying the only uncluttered spot in the office. Next to the machine were containers of sugar and milk and a large cardboard box on which was crudely written: "If you drink coffee, pay for the coffee." I saw no one drop any money into the box.

Finally Charlie Coombs slammed the phone down and said, "Jo, I heard about Harry and Mona Aspen. God, I'm sorry." He raised both palms as if emphasizing that the world is like that—full of unexplained misery and loss.

I liked the man immediately. He looked around forty-five or fifty, with a weather-beaten, aggressive face but a very kindly smile. He had thick graying black hair which went every which way, and he was dramatically underdressed considering the cold—a dress shirt without a tie, and over it a kind of hunter's vest.

Jo introduced us to each other. He leaned forward and said, "I like Jo's friends . . . under any circumstances."

I could see that he was shorter than I thought—and he was wearing red sneakers. For some reason, that made me feel very good. Imagine a man training million-dollar racehorses wearing red sneakers. It was poetic and crazy, a kind of equine *Red Shoes*, only Charlie Coombs was obviously no Moira Shearer. He was trying to give us his full attention, but it was obvious that one part of him was outside the office, focused on the horses, listening for trouble signs or whatever trainers listen for.

Jo said, "We're trying to locate Ginger Mauch."

"But, Jo, she works for you," he replied.

"She quit. Suddenly. She just went and quit."

"Well, I don't know where she is, then. Jo, I haven't seen Ginger in a couple of years."

"But she used to work for you," I said, realizing it was time for me to start leading the conversation.

"Right. She worked here for about six months. Then she quit. Then I heard she was helping out Mona Aspen on the Island. Then I heard she was working for Harry and Jo."

"Do you remember the circumstances under which you hired her?" I asked him.

My rather pretentious question made Coombs laugh. He leaned over toward me—a bit threatening, a bit flirtatious. "Before I answer that question, I want to know what business you're in."

"Why?"

"Well, it's the kind of question an IRS agent would ask."

"I'm an actress."

He stepped back, looking at me intently; it was obviously not what he had expected to hear.

Jo intervened apologetically. "Charlie, we just need all the information you can give us about Ginger. We don't have time to explain."

"The circumstances," Coombs said, skillfully mimicking my pretentious language, "were, if I remember—she came into my office and asked me for a job as an exercise rider. I told her I didn't need exercise riders, but I did need an assistant trainer to do all the paperwork I couldn't do . . . and a lot of other stupid tasks around the barn, from ordering hay to dealing with security. I told her that since I had become rich and famous I needed more time for myself. She said okay. I hired her."

"Did she tell you anything about herself?"

"Not really. I did learn eventually that she was born and raised in Vermont, that she usually came to work late on Thursday for some reason, and that she took milk and no sugar in her coffee."

I could see that he was making an honest effort to remember. "Did you ask her for references?"

"No, I didn't have to. Ginger was an exercise rider in Maryland before she came to New York. And the horse she rode was Cup of Tea. She showed me clippings."

"Cup of Tea!" Jo repeated in a startled voice. "She never told me about that."

"Who is Cup of Tea?" I asked, bewildered by Jo's response.

Charlie Coombs walked back behind the desk and sat down. He grinned wickedly at me in a good-natured way, as if I should be ashamed of myself. "Once upon a time," he began in a self-mocking, pedagogic tone, "there was an ugly little foal born on a farm in upper Michigan. He was a thoroughbred, but from a very undistinguished family. Nobody ever heard of his momma or papa. They called him Cup of Tea because his color was so murky—not bay, not chestnut. He actually looked like a cow pony, which is why he was auctioned off as a yearling for only nine hundred dollars.

"The new owner took Cup of Tea around the Midwest circuit—racing him in the cheapest races at the cheapest dirt tracks. He always lost. So he was sold to a trainer in Maryland, who wanted to make him into a track pony. Well, Cup of Tea goes to Maryland and starts accompanying real racehorses out onto the track to keep them calm.

"One day the little horse accompanies a hotshot allowance horse out onto the track for a grass workout. Cup of Tea, who probably never saw a grass track in his life, spooked, threw his rider, and ran around the grass track about two seconds faster than the world record for that distance.

"To make a long story short, the next year Cup of Tea wins the three biggest grass stakes in America, including the Budweiser Million. And right now the old boy is the most expensive and sought-after stud in the world, standing in France. It's the ultimate rags-to-riches story. It's Hollywood."

It was a wonderful story. I could see it as a movie. But who would play Ginger?

A young Hispanic man burst into the office and yelled something in Spanish to Coombs. The trainer nodded, stood up, and said, "I hope I was of some help."

He shook Jo's hand and kissed her lightly on top of her

head. Then he said to me, "I like telling you horse stories. I have plenty of them. I even have some other kinds of stories."

I leaned over the desk and wrote my number on his pad.

"His father was even nicer," Jo said after he left.

I mulled over this new information on Ginger as we drove back to Manhattan and double-parked until it was time for the alternate-side-of-the-street parking clock to change. From what I could tell, we were no closer to learning her present whereabouts than we had been before.

"What do we do now?" Jo asked.

"Wait until we can park legally and then eat. There's a Chinese restaurant right up the block, with good lunch specials."

"I mean about Ginger."

"We keep looking."

"But who else can we contact? Who else knows her?"

"That horse."

Jo laughed. "Isn't it a wonderful story? Cup of Tea is a lovable horse."

A car drove by too fast, flinging slush against our windows. Finally we were able to park. When we entered the restaurant, I realized the old woman was tired. She stared at the menu as if in a daze and then ordered exactly what I ordered.

She ate the sizzling rice soup but left the rest of her meal. I ate everything. I was hungry and cold. And I was still excited by the racetrack, by the proximity of the horses . . . and by Charlie Coombs.

"I'm just not hungry," Jo said by way of apology, appalled by the realization that she was wasting food.

When we paid the bill and stepped outside, we found that a brilliant winter sun had broken through the clouds. Everything was brighter, warmer, cleaner.

"I'm tired," Jo said. "I could use a nap."

"It's only two minutes to my apartment," I assured her.

As I looked down the street, mentally rechecking where we had parked the car, I noticed a small red pickup truck had already double-parked in front of it. Good, I thought, it would protect the windows from slush.

I looked at Jo. She was standing contentedly, her face up to the sun.

The red pickup truck in front of her car started to move. I watched it casually, the sun sparkling along its red sides. Something was wrong, though. The truck crossed to the far side of the street, where no cars were parked—the illegal side.

It began to accelerate, and one set of wheels squealed against the curb. The little red truck was coming straight at us.

I grabbed Jo's arm. I started to run, pulling Jo with me.

I heard a screaming, grinding noise behind me. Terrified, I tried to run faster. My legs started to wobble like jelly.

I heard a person scream. Showers of glass rained down. All went dark.

9

"Only one more landing to go," I said to Jo as we both hovered on the cusp between the third and fourth landings, exhausted, still dazed. Jo had a large bandage on one side of her face. I had a dressing across the top of my forehead, right at the scalp line.

Noticing that one of the tenants still had a Christmas wreath on the door, I snarled. Why hadn't it been removed? Christmas was over and done with. And as I stood there between landings, holding Jo, I remembered some lines from a play I had once appeared in. A woman faces a hated husband and says, "What I'd like on this ominous Christmas Eve is a visitation from Baby Jesus, or at least a Christ in some highly recognizable form."

What was the name of the play? The playwright? The character? I could remember nothing, only those lines.

I touched my thigh gingerly. It hurt very badly. The doctors in the emergency room at Beekman Downtown Hospital had said nothing was broken, just bruised.

The police had told us the truck had crashed into a light-post, destroyed a parking sign, smashed the windows of the Chinese restaurant, destroyed a hydrant, spun around twice—and driven off. They told us we were very lucky. Drunk drivers like that one usually ended up killing or maiming people—and both of us had been only inches from death. It was a miracle, they said, that we had escaped with only superficial wounds from the flying glass.

We started up the final flight to my apartment, Jo in front, my hand lightly on her back to make sure she didn't fall. Or perhaps my staying behind her was not altruistic. When I had gained consciousness I had seen one side of her face drenched in blood from dozens of tiny glass cuts. And her cropped white hair had been flecked with blood. The sight had made me ill.

Finally, sanctuary. We both dropped onto the sofa like stones. We didn't move. We didn't speak.

It was already dark outside and there were no lights in the apartment. I realized I should turn on a light, but for the moment I couldn't intellectually locate the switch.

When I finally did turn it on and returned to the sofa, I saw Bushy and Pancho sitting calmly, side by side, staring at us. It was a very unusual pose for Pancho. He seemed to be assessing the situation. It must be our bandages, I thought. The white bandages must fascinate him.

"Can I get you something, Jo?"

"Nothing."

I stared at Pancho. I longed to cuddle with that crazy cat. For a brief moment I contemplated making a grab for him. But I didn't. Pancho was always too swift for me. He simply didn't want to cuddle. I smiled at him. His body was less relaxed. His curiosity was almost satiated. He would get back to business shortly—flight from the enemy.

Jo laughed, and I looked at her. Her hand was feeling her bandaged face. "I was just thinking," she explained, "how ridiculous it is to come into Manhattan and almost get killed by a drunk driver. I thought all the drunk drivers were on the Long Island Expressway."

"How do you know he was drunk, Jo?"

"Well, the police said he was drunk."

"Yes, they did."

"You have to be drunk to climb a curb and run your truck into a restaurant window."

We were both alive. It was time to deal with the facts. "He wasn't drunk, Jo. He was trying to kill us."

She barked a small, nervous laugh. "Alice, how do you know that?"

How did I know that? I closed my eyes and re-created the moments before. The driver of the red pickup truck had been idling his vehicle when we came out of the restaurant. He had crossed over from his double-parked position to the empty side to gather speed and then made a straight run toward us. I had seen him. I had known he was coming for us.

"He was trying to kill us, Jo."

"Why would anyone want to kill us?" she asked, skeptical, confused, disturbed.

I didn't answer her question. I looked at the cats. Pancho was gone. Bushy was stretched out. My thigh was throbbing as if there was a frog under the skin.

The little red pickup truck had splintered all my idealistic pretensions. It had made me realize that my life was still precious to me. Sure, I had not become a great actress doing great roles, but there was still my craft, and my cats, and my apartment, and the hundreds of tiny things that constitute a life . . . and which I loved very much.

The red pickup truck had put the question forthrightly: Was I prepared to sacrifice it all to find out who murdered Harry Starobin?

No, I was not.

"Jo," I said as gently as possible, "they tried to murder us because we wouldn't let your husband rest in peace."

"I don't believe that, Alice. I have a right to find out who murdered Harry."

It was such a naive and ludicrous statement that I reacted sharply. "Don't be stupid, Jo. I'm not talking about rights. I'm talking about all that cash in your vault and God-knows-what elsewhere. I'm talking about people who murder other people. Do you want to die, Jo? Those people, whoever they are, tried to kill us. And they'll try again if we don't stop."

She didn't respond. She leaned her head back against the sofa pillows. A tiny speck of blood was seeping out of her bandage.

I knew what she was thinking, that her good friend Alice was abandoning Harry. Yes, I was doing that. I was abandoning Harry and saving my life and hers. We had both gotten in too deep. We had both scratched the surface of something that was very dangerous.

"So you just want us to stop," she said, "to leave it all to that terrible Detective Senay who doesn't know a thing about Harry . . . who doesn't care about Harry."

"Yes."

"I should just go home and forget all about Harry's papers and his death and that money, and all about Mona. Is that what I should do?"

"Just proceed with your life, Jo."

"What life?"

"Any life you can make."

"That's easy for you to say, Alice."

She started to get up, but the effort was too much.

"Please don't be mad at me, Jo. Please."

She flailed her arms in the air and then brought them to her lap. "I'm not mad at you, Alice. I'm . . . it's just that . . . poor Harry." And she began to mumble incoherently.

I covered her with a blanket and sat close to her. She had, I knew, accepted my decision, and I was relieved. I knew she was not capable of carrying on an investigation alone. We would both be safe if we distanced ourselves from Harry's corpse . . . or rather his gravel-strewn ashes. But along with the relief came no small amount of shame. I had, after all, quit. The role was too difficult for me. The consequences were potentially too dangerous. I was too old for a fling like that. Pancho flew by along the far wall, heading toward the windowsills. I was safe. We were all safe.

10

It was the first day of February, a brooding, frigid day. I had just returned from a lunch meeting with my agent and "some people." As usual, this kind of meeting had agitated me. I was not well-known enough as an actress to be offered parts like pieces of fruit, but I was too experienced and well-thought-of to be asked to read for many parts that I would have been delighted to read for. So, hoisted on that peculiar contradiction, I was always forced to have those strange, frustrating lunches with "some people" who were about to do a play or a movie or a PBS special.

The whole thing was a sham anyway, because I hadn't done any straight theater for a long time. I wasn't interested in that stuff anymore. I was looking for parts that stretched the imagination, that took reality apart, and one didn't find them with "some people." I never left a lunch with them without muttering, "God bless cat-sitting."

So there I was, sitting on the sofa, indulging my latest bad habit—touching the small crescent-shaped scar which remained on the top of my forehead after they removed the bandage.

A variant of my usual theatrical fantasy was beginning to form. I was appearing as a guest artist in some exotic foreign company like the Moscow Art Theatre. My role was minor, but as the play unfolded, I spoke my lines and exhibited such awesome stage presence that my character totally overwhelmed the major characters in the play. At the end, roses were flung at me—large bloodred roses—as if I were a ballerina. It was such an egotistical adolescent fantasy that it always embarrassed me—but it never went away. And the fantasy always afforded me, during its course, intense joy, and why not?

It was a magical, mystical, lunatic fantasy, and in each reenactment the vehicle changed. It was a Victorian costume drama. It was a sleazy detective drama. It was a Brechtian interpretation of the Theban Cycle.

"Oh, Bushy," I said, "how stupid and weary I am . . . and how bizarre my whole life has become—lunches and fantasies and kitty litter." Bushy understood. That is what cats are all about.

The phone rang. I figured it was my agent calling to tell me how the lunch had gone, how those "people" were excited by my talents. I let the phone ring a long time because I really didn't want to talk to her. She was a nice, foolish woman but she had begun to harp on my stopping all that avant-garde nonsense and going back to where I "belonged"—Eugene O'Neill? And I kept saying, "Sure, get me some skinny Colleen Dewhurst parts." Both of us were lying.

When it didn't stop ringing, I picked it up. It wasn't my agent. It was Charlie Coombs, the trainer.

He said he had something even better than horse stories to tell me. He said that an exercise rider who works for him lives in my neighborhood and will drive me out to the track in the morning to see how a great—*chuckle*—trainer like himself really trains racehorses.

I stared at the phone. For the past few weeks I had thought about Charlie Coombs many times, but only in relation to Jo and her troubles, and I had not heard from Jo since she returned to Long Island, disgruntled at my defection.

But the moment I heard his voice on the phone, I knew that we would become lovers.

I don't really know why I thought that. The theater is no place for love. Actresses can't stand actors, and vice versa. The only men I met who weren't actors or directors were bankers and lawyers and businessmen on the fringes of the theater. They were perpetually fascinated by and panting for actresses who they thought would provide a new world of erotic and intellectual excitement. It never happened that way. The magic never emerged. I was by now more or less resigned to celibacy.

But how would it be with a man who had nothing to do with the theater?

I said I would be delighted to go out to the racetrack again.

"Malacca," he said, which was the name of the exercise rider, "will be in front of your house at four thirty tomorrow morning." Then he hung up.

I turned to Bushy, who had just jumped up for some attention, and was just about to tell him about the Charlie Coombs phone call when the phone started ringing again. This time it had to be my agent. This time I had to let it ring. Or put the damn machine on, which I hated.

But what if it was Charlie with a change of plans?

I picked up the phone. It was Carla Fried.

"Alice, I'm at La Guardia. I have to catch a plane at Newark in three hours. If I go through Manhattan, we can meet for coffee."

"Where does the bus bring you?" I asked automatically, flustered by her call.

"I take it to Forty-second and Park. We can meet in the bar of the Grand Hyatt, across the street. An hour okay?"

"Fine," I said. And she hung up. God, that woman had become efficient. It was like dealing with a corporate jet.

Remembering that the bar of the Grand Hyatt was pseudo-posh, I threw on something pseudo-respectable.

Carla was waiting for me at the entrance to the bar inside the hotel lobby. She had taken a cab. The moment we sat down, she started to talk a mile a minute. She was sorry she hadn't called back after she left Atlanta. Everything about the production was going well. She wasn't going to pressure me about a decision on the part—there was still plenty of time. Then she sat back and grinned.

"I'm babbling, Alice, I'm sorry. Planes make me crazy."

We ordered drinks.

"What is going on with you?" she asked.

Her question seemed so absurd I started to laugh and then

to cry. How could I tell her what had happened? How could I tell her about the murders? She wouldn't comprehend or care. How could I tell her about the fear when that little red truck came toward Jo and me?

"What's the matter, Alice? Are you sick?"

Her face clouded over with such concern that I felt terrible at spoiling our meeting.

"No, no, a man," I said quickly, recovering.

"A man? I had forgotten all about them," she quipped. "You mean those people with the funny musculature."

"I think I'm going to have an affair, Carla. And I'm a little nervous. It's been a long, long time."

"Who is he?"

"A man I met at the racetrack. A trainer."

"It has been so long since I had an affair, Alice, that when I go out for drinks with Waring—"

"Waring?" I interrupted, not remembering the name.

"The millionaire I told you about . . . the one who funded our season."

"I'm sorry. Of course I remember. Are you sleeping with him?"

"No. That's my point. He's smart and handsome and crazy and rich. The kind of man I always dreamed of. But now I just sit and talk theater with him, and not a single erotic thought pops out. You'll see. He's in New York. I called him from the airport after I talked to you. He'll be here to have a drink with us. But I want to hear about your man."

"Well, Charlie Coombs is not rich or handsome, but he may well be crazy."

"You can't have everything," she said.

Another round of drinks came and we lapsed into one of those wonderful, surreal, lewd, revealing conversations that are basically sexual autobiographies. It was delicious. We laughed. We cried. We remembered.

Suddenly I felt a touch on my shoulder. And then I heard a voice.

"So you're Juliet's Nurse," the voice said. I turned and stared at a man.

"I'm Waring," he said, and pulled a chair to our table, sitting easily.

Is he the Pope? I thought sarcastically. Only one name—Waring. Maybe all very rich men use only their last names—even in bed. He was tall and skinny. His thinning light hair was brushed back and longish. He was wearing an old brown corduroy suit with a beautiful light blue knit tie on a dark blue shirt. He looked like an academic. His face was lined, with blue eyes. Fifty? Sixty? I couldn't tell.

"Don't worry, I'm not going to harass you about the part," he said, "because Carla has been giving me all kinds of etiquette lessons about dealing with actresses."

His voice had that funny Canadian accent, a flattish inflection which is so difficult to describe and even harder to mimic.

He sat back and beamed at Carla. My curiosity immediately turned to hate. He was looking at Carla as if she were his possession. As if her theater group were his new toy. As if, just as he owned factories and wheat fields and oil tankers and racing cars and yachts and horses and dogs, now he was going to own a little theater and he was going to apply his magic touch and—*poof*—out would come another Moscow Art Theatre. God, he sickened me. He reminded me of a hundred other theatrical backers I had met over the years, people who shared his arrogance even though they had only one-millionth of Waring's fortune.

"What's the matter, Alice? You're pale. Are you sick?" Carla leaned toward me, her voice and face anxious.

I lied.

"No, I'm fine. It's just I forgot about an appointment . . . an important appointment. Look, I have to go. Call me! I'm still thinking about the part."

Then I stood up and walked out of there.

∽

Malacca was waiting for me the next morning in a beat-up van, the back of which was filled with horse equipment, most of which I couldn't identify. He was a small man, obviously an ex-jockey, and he drove like a lunatic, sailing through lights happily, telling me his life story in violent bursts of energy, then falling silent, then erupting again.

When we reached Charlie Coombs's barn, the trainer was waiting for me. He smiled, and before I could say a word, he placed a riding hat on my head and buttoned the strap under my chin as if I were a child. Then, taking me by the hand, he led me toward the saddled ponies standing quietly.

"This is Rose," he said, pointing to the larger one.

I hadn't been on a horse in fifteen years, but Rose was

so gentle that riding her was like sitting on a pillow. Coombs climbed on the other pony and we started to pace forward. I needed a few moments to orient myself, since everything had happened so quickly, but I finally realized that all around us were racehorses—his racehorses—heading out to the track for their workouts.

As we continued to move en masse, I became unnerved. The horses were prancing, snorting, moving in often erratic patterns. Several of them looked crazed, as if they were about to bolt or rear up, and I heard the constant chatter of the exercise riders soothing them in Spanish. From time to time one of the racehorses would come close to my pony, Rose, and make contact with her. Rose was unperturbed. I was tense.

It was still dark, but there were tiny slivers of light beginning to infiltrate the horizon. Charlie brought his pony close to mine. "Okay?" he said. I nodded. He smiled. "Rose likes you," he said. He was projecting.

When we reached the gap in the track, the racehorses went out in single file. As each one passed Charlie, he gave the rider instructions—gallop such-and-such a distance, work the horse in such-and-such a time. Our two ponies drifted away from the gap and settled behind the rail.

"How do the riders know how fast they're going?" I asked, perplexed by the speeds Charlie had requested. They didn't carry stopwatches, and even if they did, they couldn't read them in the darkness.

"The clocks are in their heads," he replied.

Horses were now circling the track at different speeds. I couldn't identify Charlie's horses, but I saw from the way he was watching that he knew exactly where all of his horses were and what they were doing. Then I too began to watch carefully. The sound of the hooves pounding the track was like a beautifully precise percussion instrument. I could see white froth on the horses' mouths. I intuited the strength and skill of the riders as they perched on top of their mounts so precarious, so light. The whole scene was packed with a kind of beauty, a kind of energy. Leaning all the way forward in the saddle and laying my head on Rose's shoulders, I closed my eyes and listened to the beat.

It was all over much too quickly. We rode back to the barn and Charlie took me through the barn area and into the stalls. He showed me how the horses were stripped and cooled off and then bedded down. He introduced me to the grooms and the riders and the barn cats and dogs who roamed freely in and out of the stalls. He showed me the horses that had not worked out that morning, allowing me to give them apples or sugar cubes. He pointed out the feed problems and health problems. And then he led me back to his cluttered office, gave me some coffee and a piece of Danish pastry, and told me to wait until he finished up.

An hour later he was back, the morning work done. Now he looked exactly as I remembered him—underdressed, broad-shouldered, tousled hair, friendly manner.

But he was wearing boots.

"Where are your red sneakers?" I asked playfully.

"I don't wear them when I'm really trying to impress someone," he said.

"Well, to be honest, I found them very attractive."

"Damn," he said in mock anger, "I always make the wrong move." He sipped his coffee. Then he noted, "Jo sends her regards."

"You saw her?"

"No, I spoke to her. I called her and asked permission to call you."

"My God," I laughed, "that is old-fashioned."

"I am old-fashioned in most ways. Anyway, Jo told me you're no longer looking for Ginger Mauch."

"That's right. We gave it up." I noticed the way he looked at me, was really listening to me. I was flattered and my hand rose unconsciously to pat my hair.

"Jo told me you were both almost killed by a drunken driver."

"It was close. Very close."

"I see the scar," Coombs said, pointing to my forehead. I touched it once and pulled my hand away. I played with the uneaten Danish. I felt good sitting there. He made me feel very comfortable. His maturity was leavened with a kind of childishness. Maybe it came from working with horses.

He leaned over the desk a bit toward me. "By the way, are you a famous actress?"

"Not really. I'm more famous as a cat-sitter."

"I mean, should I know who you are? Should I have seen you in something?"

"If you were in Chapel Hill, North Carolina, in April 1985, you would have seen me do a very respectable Hedda Gabler. I'm not respectable anymore."

"My father used to tell me," Coombs said wryly, "that one

has to be respectable to make it in the world. But what do fathers know?"

"What *do* fathers know?"

He didn't answer my absurd question, but instead looked mournful for a moment. He snapped out of it quickly, though, and laughed. "Do you want me to tell you more horse stories?"

I leaned back. "Tell me whatever you want to tell me," I replied. We were flirting with each other now, I realized. I didn't want to do that. What did I want to do?

He started to play with his coffee cup. "I shouldn't have asked you to come out here on such short notice," he apologized.

"Actually I like short notices. It seems as if a crisis exists— but there is none. One gets excitement and relief at the same time."

"There was a crisis," he said.

"What?"

"You. I wanted to see you."

"Well, you've seen me."

"Yes, the crisis is over. But I was always good at crises. Actually, that's why I'm a trainer. The racetrack is about crises. Something bad is always happening. A horse throws a rider. A cinch breaks. A dog bites a horse. A horse bites a vet. A trainer makes the wrong claim. I was always good in crises."

"Is that why you don't wear enough clothes in winter?" I asked.

"Right. Stay light. Stay mobile," he replied, laughing, his rough face crinkling into an incredibly kindly smile.

"Do you come into Manhattan often?" I asked.

"About once a week."

"Where do you live?"

"I have a small room about ten minutes away from here."

I looked at his hands holding the coffee cup. I could imagine them wrapped in a rope halter. I had seen them only an hour before, running up the leg of a horse, searching for a swelling. One of his hands disengaged from the cup. He reached it across the table and placed it down, palm up. I reached across and placed my hand in his.

∽

I stood just outside my bedroom door watching Charlie Coombs sleep. I had never gone to bed so quickly with a man, no matter how much I had been attracted to him—except for my brief adventure in promiscuity, which really didn't count.

The sex had been very good. We had been very good. Perhaps, I thought, my emerging middle age was going to unflower into a new world of eros. I laughed at my own arrogance.

Two sudden darts of light on the bookcase startled me. Then I smiled. It was Pancho, awake and cruising in his particular fashion. "Go to it," I whispered to him.

I leaned against the wall and closed my eyes. The plaster was cold but I was happy. It had been a long time since I had truly experienced intimacy, that sense that one partner was looking out for the other's pleasure. Charlie was old-fashioned, as he had said. As we made love, he kept telling me how good, how beautiful, how unique I was. It was hokey and charming and ageless and very heady—like a snifter of Napoleon brandy after chocolate cake.

He had, I realized, an ability to give credence to clichés. It was a gift which, oddly enough, I should have had but didn't—because it was what made actresses great, the ability to transcend a silly fiction, a role, and transform it into something that moves an audience to view the world differently.

There was a flash in the darkness. The eyes on the bookcase had vanished. I scanned the pitch-dark bedroom. I heard a furious but nearly silent rustle somewhere.

Then I located Pancho's eyes again . . . and lost them again. Then the eyes seemed to flash off and on like a traffic light that has gone berserk. Finally I realized what was happening. Poor dear crazy Pancho was actually playing with sleeping Charlie Coombs. He was bouncing from one end of the bed to the other and then to the floor and then to the bookcase, and he was doing it all so swiftly and quietly and elegantly that the sleeping man was not disturbed.

It was a good omen. I went back to bed.

The weeks of winter began to grind down. I landed a small but lucrative part in an avant-garde German film shot in, of all places, Bayonne, New Jersey. My agent started some "promising" negotiations with "some people" for a possible role as the wife in an off-Broadway revival of Pinter's *The Homecoming*. I was asked to teach an acting course at the Neighborhood Playhouse for their summer session. And I landed two new cat-sitting assignments, one of them an overpaying job consisting of visiting and feeding a large, somewhat eccentric Siamese on nine consecutive weekends while her owners took a series of jaunts. Ah, the rich. Anyway, I like German films, I like Pinter, I like teaching, and I love Siamese cats. So things were going quite well.

And Charlie Coombs began to spend at least two or three nights a week at my apartment.

The magic, as they say, was continuing. It was odd. We never spoke about what defined us—the theater or the racetrack. We did speak passionately and honestly about the stupidest things: candles, flashlights, cats with tiger stripes, vegetarian cats, cheeseburgers, boots, uncles, and the relationship, if any, between brown eggs and white eggs.

We kept speaking nonsense to each other because we were so enthralled with each other—with the wonder of it all. It was so delicious and crazy that I even enjoyed making coffee for him in the morning.

And so it went. I was finally living the life I should have lived twenty years earlier. I mean, everyone deserves at least one fling at a sublime domestic fantasy.

The bubble, alas, burst on the first Monday in March. It was not Charlie's fault. It was mine. Out of nowhere a face from the past rose up and took me with him.

The bubble burst this way: I was brushing Bushy on the living-room floor. Grooming a Maine coon like Bushy is always a problem, given the thickness of his coat, but the coat itself was a minor chore compared to the cat. Bushy had this peculiar attitude toward being groomed. He acted as if he was about to run away, so one had to hold him firmly. What was worse, he acted as if I was literally torturing him to death.

Once it was finally done and I stared down at my perfectly groomed cat, I had a memory flash so clear and so powerful that I folded my hands like a schoolchild.

I remembered the first time I saw Harry Starobin groom one of his Himalayans.

He had combed the cat out so quickly and so playfully and with such an awesome combination of gentleness, strength, and precision that I had been unable to respond to a question he asked me during the brushing. I had been hypnotized by the perfect harmony of cat and master.

The memory vanished, as they always do, and in its wake came a profound sense of remorse, as if Harry Starobin had risen from the crushed gravel of the Starobin driveway to make a bitter accusation: I, Alice Nestleton, had allowed Harry Starobin to be forgotten.

I could see his craggy, happy, lined face. I could hear him talk. I could see him wearing those green Wellington boots.

The bizarre apparition was so real that I literally started to tell Harry that Jo and I had no choice: we had almost been murdered. But whom was I speaking to? Bushy? Pancho?

The phone started to ring. I ignored it. I went to the bedroom and lay down. When the phone began ringing again, I let it ring. I didn't care at that moment for anyone or anything.

Turning my face into the pillow, I could sense Charlie Coombs's recent presence. He had slept there; we had made love. I turned on my side, feeling bitterly that my life now consisted of making love with Charlie Coombs and cleaning up after Charlie Coombs.

The domestic fantasy was deflating quickly. It dawned on me that a single memory of Harry Starobin had negated what I had considered a profound joy.

As I turned over on the other side, I realized that nothing I had done in my life had provided the intense excitement I had felt during the few days I had spent searching for Ginger Mauch and searching for the source of Harry's secret money. Not making love with Charlie Coombs. Not the theater. Nothing.

I had to do something, I realized. I had to rectify the betrayal. I had to go somewhere.

I sat up. I laughed to myself cynically, remembering the last two lines and the final stage instructions of *Waiting for Godot*.

Vladimir asks: "Well? Shall we go?"

Estragon answers: "Yes, let's go."

The stage direction reads: They do not move.

11

I opened my eyes and found myself staring into Charlie Coombs's eyes. I started to turn away, but his hand reached quickly around my waist and pulled me even closer to him on the bed.

"It's the first time that we've made love and you've had other things on your mind," he said.

"Life is harsh," I replied sarcastically, and then added: "What's the matter, Charlie? Didn't you enjoy it?"

He released the pressure of his arm around my waist. I turned away from him.

"Hell, Alice, I train horses for a living, remember? I know when a horse is keeping her mind on her business and when she's not."

I was about to retort angrily that I was not a horse and lovemaking wasn't running—but I said nothing, because he was right. My mind was on other things. I touched him gently on the knee in a kind of apology.

My mind was on Harry Starobin. Maybe I had been wrong about the attempted murder with the pickup truck—maybe the driver had been drunk, as the police speculated.

I looked at Charlie. He still had that hurt expression in his eyes. I moved close to him and tenderly kissed him on the shoulder.

After I had made that gesture, it infuriated me. I edged away from Charlie. What was I doing? It was the same old story again. In all my relationships with men, I had always placated them. I had vowed never to do that again—and there I was, doing it. The moment a little tension had appeared, I had started accommodating his fears.

But I had to defuse the situation—it was too unimportant to keep me engaged with it. I had to defuse it . . . deflect it . . . and to do so, I indulged in a little harmless lunacy. I started to neigh like a horse. Then I asked him if I was now keeping my mind on business like I should. He found that very funny. I found it easy to do. Then we both started acting stupid together, neighing and whinnying like horses. And then we made love again.

We lay there in the dark stillness. Only faint noises from the street could be heard. Even Pancho had ceased his travels. And Bushy was curled up on the far side of Charlie Coombs's pillow.

"Charlie," I said, "I want to ask you a question."

"Ask."

"Suppose I wanted to write a book about that horse you told me about."

"You mean Cup of Tea?"

"Right."

"You didn't even know who he was, Alice."

"Charlie, just imagine I'm writing a book about Cup of Tea. Where do I get information on him—stories, pictures?"

"In both the regular newspapers and the racing press. There have been thousands of stories printed about that horse."

"What is the racing press?"

"I mean papers and magazines that specialize in the racing and breeding of horses."

"Are there many?"

"Sure. There's the *Daily Racing Form, Chronicle of the Horse, Equus, Spur, Thoroughbred Record*—hell, there must be at least fifty."

Bushy, becoming upset because Charlie had raised his voice, contemptuously vacated the pillow and the bed, walking off stiff-legged down the hall toward the sofa in the living room.

"Your cat is telling me something," Charlie said.

"Fool," I said tenderly, and then added, "Go to sleep, Charlie."

I turned away from him and waited to hear the slow, rhythmic breathing which signaled that he had indeed gone to sleep.

For my part, I was filled with anticipatory excitement. I was going to go back in time and find out about that horse called Cup of Tea whose exercise rider had been none other than Ginger Mauch. It was back again to sly Ginger, duplici-tous Ginger, dangerous Ginger. Perhaps even dead Ginger. Or perhaps even innocent Ginger—child rider, child lover, fleeing only from a broken heart.

As I lay there in the darkness, I had this tremendous con-fidence that I had made the right decision. That it was neces-sary to complete the Harry Starobin file . . . that I had to find Ginger to do that . . . and if I couldn't find her through regu-lar channels, I had to take a different path. Yes—different path—the concept excited me, like it was some kind of Ori-ental truth or something like that. But it really meant that this time I was starting with a horse—Cup of Tea.

Alice Nestleton was now engaged in writing a book on Cup of Tea. A third career.

It was ludicrous. I stifled a giggle. I was never good at composition, although I had once won a prize in the very early grades for a cat limerick that was so bad it had to win:

There once was a cat named Lily.
Her face was sweet as Chantilly.
She milked the cow
and herded the sow
But her kittens were downright silly.

The next morning, Charlie, as always, gave me a long, desperate embrace before he left, as if he would never see me again. I drank my coffee standing at the window. I was happy that Charlie had left early. The whole affair was getting strange. I looked forward to Charlie's visits. I wanted him to sleep over as often as he could. But on the other hand, I had absolutely no desire to share anything with him other than my bed. Perhaps I had been alone too long.

At ten I left the house to begin my new pseudo-career as biographer of a horse called Cup of Tea. I walked uptown toward the Mid-Manhattan Library on Fortieth Street and Fifth Avenue. It was a clear, crisp morning, and I walked easily in a denim dress and wool sweater, my hair loose. Sometimes I slipped into a long-strided gait—what they used to call shit-kicking—the only thing that remained of my childhood on a dairy farm. It was the way my grandmother used to walk.

When I reached Thirty-fourth and Fifth I slowed down and began to window-shop. Something was bothering me. My anxiety, though, had nothing to do with where I was going or what I was going to do there. I felt that someone was watching me.

Pausing in front of a store which had an enormous selection of athletic shoes in the window, I turned halfway and saw that I had a clear shot of Fifth Avenue looking downtown.

There were so many people, and none of them were watching me. I must be getting weird, I thought. Even if someone had tried to kill me, I hadn't been looking for Harry's murderer for two months.

Then a flash of color caught my eye: a fishing feather in the rim of a man's hat about two blocks away. He was turning off Fifth as I saw him. Then he and the feather were gone.

Was he the one who had been watching me? How could I

be sure? Was it only paranoia induced by the fact that I was once again dealing with the murders of Harry Starobin and Mona Aspen?

I started walking again toward the library. When I reached the entrance I leaned against an outside wall. My hands were sweaty. I didn't feel so good.

I remembered where I had seen a feather like that. At Mona Aspen's place. A hat like that had been worn by her nephew, Nicholas Hill.

I looked downtown quickly. He had not reappeared. Had Nicholas Hill been following me? If so, why? I remembered that when I had spoken to him about Ginger I hadn't liked his attitude or response. He had made me suspicious then.

As I entered the library, though, I had to shake it off. I hadn't been involved in the case for two months. Had he been coming in to New York every day to watch me go to the grocery store? No, it had to be a fluke.

The periodicals librarian, who had never heard of Cup of Tea, told me I should first search the *New York Times Index* before going to the specialty horse magazines.

To my astonishment, I found that there were literally hundreds of references to Cup of Tea. He had obviously been the darling of the *Times*'s sportswriters—there was an article every three days on average. The horse had even been mentioned prominently in an editorial.

I spent the entire day at the microfilm machine reading articles from the *Times* dealing with the horse's rags-to-riches racing career.

All sorts of innocuous bits of information were scattered

throughout the articles: Cup of Tea loved peanut butter spread over a carrot; one of his jockeys was a diabetic; his trainer had been married three times; he won his last three races, before he retired to stud, by a combined total of fifty-one lengths.

I spent two more days on the *Times* and then started on the specialized magazines. I learned much more about Cup of Tea: his stride, his breeding, his training, how he changed leads, how he acted in the barn, what he ate and why.

I really didn't know what I was looking for, but whatever it was, I hadn't found it after six days of intensive research. More important, I had not found a single reference to Ginger Mauch being one of Cup of Tea's exercise riders.

The next week I moved across the street to the main reference library, concentrating on books rather than periodicals. During the years that Cup of Tea had been active as a champion, 1978–1984, dozens of books on horse racing and breeding had been published, and a great many of them at least mentioned him.

My days became very dreary: handing in slips, retrieving books, going through indexes and tables of contents and photo lists and credits. The only reason the stultifying routine was bearable was that I often thought about Harry as I searched the books. Harry would be proud that I had transcended fear and bad faith and returned to the puzzle of his death.

Charlie Coombs, on the contrary, was unhappy. He started complaining about how even on the two nights he slept over, I left him alone with the cats and stayed late at the library. He kept asking me, "Do you really expect me to believe that you're writing a book on Cup of Tea?"

His discomfort started me really thinking about him. I remember one rainy Tuesday when the thought came to me: Where were Charlie Coombs and I going? Did he really love me? Could we live together? I started creating scenarios for both of us, from the ridiculous to the sublime—scenarios of shouting matches and furious lovemaking afterward, of stormy separations and silent reunions.

It was during one of those scenarios that I reached for a book with a beautiful blue cover. The book was titled *Great Thoroughbreds* and was one of those gushy, extravagant items for young girls who become fixated on horses during adolescence. I leafed through the table of contents—a roster of great racehorses: Man of War, Whirlaway, Stymie, Northern Dancer, Secretariat, Ruffian, Forego—it had them all.

Cup of Tea was also there, listed as being on page seventy-eight. I flipped to the page and froze.

In front of me was a picture of Cup of Tea being unsaddled after a workout. A groom was on one side, holding the horse while the trainer did the unsaddling. An exercise rider was crouching next to the horse, fixing something on her boot, helmet in the other hand.

It was Ginger Mauch.

On one side of the horse was a bucket of water, and seated beside the bucket, gazing at Cup of Tea, was a lovely calico cat. The cat had the exact same markings and appearance as the cat I had seen in the photograph Jo and I found in Ginger's abandoned apartment.

Jo Starobin had said that the cat in the photo with Harry was the missing calico barn cat, Veronica.

12

I crept up on the small coffee shop at Thirty-fourth Street just east of Third because I felt in my heart that Jo Starobin wouldn't be there as she had promised. I really don't know why I was doing something so stupid, but all the same, darted a look in the window. I saw her waiting. I felt enormously relieved. When I had called her and told her I wanted to meet her, she had been distinctly unfriendly, talking to me in a polite tone as if we were shopping together in a supermarket. She offhandedly remarked that she had to come into the city to visit the bank vault. Was Thursday okay?

I snuck another look and saw that Jo was bent over, almost as if she was in pain. I kept staring at her through the window, worried now. But when she straightened up, there wasn't really pain on her face—it was despair. It was as if the loss of Harry seemed to crush her from time to time—without warning, without explanation.

I walked inside and slipped into the chair across from her.

She had chosen a small table along the wall. She smiled at me—a broad, wonderful smile—and she stretched her hands across the table and I grasped them and we both knew that everything was fine.

When the waitress came over, I ordered an espresso. Jo ordered a cappuccino. We decided to share a piece of dark chocolate cake with cherries.

Jo started to tell me about her train ride into Manhattan, but I broke right into her monologue. I couldn't wait. I pulled out the photograph I had feloniously ripped from the book, and placed it down on the table in front of her. "I've found your barn cat, Jo."

"Veronica? You found Veronica?" Jo asked, astonished, and then leaned over and studied the photograph of Cup of Tea with the exercise rider she recognized as Ginger and the calico cat sitting beside the water bucket.

"Look, Jo," I said, "look at the markings: the exact same as the cat in the photo we saw at Ginger's apartment. You said it was Veronica with Harry."

"Alice, similar markings are very common in calico cats."

"But look at her, Jo," I pleaded.

Jo looked closely, then sat back. "Alice," she said quietly, "this photograph was probably taken around 1981 or 1982."

"So what?"

"Well, Veronica is about three years old now. She was born in 1985. I remember when she was born. It was a small litter."

I had been so excited when I found the picture that I hadn't even considered Veronica's age.

"It could be Veronica's mother," Jo continued, "who was

also a calico, if I recall. But how could she have gotten to Maryland? Those cats never left our barn. And Ginger worked in Maryland as an exercise rider before she came to Long Island. No, Alice, it's just another calico cat. And even if it was Veronica's mother—so what?"

I shook my head grimly. I had been so struck by the strange duplication of Ginger and a calico cat that I hadn't considered that someone else would shrug it off. For the past two days I had been adding up facts. Ginger had been an exercise rider for a very famous horse. Subsequently, though, she had become a stable girl on a basically nonworking farm for less than minimum wage. Wasn't that very strange? Now, however, it seemed as though I had gone off half-cocked.

Jo reached across the table, patted me gently on the arm, and said: "It's just a picture of a horse and his mascot, who happens to be a calico cat. All horses have stable companions, Alice. They live with the horses, travel with the horses, play with the horses. Sometimes a horse will go crazy or just lie down and die if its mascot is killed or runs away. Most are dogs or cats, but racehorses have had goats, pigeons, canaries, turtles—and God knows what else—as companions. I once had a carriage horse named Sam who wouldn't step out of his stall unless he was accompanied by a three-legged black cat who lived in the stall with him."

The waitress brought our coffee and placed the piece of chocolate cake equidistant between us, along with two glistening forks. Jo handed the photograph back to me. I slipped it into my bag.

"It is very good to see you," Jo said.

I smiled and nodded to show her the feeling was reciprocal. Just then I noticed a funny glint in Jo's eye, and I wondered if she knew that Charlie Coombs and I had become lovers. She probably knew, I realized, but was too discreet to say anything unless I brought it up.

"Listen, Alice, can you come out to Long Island tomorrow?"

"Why?"

"There's an auction of Mona Aspen's house furnishings and her paintings and . . . everything. She has a beautiful house."

The change in subject caught me by surprise, and I didn't respond.

"Come out, Alice. You'll love her house. I don't want to go there alone. And besides, Mona would have wanted me to make sure some of her things didn't get into the wrong hands. We can spend some of Harry's money to make sure some of them get a good home. Say you'll come. I'll pick you up at the Hicksville station at the usual time."

"I'll come," I said, caught up by her enthusiasm. I also wanted very much for our friendship to flourish again without the two-hundred dollars a day.

We played with our coffee in silence for a while. Then I asked her, "Have the police found out anything new?"

"Nothing. Whenever I ask them, they say they're still investigating. I ask them what they're investigating. They say they're trying to trace the stolen valuables from a nonexistent inventory list. I don't know who dislikes whom more. But it was my husband who was murdered."

"Have you learned anything new, Jo?"

Jo arched her eyes. "Why would you ask me that, Alice? After all, I took your advice. Remember? You told me I should forget everything and just live."

There was an awkward silence.

"But I couldn't find it," Jo said.

"Find what?" I asked, thoroughly confused.

Jo suddenly began to search frantically under her napkin, under her cup, and then under the table.

"Find what?" I asked again, now concerned about the old woman's bizarre behavior.

Jo relaxed and grinned. "Life, Alice, life. The life you told me to live."

We both laughed so loudly at the joke that the waitress threw us disapproving glances.

Mona Aspen's house was indeed beautiful. Originally an eighteenth-century farmhouse, of which the kitchen, hallway, and dining room were still extant, it had been extended several times, and even its modern wing retained a colonial feel. Jo and I wandered from room to room, staring at the lamps and chairs and rugs, each of which were tagged with the same kind of yellow cardboard on which an auctioneer's code was inscribed. A strange man in a black hat handed each of us a descriptive catalog of the house's contents with prices.

Jo seemed to want to touch everything, to gather everything in, as if she was the sole trusted guardian of her late friend's sensibility. Other people came and went, some greeting Jo, some just walking by with a smile and a nod.

"I'm going to have to sit for a while," Jo said finally. Spotting an armchair by the fireplace, I guided Jo over to it.

She said, once she was seated, "I keep forgetting that you never were in her house before. You were in the stable area that time. Well, you ought to look at Mona's bedroom. It's really beautiful. And I'll take a nap here."

I hadn't taken three steps away from her when Detective Senay slipped out of an alcove, oddly light-footed for such a large man.

"Well, well, the cat lady," he said. I didn't like the inflection of his voice. And I didn't like the way he had moved right next to me, violating the space that was necessary to maintain a conversation. That, I realized, was one of the reasons I had always disliked him—his willingness to get too close physically. I wondered whether it was a trick of the trade he had learned while interrogating suspects. Did he consider me a suspect?

I smiled and started to move on.

"I made some inquiries about you," he said.

I stopped and turned. "Inquiries?"

"Well," he said, "not really. Let's just say I spoke to some people out in Suffolk County and they said you interfered with a homicide case at Stony Brook."

"No, Detective, you and your friends have it all wrong. I didn't interfere. I just taught them the difference between suicide and homicide. They didn't seem to know the difference."

He didn't like what I said. I don't blame him. But he had

started it. "God save us from another dilettante. Tell me, do you have a psychic approach to crime?"

"Right," I said with an equivalent dose of sarcasm. "I solve murders by dissecting birds and reading their innards."

"Birds sound like your speed. Anyway, you may be interested in knowing that two kids in Manhasset tried to sell an eighteenth-century silver tea service that may have come from the Starobin place."

He grinned and started to walk away.

"Wait," I said.

"You want to tell me something?" he asked.

"Yes. I want to tell you that you're crazy if you think Harry Starobin and Mona Aspen were murdered by thieves looking for silverware."

He winked at me as if I was some kind of pathetic eccentric. He strolled off.

It took me a few minutes to compose myself after he walked away, but then I acted on Jo's instructions. I located a long hall which led to a parlor and then to a staircase which, I thought while ascending, had to lead to a dank, dark attic but which instead ended abruptly in an enormous bedroom flooded with light.

It took my breath away. For a moment I longed to be out of the city for good, to live in a room like Mona's. I could envision Bushy and Pancho staring for hours out the room's many windows in feline bliss as the squirrels and the birds danced on the tree limbs before their eyes.

Then I began to inspect the room. The furniture was old and simple and low—oak and cherrywood. The four-poster bed was tiny and fragile, graced by two frayed and no-longer-bright comforters. One of them had a sunflower design.

On the longest wall two oil paintings of horses hung side by side. Between the windows on the shorter walls hung bird prints, mostly waterfowl. One of them was a magnificent print of a loon, done in deep dull purple and black. Like the other rooms in the house, all the items in Mona Aspen's bedroom were also yellow-tagged.

"Pretty, isn't it?"

The voice came from the stairs.

I whirled toward it. Mona's nephew, Nicholas Hill, was standing at the top of the stairs. His sudden appearance frightened me. For a moment I remembered that feathered hat on Fifth Avenue. Or had it been someone else? He wasn't wearing a feathered hat now. He was wearing nothing peculiar except for a very old-fashioned tie with some kind of insignia on it.

I fought back my fear, telling myself it was stupid. Why did I think he would harm me? Did I think he was the one who had driven that pickup truck? Jo had said he was a heavy gambler, but that didn't mean he would murder his aunt. I remembered how grief-stricken he had been after his aunt's death. I remembered how he and Jo had embraced spontaneously over their loss.

He walked into the room toward one of the windows, and his slow, almost lumbering gait kept me on edge. Weren't gamblers supposed to be chipper, nervous little men? For a moment I caught myself measuring his build, wondering if he could hang people on door hooks. But no, that was silly.

If he had been following me that day on Fifth Avenue—if

the hat with the feather in it had been his—then maybe he was in the room now to finish something. His hands seemed even more powerful to me than when I had first met him in the barn, cleaning a shovel.

"Do you like those?" he asked, pointing at the two horse paintings.

I looked at the paintings again. For the first time I noticed that the space next to one of the paintings was slightly paler. A third painting had obviously hung on the wall there. Had it been sold?

"Yes, I like them, but I doubt if I could afford either one," I replied. "Or those waterfowl prints."

Nicholas nodded and edged closer to the paintings. "My aunt loved these paintings. They were done by Becker. He painted those horses as they were chewing grass in the big field behind the second barn."

"They were your aunt's horses?" I asked.

"Oh, God, no. These are famous racehorses. The first one is Lord Kelvin. The other one is Ask Me No Questions. Both are multiple-stakes winners. Mona just took care of them for a while. One had a bucked shin. The other . . . I forget. Mona nursed them back to health. When they got back to the race-track, they did nothing but win."

He shoved his hands into his pockets angrily and turned, as if he had committed a felony by reminiscing. "But, as I think I told you before," he continued, "my aunt only liked wounded things. So once they got better, she couldn't have cared less."

He was very close to me now and I began to feel apprehensive once again. I heard the sound of footsteps on the stairs. Then the steps reversed themselves and the sounds vanished.

"I have to get back to Jo," I said.

"Then go," he retorted bitterly, as if I was betraying him in some manner. I slipped past him and down the steps.

By the time I finished accompanying Jo throughout the rest of the house, I was totally exhausted. I was sorry I had agreed to come out, even though I knew that Jo had considered it a reinstatement of the friendship. I begged off on Jo's request that I come back to the Starobin house, so she dropped me reluctantly at the Long Island Rail Road station.

As the train left Hicksville station I pulled out a paperback copy of *Romeo and Juliet*, promising myself that I'd use the train ride to give some serious consideration to Carla Fried's offer to play the Nurse. But I got only as far as Act I, Scene ii, before I shut my eyes. I started to doze, then woke, then dozed again.

When the train reached Jamaica, I sat up with a start, looking around desperately. Should I change trains? The conductor assured me it was a through train to Manhattan. I relaxed and realized that while I was dozing I had dreamed about those two horses whose paintings had hung in Mona's bedroom.

What were their names? I reached into my coat pocket and pulled out the auctioneer's list that had been handed to me the moment I entered the house. I ran down the paintings for sale. There they were, at forty-seven hundred dollars each! *Lord Kelvin* and *Ask Me No Questions*.

What funny names racehorses are given! I was about to

crumple and throw the list away when I remembered the empty space on the wall next to the two paintings, where obviously another painting had once hung.

Curious, I looked at the next entry. Superimposed over the name was a rubber-stamped SOLD.

The third painting on the wall was *Cup of Tea.*

13

At noon the next day, Charlie Coombs called. It had been a good week for him. His horses were winning. He wanted to come early and buy me an opulent dinner. I suggested an Indian restaurant in the area. He said that he had never eaten Indian food in his life, but for me he'd do anything.

He came over at four and we sat around and talked to each other, then talked to the cats, then made love, and then went out to eat.

It was one of those small Indian restaurants on Lexington Avenue. The outside was innocuous, but inside was a bizarre profusion of colors: black candles, pink tablecloths, gaily patterned flower plates. Charlie studied the menu carefully, almost compulsively, but he was obviously not really interested in the food.

It was odd. I could understand his relationship to me much better than I could understand my relationship to him. I knew how I impinged on his life. But there it stopped.

Being with me, in any mode, exhilarated him. I turned him into an adolescent.

He wanted to do much more with me than just make love to me—but he couldn't bring that "more" off. He sensed that I was distant, always distant, and that I would fade away because he was essentially without the substance that bonds permanently. And he needed me forever. I elicited a kind of adolescent inferiority in him, which may or may not have been warranted. I had no idea of his worth even if I could measure such a thing in a man.

He wanted to tell me about his life, his work, his hates . . . but he always pulled back. There was always the thought that I wouldn't truly be interested . . . that I was beyond him . . . thinking other thoughts.

I knew that he loved my body, my face, my long hair, the way I cocked my head before I spoke, the way my face became blank during rapid mood swings which I couldn't control. I knew he wanted to ravage me and protect me at the same time. Poor, desperate, kindly man. I knew he hallucinated that I was aging with just the right mix of head and heart—like good horses age.

I knew all of that—but I knew little about how his feelings for me impacted on me. And what I did know I could not articulate.

Charlie decided on a dish with lamb and spinach. And a mango drink.

I selected an assortment of breads and small appetizers and avoided a main dish.

It felt good sitting across from him. I appreciated his harmless affectations, one of which was dressing like a hayseed horse trainer—short denim jacket under which were a dress shirt and tie, light-colored flannel pants, and his red sneakers.

"I have some more horse questions for you," I said after we had both ordered and settled in.

"Shoot. That's my business."

"Did you ever hear of a horse called Lord Kelvin?"

"Sure. One of my horses ran against him in Philadelphia Park—the Keystone Stakes, a seven-furlong race. Lord Kelvin won, my horse came in sixth."

"Is there anything peculiar about the horse?"

"Peculiar? What do you mean?"

"I mean like Cup of Tea—a rags-to-riches story."

"That I don't know," Charlie said, adding, "Lord Kelvin was just a good stakes horse, not a 'horse of the year.' I don't even know if he's still racing."

Other couples were beginning to enter the restaurant. A low, gentle buzz surrounded us.

"What about Ask Me No Questions?"

Charlie arched his eyebrows. He was a bit confused by those names coming out of the mouth of a lady who didn't know a thing about the racetrack.

"A pretty horse. A filly, a big gray filly, about sixteen hands high. She used to run in Gulfstream Park, in Florida. A stakes horse, she won a big filly race two years ago when she shipped into Belmont."

"Anything strange about her?"

"Other than her color, nothing at all that I know of. I remember that she didn't do well as a two-year-old; she didn't even break her maiden until she was four years old. But then she turned out real good. Billy Patchen trained her."

I nodded and concentrated for a moment on one of the appetizers which the waiter had just brought. I could sense that my casualness in stopping and starting the questioning was beginning to infuriate Charlie. He always wanted total disclosure. But there was nothing I could do. I was groping for information and I didn't even know what kind of information.

"Should I know more?"

I smiled at him but didn't speak.

"Hell," he said, his irritation rising, "I don't know much. I don't even know where you were all day yesterday. I tried to call you for eight hours straight."

My fork hung in midair. I had never heard him so upset before.

"I guess," he continued sarcastically, "that I'm not supposed to know about the travels of Alice Nestleton. I mean, after all, all we do is sleep together."

I put the fork down and stared at it.

Why had he used the word "travels"?

Had he *known* that I had been out to Long Island for the auction of Mona Aspen's furnishings?

How could he have known?

Had he really tried to get me for eight hours, or was that just a cover for his knowledge?

What if Charlie Coombs was not who he pretended to be—just my lover? It was odd that he had arrived at the same time—the exact same time—I had begun investigating Harry Starobin's murder. And it was very possible that he had known Ginger Mauch a lot better than he claimed . . . maybe as well as old Harry knew her.

"I'd like you to answer me," Charlie said in a low but threatening voice.

What if the whole affair between Charlie and myself had been orchestrated to keep watch on me?

Or to deflect my interest in the murders?

I could not dispel the growing horror I felt that Charlie Coombs was somehow tied to the whole mess—to the deaths of Harry Starobin and Mona Aspen.

The appetizers lay in a semicircle in front of me. They now looked uniformly loathsome.

"If you don't give me the dignity of a goddamn answer, Alice, I'm walking out of here and you'll never see me again."

I thought: Answer? What was the question?

His voice had started to quake with fury, and perhaps shame.

I couldn't look at him. But I felt him. It was as if he had grown larger and larger; as if he was hovering over the table—over . . . under . . . behind. I closed my eyes. Then I could feel him inside of me . . . in a sexual sense . . . as if we were making love. I could feel a kind of synchronicity, like the rhythm of love. For a moment I hated him more than I had ever hated anyone in my life. For a moment I loved him, as if my life hinged on his every move. It was a crazy few minutes. For the first time since I had known him, I was reciprocating, unconsciously, his passion. But it was all about betrayal.

"Walk," I said, smiling grimly at my fork.

And he did.

14

I stared at the contents of the tall closet in the hallway, the one that contained all my clothes. A depression was coming on, I could feel it—one of those bone-crushing, brain-deadening depressions that turn limbs and will to jelly. I had to get out of the house—to be among people.

Hour after hour I had been analyzing the breakup with Charlie Coombs. But it was too exhausting and too confusing. Of course I knew that I had provoked it by my attitude, and my attitude in turn had originated in my fear and suspicion that he was part of the conspiracy. My attitude alone, however, could not account for gentle, kindly, mature Charlie Coombs's sudden transformation into an abusive, jealous lover.

It was as if someone else had popped out of his body full-blown, like a moth. I didn't want any part of the new Charlie Coombs, under any conditions.

I pulled out of the closet a long white lace Blanche DuBois

kind of dress. I pulled from a box on top of the closet a wide-brimmed floppy hat with a black ribbon around the crown. From the bottom of the closet I pulled a pair of red leather shoes.

It was six thirty in the evening when I stepped out in my antidepression wardrobe, and I had hardly gone a block when the stares of passersby enlightened me to the fact that I was dressed oddly for my age and for the season. It was a young woman's outfit to be worn on a very hot day. The stares didn't deter me. I had a destination, a new restaurant on Twenty-third Street called Brights.

I had never been in there before. I couldn't even conceive of a single reason why I would go in there. But to fight a depression that is about to engulf you, one is forced into very strange alliances.

Brights was done in the latest minimal style; very brightly lit, much space between wooden tables. All of it was done in hard-edged style which was designed to do something, but that something was never articulated. And interspersed in all that minimal confusion, like peaches on a dessert, were a few garish wall paintings.

When I entered I saw that the end of the bar was crowded with people and the other end was empty. I slipped onto a stool midway between the extremes, removed my hat, and placed it on the stool next to me.

The bartender, a young man with well-coiffed red hair and an open white shirt, placed a napkin in front of me and smiled. The name of the restaurant was embossed on one corner of the napkin. In fact, everywhere I turned, I saw the name embossed—on the matches, on the stirring sticks, on the clocks.

"A glass of red wine," I said. Wine keeps ugly depressions an inch away. Brandy is for anxiety, but wine is for depression. It is like a yellow light in the subway.

The wine was served in a glass so huge that a full regular glass of wine would fill only one-third of this jumbo goblet. I sipped it. I listened to the laughter from the crowded end of the bar. I stared out onto the street traffic. I watched the bartender ply his trade.

When I had finished the wine, I began to relax. The danger was receding. As I ordered another glass, I noticed the empty end of the bar was filling up with men and women who obviously were stopping off after work. Who were they? Where did they work? Where did they live? I didn't know. They carried briefcases . . . they carried small posh shopping bags . . . they carried small, well-wrapped umbrellas . . . and they carried all kinds of crimes in their hearts. The last notion made me giggle a bit. It was poetic. Crimes in the heart.

Just then two old neighborhood men came in and sat beside me. What were they doing in a posh bar like Brights? Had they lost their way? Did they also need the Brights cure for depression? I removed my hat from the bar stool. One of them gallantly carried the hat to a rack behind the cashier.

I began to concentrate on what to do next. The idea of going back to the libraries with their infernal microfilm machines in order to track down information on Lord Kelvin and Ask Me No Questions as I had done with Cup of Tea made me ill. And besides, Cup of Tea had been a media star. From what Charlie Coombs had told me about the other two horses, that certainly wasn't the case.

I needed someone who knew the racetrack and horses. Charlie Coombs was out of my life now, and besides, he could no longer be trusted. Nor could Nicholas Hill. And Jo, well, I just didn't want the old woman and her newfound money involved anymore.

I stared at the second glass of wine. Was Ginger watching me and laughing at me? I grimaced at the thought.

An argument erupted at one end of the bar, and I heard a woman yell at the man seated beside her. "Don't tell me what he said. I attended the workshop, not you!"

Even as I tried to shut out the quarrel, the word "workshop" stuck in my mind and jangled there. God, it was so nice to hear that word again. How long had it been since I attended a workshop? Then a particular name popped into my head: the Dramatic Workshop. I had studied there under Saul Colin in 1970 or 1971.

Then I remembered Anthony Basillio, their stage designer. He used to bet on horses all the time. I sat back, awed at the strange way things are recalled which seem to have been lost forever. Yes, of course, crazy, wonderful Anthony Basillio would help me. I had met him at a seminar on Brecht at the Dramatic Workshop. The visiting lecturer had been none other than Erwin Piscator, the former director of Brecht's Berliner Ensemble. He was an old, brilliant, difficult man.

Basillio had sat behind me in the seminar. He was tall and skinny, with very bad skin. He was also very funny. Once he brought his cat, Fats, to the seminar in a paper shopping bag, the meanest-looking, most powerfully built alley cat I ever saw. A no-neck, low-slung beastie who was ready to claw. But Anthony told the class not to worry. Fats was really a pussycat. And besides, he was the only cat in Manhattan who could write rock lyrics and pick winners at the racetrack.

I laughed out loud at the memory, then realized the two old men were staring at me. I sipped my wine sheepishly.

The seminars, I remembered, were held at the old Dramatic Workshop studios on Fifty-first Street and Broadway, over the Capitol Theatre, and afterward a lot of us used to go to a bar on Eighth Avenue.

It was a time of great ferment in the New York theater world. Radical theater groups of all kinds were rising and falling. The seminar itself had reflected that diversity— academics, Broadway showgirls, directors, stagehands, technicians, famous actors and unknowns, junkies, critics, reviewers. All kinds of people with all kinds of agendas attended. It was that kind of time.

In the bar after the seminar, Anthony used to emote on how he was working on a series of stage designs for *Mother Courage* that would change the way the world perceived Brecht. And sometimes he would have a lot of money on him and buy everyone drinks and cheeseburgers and tell us how he had won the money playing the horses. He used to brag that the only way he could support his theater habit was to make it at the racetrack.

Once he had become very difficult and started a fight, and we were all thrown out of the bar. After the next meeting of the seminar he had apologized and said he often acted stupid because in a past life he had been a racehorse and everyone knew that racehorses were stupid because they got the same food whether they won a race or not.

Basillio would know about Lord Kelvin and Ask Me No Questions.

I paid the bartender and rushed out. A block away I realized I had forgotten my hat. I started to go back, then decided to pick it up another time.

Once in the apartment, I started to pace, trying to remember who had known Anthony Basillio then and who would know where he was now. I grabbed a pad and the telephone book and sat down by the phone.

First, names from the past: actors, actresses, directors, producers, teachers—names I hadn't thought of in years but which now came grudgingly out of the stubby pencil at first, then faster. The names first, then the faces, then the memories.

Ordinarily I would have been too reticent to call these people out of the blue, but now I had no problem at all. Just dial. And dial again. Some were delighted to hear from me. They wanted to make conversation, fill in the years, meet for lunch. Many had unlisted phones and could not be reached. Others gave me numbers of others who might be able to help.

But no one in this widening net of reemerging memories knew what had happened to Anthony Basillio, if, in fact, they had known him at all.

I stared at the clock. I had been on the phone continuously for two hours. My hand was cramped. My throat was hoarse. Each phone call, each opening line, was getting more difficult: "Hello, you may not remember me. My name is Alice Nestleton."

Then the inevitable silence, followed by: "My God—Alice. It has been so long."

At nine thirty I gave myself six more calls. On the third, I reached Winslow Jarvis, a gay man who had been part of the original Dionysus '69 group on Wooster Street. He said that of course he knew Anthony Basillio, but he hadn't seen him in years. He had heard that Basillio now owned a chain of small xerox places in the Village and the Lower East Side. He said the stores had a stupid name, something from Brecht.

"Mother Courage?" I asked.

"Right," he said.

I thanked him and hung up. That Anthony Basillio now ran a chain of small copier stores struck me as one of the saddest things I had ever heard in my life.

15

When I was a child, my grandmother had a house cat named Peter who would refuse to eat food off a plate. My grandmother was quite proud of him, saying that because he wouldn't eat off a plate, he could be trusted. It always struck me as odd logic, but that was the kind of feeling I had always had about Anthony Basillio.

Anyway, I started out to find him. The closest branch of the Mother Courage copier chain was on Second Avenue and Third Street. No, the girl behind the counter said, Mr. Basillio's office is in the Sixth Avenue store—at Prince.

I arrived there about eleven thirty. It was a larger store, and in the rear was a complex of small offices and cubicles. Three or four young men were behind the counter, servicing a continuous flow of customers. The copy machines, all sizes and makes, were humming.

I stood off to one side to distinguish myself from the rest of the customers and finally was approached by one of the clerks, who was wearing an absurd leather apron, as if he were an old-fashioned printer. It was, I recalled, the same kind of apron I had seen Jo wearing on that dismal morning we learned that Mona Aspen had been murdered. But when Jo had worn it I had thought it was a blacksmith's apron.

"Can I help you, miss?"

"I'm looking for Anthony Basillio."

"He's not in."

"Can I wait?"

"To tell you the truth, miss, Mr. Basillio has gone for the day."

"What about tomorrow?" I asked.

"Look, miss, if you really want to see him," the clerk said, exasperated, "you have to get here early. He leaves every day at about eleven for the racetrack, and he doesn't show up again until the next morning."

He paused, smiled at me, and added, "He doesn't have to. He's the boss."

I thanked him and left, promising that I would be back the next morning. He stared at me blankly.

I spent the next twenty-four hours wrapped, metaphorically, in a tourniquet—tense, tight, restricted. I could not proceed without Basillio, and it was necessary to proceed. I went to a movie. I read a few scenes from a Jean Genet play. I groomed Bushy and chased Pancho. I thought of Charlie Coombs with regret and then anger; of Harry Starobin with a kind of bitter adolescent longing; and of Jo Starobin with warmth. It was an exhausting, nerve-racking day that vanished very slowly.

At eight forty-five the next morning, I stood once again in front of the counter of the flagship Mother Courage copy shop. The clerk with the leather apron remembered me, raised one section of the counter, and waved me through—pointing to a specific office in the back. The door was open. A man sat at a desk, his chair turned to the window. Hearing my footsteps, he wheeled around.

"My God, the Swede!" He jumped out of his chair.

I smiled and held out my hand. He had always called me Swede after he found out I was from Minnesota, even though I had told him a hundred times that I wasn't of Swedish descent. It was just one of his stereotypical Hollywood affectations.

Basillio really hadn't changed at all, except for his graying hair and worse posture. He was still thin. His skin was still bad. His smile was still wicked, as if he was perpetually contemplating some kind of mayhem.

"Look, Alice," he said in a mock-serious tone, putting his arm around me and guiding me to a chair, "I refused to sleep with you then and I refuse to sleep with you now. So, do you still want to visit, or are you too brokenhearted?"

I laughed until the tears welled up in my eyes. He represented an old and treasured time for me—when the theater had been much more than just a precarious profession, when it had still been a kind of religious vocation.

"I see your name around, Swede, but not all that much."

"No, not all that much," I agreed.

"But at least you're still in it . . . and you never went show-biz," he noted with an appreciative smirk.

"I tried," I replied. And we both laughed hugely at this most hoary of all acting-class insults. We felt an enormous kindness toward each other.

"Remember what the master said," Anthony cautioned.

"Which master?"

"Which master? There's only one, Swede. Bert Brecht. He said, 'Don't let them lure you into exhaustion and despair.'"

"I see they haven't."

"Nor will they," he affirmed.

"Tony, I didn't come here to talk to you about Brecht or the theater. It took me a hundred calls to find you. I need help."

Basillio's eyes narrowed at the word "help."

"I need information on horses."

"Horses?" he asked, astonished.

"Racehorses."

"You mean you want me to give you tips?"

"No. Information on their personal lives."

"Whose personal lives?"

"The horses'."

"Racehorses don't have personal lives. They run and they die."

"Cup of Tea did."

"Cup of Tea was special."

"I'm writing a book on Cup of Tea," I said, using that convenient fabrication, "and I need information on his contemporaries. Not betting information—other kinds. I just broke up with a trainer named Charlie Coombs."

"I know of him," Basillio said, interrupting.

I continued. "So now that Charlie is gone from my life, I need someone who can talk horse talk."

"Maybe, Swede, you'll just have to hop into bed with another trainer. I mean, they're the only ones who really know horses' breeding and conformation and potential. All I know is what I pick up from other gamblers—crazy stuff that may or may not be true. Like how the horse can't run if the temperature gets over eighty degrees or if he likes beer in his feed or that the horse is really crazy unless a lady jock climbs on his back. That kind of stuff."

"That's what I want, Tony," I said, realizing that my lies were now spiraling. Charlie and I had never talked about horses—except for the first and last times we were together.

He whirled around on his chair. "Swede, if there was one woman on earth on whom I would have happily bet my wife, my kiddies, and all my copying stores that she would have never gotten involved with the racetrack, it was you. You were always too elegant, too goddamn classy. Or maybe, at most, a three-day trip to Saratoga in August with a rich lover to watch the horses run in between ballets."

He was starting to sound like my ex-husband.

"Believe me, Tony," I said, "it's not a willing involvement. This book I'm writing is a debt."

"Bookmakers?"

"No, the dead."

"The dead?" he repeated softly.

"I want to find out all the information I can about Lord Kelvin and Ask Me No Questions."

"Forget the first horse."

"Lord Kelvin? Why?"

"He's dead. Lord Kelvin was killed in a freak vanning accident in Pennsylvania about a year ago. I know because I met this guy at the track who told me he saw a small notice about it in a Philadelphia paper. He mentioned it to me because we both had made some money on that horse."

I wondered why Charlie had never told me that when I asked him about Lord Kelvin. Was it possible he didn't know?

"That leaves Ask Me No Questions," I noted.

"I've seen her run," Anthony replied. "Look, just give me a few days."

I wrote my number on his desk pad. I remembered, as I was writing, that I had done the exact same thing at the racetrack when I first met Charlie. "Thanks," I said, standing up.

"Wait, Swede," he called out with a touch of panic in his voice.

I turned back to him.

"Aren't you going to tell me how sad this all is, Swede? The Mother Courage copier shops instead of the Mother Courage stage sets? Aren't you going to say how goddamn pathetic it all turned out?"

"No," I replied. There was silence. "You told me once in a bar, after a seminar," I reminded him, "that when all was said and done, gambling was your only passion."

"I lied," he said.

I wanted to leave. I didn't know what to say. Basillio picked up on my discomfort and said, "Remember when I brought my cat, Fats, to the seminar in a shopping bag?" We both laughed so loud the customers in the front of the store were startled and peered past the counter toward us.

I went home and waited for Basillio to call. That he would call, that he would give me information I required, was never in doubt. He was a blast from the past, and the past is always good.

Sure enough, he called me two days later. He said he was going to the racetrack, but he would meet me in front of the Plaza Hotel at eight that evening and buy me seven dozen littleneck clams, three dozen cherrystones, nine brandies, and a piece of cheesecake in his favorite place—the Oyster Bar.

"Can't we meet in a coffee shop somewhere?" I asked.

His voice was happy, playful, manic: "Don't provoke me, Swede. It's the Plaza or nothing."

At seven forty-five I was standing in front of the Plaza Hotel. I felt stupid and ill-at-ease; I had provoked another male into adolescent gestures. I was wearing jeans and a sweater, just to be perverse, I imagine.

He arrived a half-hour late, flushed, excited. Grabbing my arm in a tight grip, he led me up the steps of the hotel, across the lobby, and then into the Oyster Bar by the back entrance, where we were seated by a man who looked like he had survived prewar Vienna only by the skin of his domed head.

"Look at the bar, Swede. Don't you love it? It's square. I mean, did you ever see another bar with corners?"

Once we were sitting across from each other, I could tell that he had been drinking before he met me.

"How did you do at the racetrack?"

"I lost heavy."

"Easy come, easy go," I said by way of a gentle criticism.

He smiled at me. He ordered clams and brandy and ale. "So," he said after it was all settled, "what I found out, you probably already know."

"Try me," I said.

"Right. Ask Me No Questions was a big, hard-running gray filly. Not much breeding, but she ended up a multiple-stakes winner."

"Like Cup of Tea," I said, remembering that Charlie had told me there was absolutely no similarity.

"Sort of, but not really," Anthony hedged, staring at the two plates of beautiful littlenecks and one plate of cherrystones. He began to prepare them carefully—lemon, horseradish, a tiny dollop of hot sauce.

He explained, "No one ever went from nowhere as far and as fast as Cup of Tea. He went from a dirt track to become the world's champion grass horse and sire. Ask Me No Questions never started that low or went so high. She won grade-two stakes at best, not the Arlington Million like Cup of Tea."

"But something did happen. I mean, there *was* a transformation, wasn't there?"

"Right. Something sure as hell happened. She lost her first twelve races. They sent her back to the farm. She came back as a four-year-old, lost six more races; then went back to the farm with another injury. The next time she raced, four months later, she won an allowance race by ten lengths at odds of sixty-five to one. And she kept on winning."

I sat back, exhausted suddenly by the realization that I had at least put one firm piece into the puzzle. "Thank you," I said.

He grinned at me wickedly and pushed the clams across the table. The one I ate was cold, tart, delicious.

"Do you want to see her?" he asked.

"Of course! Can I see her?" It had never dawned on me that I would have access to Ask Me No Questions.

Triumphantly he pulled a small piece of paper out of his shirt pocket, unfolded it, and slid it across the table to me the same way he had slid the clams. It read: "James Norris Stables, Far Hills, New Jersey."

"They retired Ask Me No Questions to become a brood mare. But there was something wrong with her. She couldn't conceive, and when she finally did, she couldn't deliver a live foal. So they sold her to that stable in Far Hills. They're going to make a Grand Prix show jumper out of her—you know, going over seven-foot fences for ten thousand dollars first-prize money contributed by Volvo or BMW. For all I know, she's a jumper by now."

"You told me what I need to know," I said thankfully.

"I wish you'd stop thanking me, Swede. After all, I'm not a happily married man and you're going to damage what remains of my libido. Besides, you don't think for a minute that I believe all that nonsense about you writing a book on Cup of Tea."

I was barely listening to him now. An absurd little ditty was bouncing around my head:

Three little racehorses
Hanging on a wall
Two hung straight
But the third took a fall

I wasn't finished with Anthony yet. "Did anyone mention to you an exercise rider named Ginger Mauch?"

"You mean someone who used to ride Ask Me No Questions?"

"Yes."

"Never heard the name. But, then again, exercise riders are anonymous unless they're name jockeys and doing a favor for the trainer. Is this Ginger a jockey?"

"No," I answered, trying a cherrystone this time, remembering that Dr. Johnson used to feed oysters to his cat. I started wondering if Bushy and Pancho would like clams, speculating how best to remove them in their half shells from the Plaza.

Basillio started a monologue about how the racetrack was the closest thing around to Brecht's conception of theater. The brandy was obviously getting to him.

"How do I get out to Far Hills?" I asked him.

"By car. Take the George Washington Bridge. Then some kind of highway you pick up there—84 or 80 or 287—I forget which."

I began to look around for the first time since I had sat down. There were only out-of-town faces, like mine had been so many years ago.

"Do you know what, Swede?" Basillio asked, now desperately trying to get a waiter's attention for coffee.

"What?"

"I think you're going to ask me to do you another favor. So, before you ask, I'm going to offer it. Not because I'm a good guy or anything like that, but because it was so damn wonderful to see you again and I don't want it to be another seventeen years before we see each other again. So, I'll take you to Jersey. No big deal. I live in New Jersey—Fort Lee. I'll take you to see Ask Me No Questions."

⌘

"You going to interview the horse with a tape recorder?" Basillio asked, chuckling.

I nodded absentmindedly, staring out the window of the late-model Pontiac. Actually, I didn't know why I was driving out to see the horse. But I was going. For that was the way the thing was developing. One tiny, stupid step at a time. Ask Me No Questions was a real live thing that I could see and touch, not a painting on a wall or a photograph in a book. I was going to see a horse.

Basillio started asking me theater questions—about old friends and colleagues: Where was L? What about R?

I answered the best I could. The traffic was thinning. The motion of the car soothed me. Basillio was a good driver, fast and safe. Snatches of a poem I had studied in school came to me: "That's my last Duchess painted on the wall." Was it Browning?

A little more than an hour after we crossed the George Washington Bridge, we pulled up to the Norris stables. The place was a large complex with indoor and outdoor rings and dozens of young girls standing around with riding helmets and whips. There were jump courses on which classes were being held, and a steady stream of lathered horses being led from ring to stable.

"Well, it isn't Belmont Park," Basillio said.

We parked the car and entered the main office.

A tall, elderly man wearing a sheepskin vest greeted us. I proceeded with my fiction, slanting it a bit: I was writing a book on lady racehorses who had beaten the boys. I wanted to take a look at Ask Me No Questions, who had done just that many times.

The man smiled and said, "She's going to beat the boys in the jumping ring also."

Basillio whispered in my ear, "You keep changing your story about what kind of book you're writing. Why don't you stick to one story?"

I ignored his comment. The elderly man leafed through some index cards and then said, "She's being schooled now on course number three. Why don't you take a walk over?"

He led us to a window and pointed out the path to the course.

As we headed that way, I began to search the faces that passed us. Would Ginger be here? Was that why I had come?

When we reached the course, a large gray horse was being led over very small jumps at a very slow pace. Most she took easily, hesitating just a bit when she was forced to jump after coming out of a tight turn. The girl on her back encouraged her, crooned to her, patted her neck constantly. Then the rider pulled up, slid off, and started to lead Ask Me No Questions out of the ring.

"What a beautiful lady," Basillio whispered in awe.

I could not respond. I, too, was mesmerized by the rippling, delicate, gathered beauty of the mare. But I felt something else: I was finally about to make contact in some way with the ashes of Harry Starobin.

My hands were trembling as I told my story to the rider, a chunky girl of about twenty, who then invited us both back to the barn, a bit proud that someone was going to put Ask Me No Questions in a book.

As we all walked back together, Ask Me No Questions playfully swung her head and hit Basillio on the chest.

"She's paying me back for the time I bet against her," he said.

As we reached the entrance of the large barn where she was stabled, Ask Me No Questions suddenly stopped, planted her feet, and would go no farther. The girl smacked her on the rear end. But Ask Me No Questions would not budge.

"Hell," said the girl, "I forgot that she won't go in until Marjorie comes out."

"Who is Marjorie?" Basillio asked.

The girl laughed. "You'll see. Oh, here she comes."

As we waited there, sweat started beading on my face. It will be Ginger, I thought, here she comes!

"There's Marjorie," the girl said happily, and the horse moved forward.

Lumbering out in front of the barn, yawning, was a large, beautiful calico cat.

16

I showed the wine bottle to Bushy, as if I was a waiter and the cat was a patron. Bushy ignored it. I opened it quickly and poured myself a glass of good Bordeaux—a St. Emilion.

The wine was for my confusion. I sat down on the sofa, my legs drawn tightly together. The search had ended in a calico cat named Marjorie strolling out of the barn. Ginger had not been there. Of course she hadn't. Why had I ever thought she would? Only a calico cat. And a different calico cat from the one in the Cup of Tea photo, which in turn had been a different calico cat from Veronica the barn cat, according to Jo. Just a calico cat. A horse's mascot.

I went into the kitchen, opened the refrigerator, took out some St. André cheese, and spread it on a rice cake. Pancho was high on a cabinet, staring down at me. He loved cheese.

I walked back to the living room and ate the snack, staring out the window onto the street.

"Poor Ginger," I muttered. I put the wineglass down on

the sill, stiffening a bit. Why had that popped out? Lately I had found myself muttering out loud from time to time. But usually it was "poor Harry" or "poor Jo." Why in God's name would I suddenly be feeling sympathy for Ginger Mauch. Ginger was the enemy. Wasn't she?

It was suddenly apparent to me that Ginger was probably just a frightened girl. She had been running from the murderers before they caught up with her.

∽℮

The next morning, as I made coffee, I conjured up an image of a short, chunky red-haired young woman, physically strong, with a nervous way of speaking, dressed in work clothes. Where would Ginger run to?

Not to the racetrack. It was too well-regulated. Everyone knew everyone. People walked around with identification badges.

Not on Long Island. Too many people knew her.

She might be a thousand miles away, in some Midwest or Southern hamlet, but in that case I'd never find her. I had to proceed on the assumption that she had melted into the one place where her face was one of millions—the perfect camouflage. She was right here in Manhattan. In New York City she would be just another young woman seeking a job.

And where would an exercise rider with a lifelong passion for horses get work?

My hand holding the coffee cup began to shake ever so slightly. I knew where Ginger would be working. Of course.

At the last remaining riding stable in Manhattan—at Claremont on West Eighty-ninth Street.

I had been there many times when I first came to New York. I used to take long walks on the bridle path in Central Park and follow the horses and riders home to the stable, marveling at how the experienced horses could gingerly pick their way through the traffic-choked, double-parked streets once they left the park.

I dressed quickly, without thinking, and only after I was fully dressed did I realize that I was wearing the clothes I usually wore only to acting classes—jeans and an old sweatshirt on which was printed PROPERTY OF ATHLETIC DEPARTMENT/ UNIVERSITY OF VIRGINIA. I never knew where or how I had obtained that sweater—it had just appeared.

My instinctive clothes selection was a good omen, I thought. One always attempted to diminish one's natural beauty in acting classes, since it was looked upon as fakery. The ability to go deep inside a character was what was treasured. And wasn't I doing that? Wasn't I going inside of Ginger's head?

I was catching a character, a role—I was intuiting another's movement. I was a bloodhound . . . a choreographer . . . a nonsensical forty-one-year-old actress on the move. Chuckle. You know what they say: Bedouins sharpen their vision by painting the whites of their eyes blue.

I folded the only photograph of Ginger I had—the one with Cup of Tea and an unidentified calico cat—and placed it carefully in my bag. Then I left the apartment, cautioning the cats against any bizarre behavior, took the Third Avenue bus to Seventy-ninth Street, and walked west through the park.

The riding stable had not changed. On either side were the same crumbling brownstones. There was the same small, low-ceilinged ring with posts scattered throughout. The same treacherous ramp led from the ring to the stall area on the second floor. The office area was still as crowded as a subway car, even though it was late-morning on a weekday, with children, parents, instructors.

I finally cornered a man who seemed to have managerial responsibilities and gave him the current fiction: I was writing a book about the great racehorse Cup of Tea, and I had learned that one of his exercise riders was now working in his stable.

The man, who wore a whistle around his neck and riding boots in which white carpenter jeans were stuffed, folded his arms impatiently, as if I was a saleswoman about to launch into a long pitch. "That's news to me," he said in a heavy foreign accent which I could not identify.

"Her name is Ginger Mauch."

"No Ginger Mauch works here."

"Well, maybe she's a groom."

"No groom named Ginger Mauch works here. No instructor either."

I pulled the picture out and shoved it under his face, signifying but not saying that she might be working under a different name. It was too gloomy in the ring to see the photo clearly. Angrily he took the photo and strode to the stable entrance, flooded by the morning sun. I followed.

He stared at the picture, then handed it back. "No," he said, "I've never seen that woman here, and I've worked here for the last nine years."

I walked out of the riding stable so bitterly disappointed that my lower lip started to quiver like a child's. It never had really occurred to me that Ginger wouldn't be there. I knew she would be there. The doors of perception had shut on my arrogance like a steel trap.

I walked to Broadway, found a coffee shop, and collapsed in a booth. I ordered a cup of tea and a piece of coconut custard pie.

Everything connected with the murder of Harry Starobin seemed to recede . . . to have taken place fifty years ago. I wanted to push it even further back . . . to get away . . . to go to the shore . . . to the mountains . . . anywhere. I wanted out of those tiny compulsions which were leading me from one cipher to another.

"Poor Alice," I mocked myself, "too old to really enter a part."

I ate the pie slowly and doggedly, determined to get some energy. I sipped the tea. When the coffee shop began to fill up with a lunchtime crowd, I left, contemplating for a moment a cab . . . then deciding it would be best to walk.

I went back into Central Park and walked downtown. It was a glorious spring day. Everyone was out walking, jogging, bicycling. Even the homeless derelicts, huddled among the trees, seemed less desperate, less aggressive than usual.

When I reached the Tavern on the Green, I stopped and stared, discomfited, tense. Years ago I had eaten brunch there with my husband on a Sunday morning. The marriage was already in the last stages of dissolution and the brunch had become ugly. The dialogue between us was late-Gothic-bitter—

and centered around that most absurd of things, cream for the coffee:

He: I want half-and-half for my coffee. They gave us plain milk.

Me: Ask the waiter.

He: You ask the waiter. He keeps smiling at you.

Me: Are you jealous?

He: He can have you. All I want is the half-and-half.

I wondered why I had always remembered that stupid exchange—word for word, nuance by nuance.

I exited Central Park at Columbus Circle and turned east onto Central Park South. There were the carriage horses lined up in their accustomed spot, waiting for tourists. Their drivers, bizarrely outfitted, sat high up on their boxes, calling out to people passing.

I kept well clear of them; I was sick of horses.

The Plaza came into view. It was where I had had the clams with Anthony Basillio. He had been a good friend.

Suddenly there was violent barking. A woman held a dalmatian on a leash and the dog was pulling at it violently and barking at a big white carriage horse parked by the curb, whose nose was hidden in a feed bag.

The woman holding the dog was yelling apologies to the driver. The driver just smiled and nodded her head. The horse seemed totally unconcerned.

I started to cross Central Park South to continue in a downtown direction. The light was with me.

I stopped suddenly and let the light change.

My heart was beginning to jump, to beat with a funny little flutter—quickly, lightly, but pronounced.

My hand grasped my shoulder bag tightly and then released it.

The city became silent. I was frozen in time and space.

The carriage driver behind the big white horse was Ginger Mauch.

17

The watch on the waiter's thin wrist read two twenty. It seemed to be a very old watch. Maybe it had been his grand-father's. Maybe he was an out-of-work actor and he had come to New York from Minnesota, from a dairy farm, and the watch was the only rural memento he had left. How could a watch be a rural memento? Stupid thoughts.

I had been sitting in the outdoor café on the corner of Sixth Avenue and Central Park South for more than an hour. I had kept my eyes glued on the carriage with the big white horse.

The carriage was moving slowly but inexorably westward, toward me. Each time a carriage was hired, the others moved up—like a taxi line in front of a hotel.

An untouched Bloody Mary was in front of me. The waiter was bothersome, continually asking me if I wanted anything else. Business was slow. It was just a bit too early in the spring for café sitting.

There could be no doubt that the carriage driver was Ginger Mauch. Her hair was short now and dyed brown. But it was her. I had seen her in the flesh three times before this: once when I arrived by taxi at the Starobins' place on that terrible day; once when we were being questioned by the police; and once that same night, when I had stumbled on Ginger weeping behind the cottage.

No, this was not a mistake. This was real. This was Ginger.

In retrospect it was all so logical. Ginger had taken care of the old Starobin carriage horses. Of course she would seek work in Manhattan with carriage horses.

The longer I sat there, the more frightened I became. It wasn't physical fear of Ginger; it was something else. Something to do with the fear that even finding Ginger would yield only another dead end . . . a wall . . . a blinking image of a calico cat.

Ginger's carriage moved another space. I realized I would have to make my move soon. I placed a ten-dollar bill on the table in a manner which mutely showed that the waiter could keep the change from the drink—a very substantial gratuity. The sight of the ten-dollar bill calmed the waiter; he stopped hovering about me.

What happens if I wait too long and someone else hires the carriage? The thought panicked me.

I left the café swiftly, walked to the corner, and waited for the light to change.

Then I crossed the street to the carriage side and waited, turned away from the line of view. It suddenly occurred to me that since I was wearing my acting-class garb, Ginger would never even recognize me.

It was only by chance, instinctively, that I had selected that particular garb. In fact, everything had ended up without reason. I had found Ginger by chance, and only by chance. My reasoning, my "getting into the part," had gotten me nowhere, it was a chance walk at a chance time in a chance place—and a dalmatian dog barking for no bloody reason.

The absurdity of it all gave me strength.

I whirled around, walked ten steps, and was about to climb up into the carriage.

I froze before the carriage steps. Ginger's head was in repose.

I turned and walked quickly away, five steps, ten steps, then stopped. Not the carriage. Not the carriage now. It was wrong. It was childish. What was I going to do in the carriage? What was I going to say? Where were we going to ride?

It wasn't a confrontation that was needed. It was information. Where was she living? Whom was she talking to?

I took ten more steps away from her. What if Ginger wasn't a victim? What if she wasn't running but was pursuing?

I walked toward the low wall that separated the sidewalk from the park. I turned. A couple had climbed into Ginger's cab. They were pulling away. Fine. Ginger would be back to deposit her fares after the ride was over.

I leaned against the wall and waited. From where I stood I could dimly see the waiter in the street café I had vacated.

Ten minutes. Twenty minutes. She and her carriage would be back. Thirty minutes. Sixty minutes. The big white horse poked his nose out of the park, moving leisurely toward the line again. Ginger pulled the carriage up about ten yards from me and helped her fare down graciously.

Then she climbed up again and started to move. But this time she didn't rejoin the line. She pulled out into the street and headed west on Central Park South.

She was going back to the stable. She was through for the day. I started to walk, easily keeping her in view, staying as far away from the curb as I could. Her pace was painfully slow, as if she was allowing the horse a leisurely stroll.

The horse and carriage turned south on Broadway and then west again on Fifty-fifth Street, then south on Eleventh, and then stopped in front of a long, low, decrepit stable in front of which were dozens of broken-down, horseless carriages. Ginger climbed down and led the horse and carriage inside. I could see her disengaging the horse from the carriage and leading him into a stall. I moved away from the stable and waited near the corner, in front of a busy taxi garage.

She was in there forty minutes. When she came out she walked briskly to a white stone house on Forty-ninth Street and Ninth Avenue.

I climbed the stairs into a cramped, filthy lobby. There were sixteen plastic buttons and under each one a nameplate. There was no Ginger Mauch. What name was she using? I didn't know, but it had to be one of the newer plates. There were three of them: L & H Martinez; Jon Swan; M. Lukas. It had to be Lukas. Ginger Mauch was now M. Lukas. I walked out of the lobby and down the steps. Right next to the building was a small bodega. I walked inside, ordered a container of black coffee, and sipped it dourly, standing inside the store, by the front window.

What was I waiting for? I had postponed the confrontation in the carriage. And now I was doing the same thing: waiting . . . making excuses. Now was the time to confront her. Now was the time to ask her all those questions I had stored up in my head: about Harry; about those damn calico cats; about Veronica the barn cat; about Cup of Tea and Ask Me No Questions; about her life on the racetrack and her life with the Starobins; about whom she was running from or running to.

Why was I equivocating? What was I afraid of? Why couldn't I confront her? What was the point of the whole investigation . . . what was the point of tracking her if I couldn't finish it up?

The coffee was horrible—bitter, with a funny taste, as if someone had poured some kind of syrup into it. I dumped the container into a carton of trash. But I stayed where I was and stared out onto the street. Children in parochial-school outfits were talking in front of the bodega. I could hear them dimly, but their words made no sense. Then I realized they were speaking in Spanish. I started to laugh at myself. I walked out of the bodega, up the steps of the house, into the small lobby, and pressed my finger hard against the M. Lukas bell. There was no answer. Maybe the bells didn't work. The landlord had obviously long since given up on the building. Realizing this, I pushed at the lobby door. It opened easily. The lock was still in the door but was totally corroded. I cursed myself for not trying the door the first time.

M. Lukas lived on the third floor. Up I went, slowly, trying to think of opening lines that would get me inside that apartment.

A burly man walking down the stairs greeted me warmly. A woman passed me and didn't say a word. The ceilings above the stairs were filthy. Chips and pieces of paint seem to flutter down in a steady stream, jarred loose by footsteps on the stairs.

The first door I saw when I reached the third floor was 3E. Was this M. Lukas? The door was ajar. At the top of the landing I stared at the open door and felt an incredible sense of déjà vu. When Jo and I had traced Ginger to her apartment in Oyster Bay Village, we had found the same thing. The door ajar. Ginger gone. Was there a back door to the building? I wondered, cursing myself.

I stopped at the doorway. "Ginger, Ginger Mauch?" I called into the opening. The sound of my voice was strange to me, as if someone else was calling.

There was no answer.

I pushed the door open and stepped inside. "Ginger," I called again, more softly.

The apartment was a studio. And it had been ripped apart. Clothes and books and papers were flung all around. Things had been shattered. A tiny kitchen had been totally ransacked. The apartment stank of something I couldn't identify.

Then I noticed that the bathroom door was closed.

I walked to it swiftly, my feet crunching objects on the floor. I pushed the door open with my foot.

And then I sank to my knees. Ginger Mauch was sitting in the rusted bathtub. The red roots in her brown-dyed hair were visible. Torrents of blood had flowed and dried on her naked body. The cut across her throat was a jagged white road.

I remained kneeling on the floor, half in and half out of the bathroom. I knew what I had to do. Stand up. Go to the phone. Call the police. But I was paralyzed.

I started to cry for Ginger. Not because she was dead, for death seemed to be irrelevant in that room. Because she had suffered. Because she had felt pain. Because some animal had slit her throat. I could see her as I had seen her that first time, in the cold gleaming morning, from a distance, brushing the aged horse on the Starobin farm.

I stopped sobbing. I crawled out of the bathroom and found myself surrounded by her trashed belongings. What had they been looking for?

A heap of books had been pulled off the bookcase and lay in a crazy pyramid. One of them caught my eye. I knew it. I was staring at a copy of the book I had found in the library, the one containing a photo of Ginger and Cup of Tea. The thought chilled me. My eyes swept in fear around the room. Not for her killer, but for the calico cat. There was none. Poor Ginger. The book was probably a precious memento.

I reached out and pulled it to me. As I did, a piece of old thick cardboard slid out. It was taped around the edges to thicken it, like boys used to tape their baseball tickets.

I found myself reading some kind of list or inventory on each side. The letters and numbers were indecipherable, written in red and black crayons and smudged.

But I knew one thing. I was staring at something written by Harry Starobin. His scrawl had been indelibly imprinted on my brain, after sorting through hundreds of his papers at Jo's request.

Harry Starobin and Ginger Mauch had been part of some kind of conspiracy, and I had found the codebook.

☙

I was awakened by strange sounds. I stared at the clock in my bedroom. It was one in the morning. I had slept almost seven hours. The police, I knew, would have responded to my call in minutes and Ginger was by now a statistic, her apartment contents cataloged, her walls and furniture swept for prints.

Those strange sounds that woke me were the cats. They wanted to be fed. I climbed slowly off the bed, the back of my neck and shoulders stiff.

After I fed them, I made myself a cup of coffee and then went into the living room, where the strange piece of taped cardboard lay on the long table.

I sat down and stared at it.

The front was a fourteen-line list:

78/TTQQCC
79/TTQCCC
80/T CC
81/TQCCC
82/TC
82/QQCC

83/TTTQCC
83/TQQC
84/TQQCC
85/TQC
85/TTQC
86/QCCC
87/QCCC
88/TTTTTCC

It was obvious that the numbers were years: 1978–1988. There was only one line for each year except for the years 1982, 1983, and 1985—where there were two entries each.

But what were those funny capital letters after each year—T or Q or C?

They must mean something. They must be important. Ginger had carried them with her during her travels.

Bushy sauntered into the living room and hopped up on the sofa, quite content with his meal.

Pancho flew by once, paused, stared at me, and continued his journeys.

I was chilly. I wrapped a blanket around my shoulders.

I stared at the markings on the cardboard again. It was obvious that Harry was tallying something that happened in each year. It was an inventory . . . a count . . . like someone saying an apple tree produced eighty barrels of apples in 1986. Or a farm produced thirty barrels of peaches, twenty of plums, ten of pears, in a given year.

But what had he been counting?

I leaned back and closed my eyes, thinking of Harry.

What had defined him? Humor. Kindness. Boots. Animals. Cats. Horses.

But he didn't grow any of those things. He didn't produce.

Harry wasn't a breeder of anything. His farm was totally nonfunctional.

Except . . . except . . . except for the Himalayans. No, he hadn't bred them.

Except for the barn cats. Jo had said there were always litters of barn cats. Veronica had vanished with her litter.

I stared at the letters.

Why would Harry list in coded form litters of barn cats over the years? And what did the letters mean?

Of course! I flung my hand up to accentuate my own stupidity. T stood for tom—a male cat. Q stood for queen—a female cat. Old names that people didn't use anymore.

My fingers were trembling ever so slightly.

According to my analysis, in 1978, the first year of the inventory, the barn-cat litter consisted of two male kittens, two female, and two Cs.

But what was C?

Calico. A delicious chill went right through me. I had broken the stupid code.

Then I pulled back my enthusiasm. If my analysis was correct, there were calico cats in each litter, in most years more than one, and in some years more than half the litter.

That was impossible. I had read a lot about calico cats over the years.

There are only three multicolored cats, found only in

females—blue cream, tortoiseshell, and calico. Calico is the most difficult to reproduce.

To obtain a calico, one breeds a male with a dominant white color to a tortoiseshell female. The white male is crucial because calico is really only tortoiseshell plus the color white. White, in fact, is the dominant color of the calico cat.

If the mating is successful, a calico female may appear in the litter—possibly even two.

But over the long run, calico is very hard to produce. The accepted probabilities are one calico female out of every seventeen kittens.

I stared down at the list again. How could Harry have bred so many calico cats in each litter of barn cats?

Was Harry a magician? Had he somehow done what cat breeders considered impossible?

I turned the cardboard over. This side contained dozens of entries, many of them faded.

Among the ones I could make out were:

RS/87C

NA/83C

LBD/86C

COT/78C

LK/81C

ANQ/82C

FG/84C

GB/84C

R/79C

BB/79C

The second part of each entry I now understood. C meant calico; 84 meant the 1984 litter; 84C meant a calico cat from the litter in 1984.

But what did it refer to? What referred to it? What did FG/84C mean?

It was the LK/81C entry I focused on most. For some reason it infatuated me. The letters LK meant something to me, or reminded me of something.

I began to make up possibilities. Ladybird. LK. Ladybird in Kansas. LK. Larry Koenig. Lucifer Kills. LK.

I kept at it . . . from the stupid to the sublime . . . from the known to the unknown. And then it tripped off my tongue— Lord Kelvin.

Lord Kelvin! I looked down the list. If LK was Lord Kelvin, then there should be COT—Cup of Tea. He was there. And Ask Me No Questions. She was there.

It was a list of abbreviated horse's names and after each one was the year the calico cat it had received as a mascot was born.

It was a list of horses that had had Harry's calico cats as mascots.

I stood up quickly and walked to the window. My arms were folded across my chest. I knew what Harry had done. The enormity of it . . . the scope of it . . . the sheer intellectual audacity of it was staggering. Harry had, indeed, changed his world. His laughter rolled gently over me. How I missed him!

18

Jo Starobin sat in her rocking chair. One Himalayan was on her lap. One was on her shoulder. The others were scattered about, at least one stalking the slow, steady rock of the wood.

I was standing behind her. We both watched Detective Senay. He was holding up the piece of taped cardboard.

"Sure," he said, "I looked at it. I looked at it pretty damn carefully."

He held it at arm's length, as if it was something ugly.

"Let me get straight what you're telling me, Mrs. Nestleton."

"I'm not married," I corrected him for the fifth or sixth time.

"What you're saying is this," he continued, brushing aside my objection, his voice rising just up to the limit of anger. "What you're saying is that Harry Starobin was not the sweet, kindly man everybody thought he was. He was a kind of magician. He discovered a new way to breed calico cats. He found a way to get a whole slew of calico cats in a single litter because he had these special kinds of barn cats. But that was only the beginning. Not only was he a magician, but these calico cats were magicians also."

He looked at me, arching his eyebrows, grimacing, shuffling his body. The poor man.

He continued. "If one of these calico cats starts to live with a racehorse as the horse's mascot, that broken-down three-legged horse will turn into a champion runner sooner or later."

He stopped again, held out his hands, and asked, "Do I have it right so far?"

"You have it right," I said.

"So Harry began selling these magical calico cats to horse trainers and owners. And he made a lot of money. But we don't know where all that money is, do we?"

Jo looked at me quickly. I said nothing. She knew I had said nothing about the money in her safe-deposit box. I would never say anything about that.

Senay continued. "According to you, what happens next is something like this. Someone wanted this magical line of cats. That someone murdered Harry to obtain them. That someone ripped apart his house to make it seem like a robbery. And that someone killed Mona Aspen and Ginger Mauch because both of them worked with Harry on this scheme. Mona was the one who introduced Harry to the trainers and owners who needed the cats to turn lousy horses into champions. And Ginger was the bagman."

He walked to the sofa and sat down. There was silence for a long time.

Then he grinned. "One of us is crazy, lady. Or, to put it another way, what you told me is very difficult to believe."

I grinned back at him, stiffly. I was not going to let him bait me.

Senay said, "The real problem with stories like these is that when all is said and done, when all the smoke and fire and belief and nonsense clear, there's simply no way to corroborate them."

It was the moment I was waiting for. I knew that Senay would bring up the paucity of demonstrable evidence. I knew that Senay would have to be cornered and recruited, otherwise there would be no chance.

"They can be corroborated," I said quietly.

Senay exploded. "You mean we do a statistical study of racehorses that have calico cats for mascots? Or we subpoena the financial records of every trainer who has a calico cat to see if he paid ten thousand dollars for it when she was a kitten? Who gives a damn whether all that calico-cat nonsense is true or not? I'm investigating murders. Do you understand? Murders." Senay had temporarily lost his cool; he was almost shouting at the end of his little speech.

I handed him a small folded piece of paper. White memo paper.

He opened the paper and read: CALICO KITTENS, NEW LITTER, VERY REASONABLY PRICED, IDEAL FOR BARN AND STABLE. WRITE: STAROBIN, P. O. BOX 385, OLD BROOKVILLE, LONG ISLAND, NEW YORK.

"I don't understand this," he said. "What is it?"

"An advertisement," I replied, "that, with your consent, will be placed in the classified sections of all the leading thoroughbred racing and breeding magazines."

"But what's the point?"

"Whoever murdered Harry and Mona and Ginger and stole Veronica and her litter will think that there exists another line of magical calico cats. The murderers will find that unacceptable. They will try to get this new litter."

"You mean we create a litter of calico cats?"

"We fake a litter. The litter box will be empty."

"And wait for the thief to show up in the barn?"

"Exactly."

"And the thief is the murderer?"

"Or has been hired by the murderer."

"Did it ever dawn on you, lady, that you have been watching too many Miss Marple mysteries on Channel Thirteen?"

"No. My television set went on the blink two years ago and I never fixed it. But did it ever dawn on you, Detective Senay, that you know absolutely nothing about these murders after all this time—except what I told you today?"

I let that sink in, then continued. "If the killer is truly a madman, and I believe he is . . . if he is willing to murder to win races . . . then he is not going to let these mythical calico kittens go elsewhere."

He stared at me. I could tell his defenses were beginning to crumble.

"What kind of departmental response are you talking about?" he finally asked.

"Nothing," I replied, "but one police officer at all times in the barn between six in the evening and six in the morning. In plainclothes, in the old hayloft."

"Does it have your approval, Mrs. Starobin?" Senay asked. Then added, "After all, it is your property."

"I suppose so," Jo said.

"Then I'll set the damn thing up," he half yelled, and strode out of the room as if I had offended him greatly.

When we were alone, the old woman pointed a shaky hand at me and said, "How dare you tell that policeman all those stories about Harry! How can you believe them?"

"You told me yourself, Jo, in the bank, that Harry must have been involved in something criminal. You asked me to help you find out."

"But, Alice, not this . . . not selling kittens for exorbitant prices on the grounds that they make horses champions. It's a fake . . . and Harry wouldn't have had anything to do with it. Harry would have robbed a bank if he was desperate enough— and our financial situation *was* desperate—but not this."

I lowered my voice. I couldn't bear Jo's anguish.

"What if it wasn't a fake, Jo? What if Harry really had bred such a line of kittens? What if all those racehorses began winning suddenly because of their mascots—the calico barn cats . . . what if somehow, in some way, Harry had pulled off a miracle, something that really can't be explained scientifically? What then, Jo?"

Jo didn't answer. She started to weep. The cats seemed to sense her grief and started an orgy of playfulness, as if trying to cheer her up.

LYDIA ADAMSON

❧

Even in springtime the Starobin house was cold and damp in the evening, so Jo and I wore shawls as we spent each evening together, complementing the police officers who split two six-hour shifts in the barn.

I had moved into the cottage again, and slept there, with Pancho and Bushy.

There was a strange enmity between Jo and me—a silent one, as if we had both agreed to a truce in some long-standing struggle.

I didn't understand why Jo avoided speaking to me, or I to her; I didn't understand why the name Harry no longer was mentioned.

Three days after we had begun that evening vigil—after the advertisement had been placed in the six daily and weekly publications and we all waited for a murderous thief to attempt to steal a litter of nonexistent kittens—Jo broke the truce.

She turned on me with a suddenness and a ferocity that made me cringe.

"Don't you think I know what went on between you and Harry?"

I didn't know how to reply. Harry and I had not been lovers. Ginger had been Harry's lover. And she was dead. For all I knew, Mona also had been his longtime secret lover. That might explain her fatal involvement; she might have helped him for love and not for money. And maybe there had been others—maybe there had been hundreds of others. But not I.

Had Jo, in her wisdom, intuited my secret fantasy passion for the old man . . . a strange oedipal passion that I had never articulated to anyone?

I didn't answer. I bowed my head. She construed it as an admission of guilt and she was happy—she forgave me. The air cleared. The hostility dissolved. She mumbled and turned away, making a motion with her hand to signify that it meant nothing.

On the fifth day, as we were keeping vigil in the large house, Jo mentioned that she had spoken to Charlie Coombs and he had asked after me.

"How is Charlie doing?" I asked calmly, academically. It is the proper way to speak about old lovers.

"Okay, I suppose. Did I ever tell you about his father? His father was a wonderful man. He used to sleep in a stall with a horse if it was sick."

I smiled. I wondered how Charlie Coombs was really doing. Had he bought a new pair of red sneakers? Had he cleaned up his cluttered desk in his small racetrack office? Were his horses winning? Did he miss me? But I could not muse abstracted for long on our affair without that old suspicion beginning to grow again—that Charlie Coombs was part and parcel of the whole mess—that Charlie was on a calico tightrope.

Jo changed the subject: "Should we get coffee for the policemen in the barn?"

"They're being paid," I noted.

"It's been bothering me since the first night they started to stay in the barn. Shouldn't we make them coffee? Amos can do it." Jo was beginning to worry over trifles.

I laughed. "Amos couldn't deliver an empty cup, much less one filled with coffee."

"He's a fine man." Jo leapt to his defense. "It's just that he really wasn't cut out to be a handyman . . . He gets confused."

My mind really wasn't on Amos. I was thinking about what was coming. I was thinking that it would be someone close . . . perhaps Charlie . . . perhaps Nicholas Hill . . . it would be someone I knew who would try to take the nonexistent litter.

I was beginning to experience a profound sense of inadequacy and almost shame, as if, in the face of the bizarre and inexplicable conspiracy of magical cats and triumphant horses created by Harry Starobin, it would be best if the advertisement was ignored . . . it would be best if the guilty would not act and let time dissolve the memories.

"Harry used to love peaches," Jo said, startling me with a comment that had nothing to do with anything. "We used to buy bushels of hard, unripe peaches on the roadside in front of the Mannigalt farm."

It dawned on me that Jo was probably speaking about a farm that had closed its doors twenty years ago. She was talking about a Long Island that had long since vanished.

On the eighth day, at ten thirty in the evening, Jo began to act strangely again. We had nothing to do but play rummy together. Two or three letters had dribbled in about the nonexistent kittens and there had been a few phone calls. But the barn was still inviolable.

Suddenly Jo whispered, "Why calico?"

"What?"

"If what you say is true, Alice, if Harry did what you said he did . . . why did he breed calicos?"

"I don't follow you, Jo."

"Why not seal point or red tabby or silver mackerel? And why a short-haired barn cat? Why not a Persian or a Manx or a Maine coon or a Himalayan?"

Her questions were becoming hysterical.

"Calm down," I said, gently but firmly reseating her.

Then I said, "Maybe he thought calicos were special. Maybe he loved them because they were so hard to breed."

"Harry never told me that," Jo said, her voice rising again.

I tried to be rational. "I don't think he knew about their special qualities until Cup of Tea. I think he just bred calicos at first because he wanted to show that he knew more about cats than the people who wrote books about them. He wanted to do things that people said he couldn't do."

Jo picked up the cards again and started to play. She kept nodding her head and forming words with her lips—mutely, as if she was carrying on a very important internal conversation.

Then she stared at me and said, "Ashes."

"What do you mean, Jo?"

"Ashes. Our marriage was ashes. It turned out in the end to be ashes."

"He did it for you, Jo—for the money, for the house, for the way you lived, for you, Jo, and what you had been to each other all those years." I don't know why I said that. I didn't believe it. If he did it for anyone other than himself, it was Ginger or Mona. But that was too sad to speak.

"It's all over. And it's all ashes. Just like Harry's ashes on the gravel roadway," Jo said, and her body began to be racked with chills. I wrapped a blanket around her.

I was beginning to intuit that whatever else was going on, we were performing a wake for Harry Starobin. The old man had burned his own peculiar life in each of us. He was a lover, husband, father, breeder, Merlin. A bizarre man none of us really knew in the end.

I closed my eyes. I could see him rising from the ashes of the roadway—funny, potent, sad, compassionate, inquisitive. And, above all, wise. Was it his supposed wisdom that so infatuated all of us, why we still hung on to his memory like drowning people?

I wanted to leave the house. I wanted to talk to Bushy and Pancho in the cottage. They didn't like it there.

"If you don't mind, I'll turn in before the curfew, Jo." It had been decided that we would stay together in the living room of the house from the moment it got dark until midnight, and then leave the vigil to the police officers hiding in the barn loft.

Jo nodded. It was fine with her. I left quickly and walked back to the cottage. Poor Pancho. Poor Bushy. All alone in a strange cottage again.

I had just reached the door of the cottage when a scream split the night air.

And then a crack, as if something had been broken in a sound chamber.

I turned, petrified.

I saw lights switching on in the large house and the barn.

Jo was walking toward the barn as fast as she could.

I started to run.

When I reached the barn I saw the police officer crouched against the barn door, blood streaming from a wound on the side of his head. His gun was drawn. He seemed crazed, disoriented.

He shouted at Jo, who was pressing what seemed to be a dish towel against his wound: "I got him! He hit me with a flashlight! But I got him!"

I could now see blood all around in the flickering lights. Blood on the officer. Blood on the barn door. And a trail of red blotches leading from the barn into the overgrown field, as if someone had placed red doilies on the ground.

"Get him," the officer pleaded, unsteady. "He's hurt bad. Get him!"

Jo and I walked into the field, holding each other. Then we stopped. Where were we going? It was dark. How could we find him? What would we do if we did find him?

We huddled together. We waited. We stared back at the barn lights.

Something came to us on the night breeze.

It sounded like a cricket. No, it sounded like a night warbler.

No, it was a human sound. A moan. At first we thought it was the wounded policeman, but he was too far away.

We moved toward it, our shoulders touching.

Now we could see something alien in the grass; a heap.

Jo's foot kicked something metallic.

"Flashlight," she whispered.

I picked it up and flicked it on, grabbing Jo's hand with my own free hand.

The heap was a body. Alive. Knees brought up to the chest in pain. A blood-soaked thigh.

We moved closer.

It wasn't a man. It was a woman. The beam of the flashlight was full force on her face.

I stared in horror at her writhing.

My legs could no longer hold my body. I sank beside her.

I placed my hand on the face of my old friend—Carla Fried.

Then there were sirens. And feet crashing through the field.

People surrounded us, loaded the woman on an aluminum rack, and wheeled her out of the field.

Senay helped me up. Jo was hanging on to a uniformed policeman. I felt affection for Senay—an impossible-to-explain affection.

I said to him very slowly and precisely, "The man who sent her . . . the man who sent others to murder . . . the man who now has the barn cat Veronica and her calico litter . . . is a Canadian millionaire named Thomas Waring."

Senay said, "Yes, I've heard the name."

I added, "He's also a patron of the arts," and then began to laugh hysterically at the dirty little joke. But the laughter died in my throat when I saw someone wrap a blanket around Jo and lead her very slowly and very tentatively out of the field. I was suddenly frightened that she would have to walk over Harry's ashes to reach the house.

19

"How is Mrs. Starobin?" Senay asked.

"Fine. She's fine."

I sat down on the sofa. Jo was upstairs, tucked into bed and sleeping. The first rays of morning sun were beginning to filter through the house.

In front of the rocking chair on which Detective Senay sat was a large paper bag. He reached in, brought out a container of coffee, leaned over, and handed it to me.

Three of the Himalayan cats quickly surrounded the paper bag and inspected it carefully.

"This is out of my own pocket," he noted ruefully.

Then he reached into the bag again and came out with a toasted corn muffin wrapped in aluminum foil. He handed that to me also.

It was, I suppose, the only way Detective Senay could apologize to me for his past behavior toward me. I wanted to be gracious. I was too exhausted to be anything else.

We sipped our coffee, nibbled our muffins, and stared at each other and at the Himalayans.

Finally he said, "So this woman Carla Fried is a good friend of yours."

"An old friend," I replied.

"Well," he noted, "if she lives, which she probably will, she'll cut a deal. All she has to do is name her associates—she couldn't have murdered Starobin and Mona Aspen and the young girl alone. And then finger that Canadian, Waring, as the man who pulled all the strings. When all the smoke clears, she'll end up doing five years . . . if that."

"How can we be sure she'll talk?" I asked.

"Simple. If she doesn't, we'll hang an attempted-murder charge against her for attacking the cop in the barn. No, your friend will play ball with us. She has no other option."

He finished his coffee, crushed the container, and dropped it down beside the paper bag for the cats to play with.

Then he straightened up on the chair. "What's right is right. You did a helluva job, lady. You broke the case."

I didn't respond. He grinned and added, "To be honest, when you set up that calico-kitten trap, I thought you were a stone lunatic."

He was starting to squirm. Poor Senay.

I closed my eyes. He was right. I had broken the case. But never in my wildest dreams had I suspected Carla Fried.

She had pulled the wool over my eyes completely. I had thought she was visiting me and calling me only because of the part, or because we were old friends . . . but in fact, she was in New York to orchestrate a different kind of drama—murder and theft for her patron.

I had thought she was flying in and out of New York, but all the while she was probably in town, keeping tabs on things, telling her associates just when it was the right time to run her old friend down with a red pickup truck because she was getting too inquisitive.

And I really had no idea why she had done it. Had it been a quid pro quo? Had Waring said: I'll give you 1.5 million dollars for your theater if you do something for me? Or had Waring and she been lovers?

Had the promise of a well-funded independent theater company been so important to Carla that she would participate in murder?

How could she, in fact, have anything to do with a man who was so obviously obsessed with winning at all costs—even horse races?

Why? Why? Why? What made Carla run? Passion? Ambition? The promise of artistic freedom? A whim? Psychosis? All of the above?

The more I thought about it, the more I had to face the nagging, hard-to-accept, but harder-to-deny possibility that Carla Fried was just another talented woman who had been crushed to death by theatrical fantasies . . . who had become so deranged and so confused by the need to achieve something in the theater that she would do anything to fulfill that need. Anything!

"You know," Senay said quietly, "your crazy friend

probably didn't even know Harry Starobin or Mona Aspen or Ginger Mauch."

I opened my eyes. He was right. And that was the most pernicious and ugly fact of all.

As for Waring! How obsessed with winning he must have become. And how twisted. With his money, he could have bought the cats from Harry, like others had. But no! Waring had to be the sole possessor of the cats. He had to guarantee exclusivity by having Harry and Mona and Ginger murdered. He had to relish the sense of secret power as his thoroughbreds began to win . . . and only he would know the reason why. His wealth had not brought him virtue or wisdom. It had turned him into a murderous, psychotic fool.

"Maybe she didn't even like cats," Senay added.

"She liked my cats."

"Do you have calico cats?"

"No."

I stared out the front window of the Starobin house. Amos, the old handyman, was walking slowly up the drive. I shivered and reached for one of the blankets on the sofa. Amos was walking over Harry Starobin's ashes.

"How about another muffin?" Senay asked, reaching down into the paper bag.

"No thanks."

"Danish, then?"

"No thanks."

Senay sighed wearily and commenced to rock.

The Himalayans abandoned the paper bag. They had found nothing of value there.

Amos walked into the house, through the large living room, and into the kitchen. He didn't greet us.

I heard all the Himalayans moving toward him. They were hungry. I heard him preparing their food. Before I fell asleep on the sofa I remember thinking that they sure feed cats early in Old Brookville.

20

I opened the cat carriers the moment I closed the apartment door behind me.

Bushy ambled out. Pancho flew out to begin his frantic dashes in order to find, identify, and flee from the many enemies that had invaded Manhattan while he was away.

I walked into the kitchen, opened the refrigerator, took out a container of low-fat milk, and poured myself half a glass. I sat down at the tiny table. My body felt as if all the musculature had been sucked out.

The green light on the phone machine indicated there had been messages while I was away. Pancho's enemies. I ignored them.

I sipped the milk. My hands were shaking. I was becoming agitated.

Reaching for pencil and pad, I made a soothing list:

1. Pick up hat left in bar
2. Write nice note to Charlie Coombs

3. Call Anthony Basillio and thank him again
4. Buy saffron rice for Pancho
5. Cash check
6. Buy toothpaste and regular cat food

I put the pencil down. It was musty in the apartment. I left the kitchen and walked to the windows in the living room—heaving both of them open as far as the cracked wood allowed.

Turning back, I saw the paperback copy of *Romeo and Juliet* on the long table.

Poor Carla Fried, willing to do anything for anyone to fund her dream of a theater. Poor, sick, crazed Carla.

I went back to the kitchen to finish my milk.

Strange thoughts came to me as I sat there.

What if Carla's theater group in Montreal had already been funded?

What if, in spite of the fact that Thomas Waring and his associates would be convicted of murder, the funds were already in place, in possession of the theater group, inviolate?

What if the season would go on as planned . . . without Carla Fried . . . without Thomas Waring?

What if they would still need an actress to imaginatively interpret the role of the Nurse in a Portobello production of *Romeo and Juliet*?

I picked up the pencil and added another item to the list:

7. Contact Carla's theatrical group in Montreal

A part is a part, I said to myself grimly.

And Portobello would appreciate my interpretation of the Nurse as a middle-aged woman whose eccentricities hid the fact that she loved Romeo just as passionately as Juliet loved him. Portobello would find the idea intriguing . . . chewable . . . dramaturgically innovative.

"I'll discuss it in detail with Bushy before I discuss it with Portobello," I said to the pencil in my hand. Then I walked into the living room to join Bushy on the sofa.

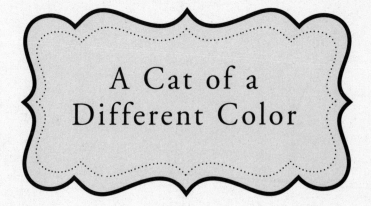

A Cat of a
Different Color

1

The woman, whose name was Francesca Tosques—she was vaguely attached to the Italian legation—had told me before I started the cat-sitting assignment that Geronimo was a lovely cat but he had some peculiarities.

"Don't go near the fireplace," she said mysteriously. "Fine!" I replied. Francesca was going to be away for three days: Sunday, Monday, and Tuesday. All I had to do was go up to her large old apartment on West End Avenue and Ninety-seventh Street in Manhattan . . . feed Geronimo . . . talk to Geronimo . . . kill some time. That's all. A very good assignment as these things go.

I arrived on Sunday at three in the afternoon, walking all the way from my East Twenty-sixth Street apartment, through the park. It was hot outside but the apartment was cool without air-conditioning, utilizing only one large, slow ceiling fan. The view from the apartment was spectacular: out over the Hudson to Jersey, or north up the Hudson, or downtown.

Pick a window, pick a view. She had left me twenty-three notes on the dining-room table, complicating the simplest procedures. But I was used to that.

As for Geronimo—I was expecting a Balinese or a Cornish Rex or some other exotic feline, but when I finally met him—he was lying on the Formica kitchen table—well, Geronimo was simply an old-fashioned black alley cat. You couldn't call him anything else. He was big and brawny and ugly, with scars up and down his flanks, and he walked—when he did walk, like alley cats do—as if he had some kind of testicular problem, to put it kindly.

That first day, I stayed in the apartment about an hour, talking to Geronimo, who really wasn't listening. After eating, he had gone back to the Formica table and I had to almost shout to get my points across. I joshed him, telling him that I was a famous actress, a famous sleuth, and above all, a famous cat-sitter, and I'd be damned if he was going to be standoffish. I just wouldn't tolerate it.

On the third day, we weren't any friendlier; it was live and let live. Anyway, on that third and last day of the assignment, Geronimo was beginning to irritate me. And my pride was hurt. Everyone always said I had a magical way with cats. Ask my own cats—Bushy and Pancho. They'll tell anyone. So it started to bother me about what his mistress had told me— that I should not go near the fireplace. Very strange. The fireplace was an old large one, set in the north wall of the apartment. It was obviously a working fireplace but it was also obvious that it hadn't been used in a long time. I had kept away from it because of what she had told me and because it was in a far part of the apartment. I mean, one really had to want to go there to end up there. So I sat and stewed at the living-room table, staring at Geronimo, who was staring at me from the kitchen table. Instead of a forty-one-year-old woman, I was thinking like a twelve-year-old adolescent. Something had been denied me. Authority had spoken. It was necessary to subvert authority. It was a decidedly adolescent impulse.

I got up slowly, theatrically, elegantly, and sauntered over to the fireplace. Reaching it, I placed one hand gently on the mantelpiece and smiled.

A moment later a blur seemed to explode across the room. And then I felt a short intense pain in the thumb of the hand resting on the fireplace.

Startled, I looked down. Geronimo was standing there. He had flown across the room and bitten me. Can you imagine that?

Then the cat turned and sauntered back toward the kitchen table, very much the macho alley cat.

In a state of semishock from the attack, I stumbled into the bathroom and let running cold water clean the small wound. Geronimo stared at me from his kitchen table, bored, implying that I had been duly warned and that since I had obviously wanted to play with fire, it was simple justice that I got burned.

After I washed and dressed the wound I felt exhausted. I walked into Francesca Tosques' bedroom and lay down on the bed, closing my eyes and flicking on the radio. The station was set on 1010 WINS—news all the time.

I lay there wondering why Geronimo attacked people who

stood in front of the fireplace. It was very perplexing. I must have dozed off and then awakened with a start. My mouth was dry. A bad dream? No. A name on the radio was being repeated, and I knew the name. The announcer was saying that one of the last famous Greenwich Village bohemians was dead. Arkavy Reynolds had been shot to death on Jane Street. Reynolds, the announcer said, was a well-known denizen of the lower Manhattan theater scene. He was a producer, publisher of a theatrical scandal sheet which he hawked himself from coffee shop to coffee shop, and one of those outrageous individuals who at one time were so much a part of bohemian life in New York. The announcer ended with the comment that the police were investigating the murder but had no leads or witnesses at this time.

Poor Arkavy! I had bumped into him often over the years and we always chatted, or rather I listened to his monologues. He was a huge fat man who seemed to roll down the street. In all seasons he wore the same outfit: a cabdriver's hat, white shirt and flamboyant tie, vest, farmer's overalls with shoulder straps, and construction-worker shoes. Of course, he was quite mad. Rumor had it he came from a wealthy family. He was always looking for space to perform some play far off-off Broadway. He was always talking about some brilliant new playwright whom no one had ever heard of. And his newsletters were often about people who simply didn't exist. Each issue of his newsletter also carried reviews written by him, which were filled with typographical excesses—he loved asterisks and exclamation marks and dots and dashes.

I got up from the bed and walked into the kitchen. There

was Geronimo. He no longer interested me at all. I ignored him. I opened and closed the refrigerator a few times absent-mindedly, thinking of Arkavy, trying to remember the exact time I had last seen him. It might have been on East Fourth Street and First Avenue one night in the fall of 1989. I was going to a dramatic reading by an East German woman. Yes, it might have been then.

I left the kitchen and walked back into the living room, where I fell wearily into a chair. My wound was beginning to throb. Geronimo was still looking at me. It dawned on me, right then, that if Arkavy and Geronimo had by chance met, they might have become the best of friends. After all, poor Arkavy was a man who had spent his life looking to be bitten.

2

It was ten o'clock in the morning. I was standing in front of the public school on Eighty-first Street and Madison Avenue, staring across the street at the Frank E. Campbell Funeral Home, where poor Arkavy Reynolds' body could be viewed in the coffin before burial. The public had been invited to pay their last respects. Well, that was what I intended to do. He perpetually had been a fresh breath of lunatic air in the New York theatrical world. Time had passed him by . . . the New York theater was now showbiz or high finance—all aspects of it—and I owed it to him to stare at his corpse.

The *Times* printed a small article about him in the theater section, not the obituary section. The reporter had called it just another senseless New York tragedy. Arkavy, it seems, had fought with a panhandler at Sheridan Square on the morning of his death. The police speculated that the panhandler got a weapon, went looking for Arkavy, found him on Jane Street, and shot him five times in the chest. The reporter said Arkavy

Reynolds' last-known residence was a seamen's shelter down near South Street Seaport. And then the article went on to recount some of the more colorful "Arkavy" stories—such as his predilection for taking cabs and then paying the meter with off-off-Broadway theater tickets from shows that had closed years ago.

Why didn't I just cross the street and walk inside the funeral parlor? Why was I hesitating? I don't know, but I dawdled there for the longest time. The morning was sunny and warm but without humidity, and there was a gentle early-August breeze blowing up Madison Avenue.

I waited until I saw a group of people who might be theater folk enter the funeral parlor and then I crossed quickly against the light and went in on their heels. I had my long gray-gold hair pulled up in a bun and I was wearing leather sandals and a long loose white dress with marigolds on it.

Inside was all marble and gentility. A well-dressed man with a carnation inquired as to the name of the deceased and, once given, pointed me to the stairs. I walked up swiftly and found the room.

Arkavy Reynolds was laid out in a brass coffin. There were only eight or nine people in the room, moving awkwardly from wall to wall. Great bunches of flowers were present, still wrapped in their cellophane delivery shrouds.

I walked to the coffin, close up, and stared down. Arkavy was lying there in some sort of garment. He looked so thin in death. He had little hair on his head, which surprised me, but then again, I had never seen him in life without his hat. The moment I looked at him, I realized how stupid and sentimental I had been in coming. Arkavy would have found it too funny for words.

"A nice man," I heard someone say very close to me.

I turned. An old woman with a pink straw hat was standing with the help of a cane and looking past the coffin at the wall.

"A very nice man," she repeated, and then added, "and he was so good to his mother before she died. Did you know his mother?"

I shook my head.

"Did you know his family is from Albany?" she asked.

"No."

"Yes, Albany," she affirmed, smiled, and then hobbled away. I looked at the coffin again. It was all too sad. Who knows what dreams Arkavy had when he arrived in New York all those years ago from Albany . . . thirsting for the theatrical life, which was then the bohemian life . . . for beauty and truth through artifice . . . for *épater la bourgeoisie*. Did he really think New York would be like the Paris of Baudelaire? The fool. I turned away and walked quickly out of the viewing room to the stairs.

I hadn't gone three steps down when a young man walking up loomed in front of me and barred my path.

He had thick black curly hair and equally thick eyebrows laying over very radiant blue eyes. He was wearing the ugliest Hawaiian sport shirt I had ever seen, hanging loose over his belt. My first thought was: How did they let him in?

He grinned at me and didn't move aside. He said: "Beneath this rock there doth lie all the beauty that could ever die."

I stared dumbly at him. Something about him was very familiar.

"Ben Jonson," he said, identifying the quote.

And then I uttered a long, exasperated groan. Of course I knew him. What bloody bad luck! I had just started teaching a course in the second summer session at the New School. The class had met only once so far. And this young man had already become a pain in the posterior. A severe pain. It was just the introductory session of the course, so I had thrown out to the class a childish bone—what came into their minds when the word "theater" was mentioned. This young man, the one now blocking my exit, had leapt up and launched into a long violent diatribe about the American theater, quoting and approving and expanding upon Brecht's comment that Broadway was simply one segment of the international drug trade. He had immediately alienated all the other students to such a degree that they started yelling at him . . . and my fine, gentle introductory session had turned into a shambles.

"What are you doing here?" I asked him.

"Paying my respects to a madman, Professor, just like you."

"May I pass?" I asked, my voice growing angry.

He stepped aside and bowed low in an Elizabethan flourish, his grotesque shirt billowing, showing the lean muscular stomach underneath.

"May I introduce myself?" he asked, grinning.

"No need," I replied, and walked swiftly down the stairs and out of the building.

Once outside, on Madison Avenue, I breathed deeply. What a fiasco! I wanted very much to be back in my apartment with Bushy and Pancho. I wanted very much to be far away from that sad dead man and that obnoxious young man. So I took a cab home.

3

One cannot control one's students. At least I never could. Worse, I inspire them, always, the wrong way.

"Is it true that most actors are lousy lovers?"

I stared at the heavyset girl in the second row who had asked me that question. Was she serious? Was it a serious question?

I tried not to make a face, but I was disgusted with the question. This was a summer-school course at the prestigious New School for Social Research—an elite institution. It was supposed to be a serious course; about the theater and the actress in New York City . . . how they interact . . . how each enlightens, cripples, and modifies the other.

But all I had gotten during the first three sessions was a series of stupid questions. In fact, there were only six sessions left. When would I gain control of the course? When would I be able to move the students to a higher level? I had taught a few classes in the past . . . in acting schools . . . and some at

City College. Some of them had turned out to be memorable. A professor at City College once told me that my lecture on *Waiting for Godot* was the best and most exciting piece of Beckett analysis he had ever heard. I had brought a homeless woman to the class to show my students that Beckett's portrayal of tramps had nothing to do with any reality whatsoever . . . that the tramps in Beckett's great play were in disguise. And then, with the class's participation, I began to peel off the disguise . . . to discover who those tramps really were. Where had they worked? What were their medical problems? What country were they from? The class was in an uproar. It was the most remarkable explosion of good chemistry I had ever experienced. But that was then. And the times were different. And the milieu was different. And perhaps I was different. None of that good chemistry had emerged so far in the New School class.

Maybe it was futile, I thought, as I also thought of a way to answer the lousy-lover question. I had obtained this teaching job, in fact, only because of a stupid article about me buried in the theater section of the Sunday *New York Times*. So maybe they expected me to field stupid questions. Anyway, the opening paragraph of that article had read:

> At forty-one, Alice Nestleton is still an unknown to the general public, but in the inner circle of the New York theater world her recent interpretation of the Nurse in a Portobello production of *Romeo and Juliet* in Montreal is

considered a brilliant dramaturgical explora-
tion. In addition, Miss Nestleton has a very
interesting hidden life—crime. She has recently received a commendation from the
Nassau County Police Department for her
help in solving several grisly murders on the
North Shore of Long Island, which took her
into the rarefied atmosphere of the thorough-
bred-horse world.

The article then went on to briefly document the roles I
had played in the past and to discuss my interpretation of the
role of the Nurse.

Let's be honest. It was that damn article that got me the
job and, believe me, what the New School pays buys a lot of
cat food.

"I haven't had too many lovers who were actors," I said to
the class, "so I really can't judge them. The ones I did have
were medium-rare."

Laughter in the class. The air-conditioning was breaking
down again. One of the students had opened the window in
the rear; a sticky, hot, and humid August air seemed to envelop
us. It was a night class. The students worked during the day.
They were paying their hard-earned money for insights into
the life of the actress in New York, but they hadn't given me a
chance yet to explore it with them. They were fixated on bizarre things: Who did I sleep with? . . . Where did I buy my
clothes? . . . How did I support myself between parts? None of

them really relevant to *the* problem, which was the structure of the theater itself and how it destroys the actress like a sausage-making machine.

I stole a glance at the right rear of the classroom. That was where my nemesis always sat—the young man in the Hawaiian sport shirt who had accosted me in the funeral parlor. His classroom behavior had continued to be unbelievable. I seemed to irritate him severely. I seemed to lack the dedication he required. I seemed to be his ogre of a decaying theatrical class. He challenged. He emoted. He screamed. He wept. He was wearisome. But sometimes he looked at me with such a strange, fierce look, I had the feeling that he and he alone in the class knew I was a very good teacher when the time and place were right. And always, from the first moment he walked into class, I felt that he was watching me, studying me, waiting to pounce on me, and wanting very much to anticipate the things I would say and the movements I would make.

His seat was empty! Thank God! Maybe he had withdrawn from the course. It was a cheering thought.

I looked at my watch. Eight thirty-two. The class was supposed to run until nine.

How does one abort a class? Would the students be happy? Or would they feel cheated?

A middle-aged woman with startlingly gray hair raised her hand. I acknowledged her.

"I want you to address Portobello's concept of Shakespeare."

God bless you, lady, I thought. I was about to do it, but

suddenly I became weary . . . very weary. I wanted to go home . . . I wanted to feed my cats.

I smiled at her. "Why don't we quit early tonight, and I'll start the next class with Portobello." I was suggesting, asking, begging.

They leapt at the chance. Without another word, they gathered their packages, half-eaten sandwiches, carryalls, and paperbacks. They were as happy to leave as I.

One girl remained as the others flew out. She was an actress. I just knew it. I couldn't handle her worshipful gaze, as if I had truly "made it." I hadn't. My income was still primarily from cat-sitting, from playing games with oftentimes borderline psychotic felines like the beloved Geronimo.

"At least," she said, "that idiot didn't show up."

She was wearing a tank top. She had short brown hair and incredibly intense green eyes.

"That's for sure," I replied, smiling, thinking of the blessed absence of that young man who had tormented me maliciously during the first few sessions. Then the girl became shy and said nothing. An awkward minute passed. Then two minutes. Finally, she left.

I waited sixty seconds and was starting to exit when two men entered the classroom. They didn't come all the way inside, hovering near the door and smiling at me. They introduced themselves. Cops. Detectives Felix and Proctor. They were attached to some task force with an incredibly bizarre bureaucratic name. Young men, clean-cut, vacant eyes.

"You are Alice Nestleton?" the one named Proctor asked.

"Yes." I had no idea what they wanted.

They laid out on my desk in a scattered pattern about twenty photographs. I looked at them. In most of them the backdrop was the inside of the Frank E. Campbell Funeral Home, where Arkavy Reynolds had lain in state.

"You took pictures at the funeral home? Why?" I was astonished.

"Arkavy Reynolds was a good snitch. An informer. He helped us. We helped him. We don't like it when one of our own gets blown apart by a semiautomatic twenty-five-caliber Beretta in broad daylight."

Arkavy a police informant? My God! It was too bizarre. What did he inform about? Dressing-room sex at the Public Theater?

The one called Felix, who was wearing an old-fashioned button-down shirt, asked me to go over the photos. I identified myself. I identified the obnoxious student. I identified a few other people—theater people—whom I hadn't seen in the funeral parlor because they arrived earlier or later than my visit. The detectives made notes on the backs of the photographs I had identified.

"What time was he murdered?" I asked.

"Late morning," Proctor answered.

"Were there any witnesses? Do you have any suspects?"

"We're working on it, lady," Felix answered testily.

"Did you check out his room? I think he lived in a seamen's shelter downtown."

"We know where he lived."

"Did you check out his coffee shops? He used to go to one

on Fifth, just east of Second and the Polish coffee shop on Tompkins Square Park."

"We know where he hung out," Proctor replied.

I was about to ask another question when Felix exploded: "What the hell is going on here? Are you a cop? Who is interrogating who?"

"No one is interrogating anyone," I replied softly, then let the dust settle before I asked another perfectly plausible question.

"Why would the murderer show up at the wake?" I asked.

"You never know," Detective Felix said, then gathered up the photographs, thanked me, and left. I had the sense that the two men were oddly foreign . . . like they were from Belgium or someplace like that.

One of them stuck his head back through the door. "By the way, we found you because one of the ushers at the funeral home saw you once in an off-Broadway show. He said you were very good, but he didn't remember the name of the play."

∞

It was almost ten when I finally began climbing the five flights of stairs to my apartment. I was carrying a large bag of groceries, which included various tidbits for my Maine coon cat, Bushy, and my nearly tailless ASPCA contribution, Pancho.

The hallway was stifling. But there was only one more landing to go. The stairs were so familiar that I had lost my sense of climbing and thought only of the cats waiting for me . . . waiting in the darkness . . . each doing his own thing. Bushy was probably stretched out on the sofa, one eye open, his stomach purring softly at the thought of the coming food. Pancho was probably just finishing one of his lunatic dashes from cabinet to cabinet in the kitchen, running from shadowy enemies.

In fact, I was so wrapped up in the cats, I never saw the figure sitting at the top of the landing until he said: "Happy Birthday, Professor."

I froze in fear—staring through the dim light.

"Happy Birthday, Professor," the voice repeated in a mocking tone.

The outline of a man, a young man, sitting calmly.

Next to him on the stairs was a large carton wrapped in paper, with ribbons hanging from it.

A thief? A rapist? A psychotic derelict? I didn't know. I wanted to run, but my feet remained rooted.

My grocery bag, I thought. I can fling my bag at him and run down the steps. But I didn't.

"Who are you? How did you get in? What do you want?"

"Theater!" he shouted dramatically.

Oh, God! My fear abated for the first time. It was my nemesis: the obnoxious student from the back of the class who had not showed up for the most recent lesson, thankfully— the same one I had met in the funeral parlor.

"What are you doing here?" I yelled, anger replacing the initial fear . . . anger at his arrogance and stupidity and craziness. I was so weary of him.

"I brought you a birthday present," he replied.

"It's not my birthday."

The young man stood up for the first time. Even in the bad light I could see that he was wearing one of his ghastly loud sport shirts. He was taller than I had remembered, and older. He had a small blunt nose and his large eyes seemed green in the hallway—not blue. His skin was very white.

I was tired. I was angry. I snapped at him: "Please move aside with your box and let me get into my apartment."

I had spoken to him as if I was a kindergarten teacher and he was a recalcitrant tot.

He didn't move. He didn't speak.

The clock was ticking. Tick-tock. His shirt was drenched with sweat; large stains moved from his arms to the center of the fabric.

Then he moved quickly, down the steps, toward me—so quickly I couldn't respond at all.

At the last moment he sidestepped, just brushing me with his face, whispering: "I love you."

And then he was gone to the next landing below. His steps were like a receding train . . . quicker and lighter in the distance.

"Your box," I yelled out after him, pointing at the item he had left behind on the top of the landing.

But it was too late. He was gone.

Oh, God, I thought. All I needed now was a crazy student who had fallen in love with me. But there was a more immediate problem. I had to open my apartment door with an extra-large package in addition to my shopping bag—without the cats getting out.

I reached the top landing and began to push the large birthday box toward the door of my apartment with my foot.

Halfway there the box began to vibrate furiously, ribbons flapping and unraveling.

I stepped back, startled.

Before I could do anything, the box turned over on its side.

Out leapt a very large and very beautiful snow-white cat with a black-spotted face and a black-spotted rump.

The cat leapt onto the banister and stood there—eyeing me malevolently.

4

I stared at the creature from the box with a kind of shocked disbelief.

It was one of the most beautiful cats that ever hissed at me. My first thought, as I moved toward it slowly, was that it was an Abyssinian; it had that long-legged cougar look which so distinguished the breed.

But then I realized my identification was nonsense. There is no such thing as a white Abyssinian. And, to make matters even more absurd, this cat, now elongated against the banister as if it was about to spring, had black spots on its face and rump.

"Now, be reasonable, Clara," I said to her as I inched my way forward, not having the faintest idea why I called her Clara. She wasn't impressed. When I was about ten inches away, she leapt lightly off the banister and came to a stop in front of my door. She sat and stared at me.

Inside my apartment, my cats were scurrying. I could hear

them through the door. Reality dawned on me. I could not take Clara into the apartment with my own cats. It was too dangerous . . . too problematic—God knows what would happen!

I stood still and silently cursed that idiotic young man who had left me Clara. Was this the way he expressed his adolescent love? God help me if he falls out of love, I thought—he'll deposit a real cougar on the stairs, gift-wrapped also.

What were my options? Well, I could just leave the cat in the hallway and hope that it would wander to a different floor and someone kindly would give it a home. Or I could take it to an animal shelter. But that was dangerous—cats in shelters are two cans of tuna fish away from the gas chamber. No, Clara couldn't go there.

Clara stared at me. I stared at Clara. The solution was obvious. Board Clara out until the next class at the New School, when I could demand that the retarded Lothario retrieve his poor cat.

But with whom could I board her? I knew only one person close by . . . only one person well enough for me to have the audacity to ask.

I walked quickly down the hallway to the last door on the left and knocked, calling out: "Mrs. Oshrin. It's me, Alice Nestleton. It's all right. It's me." I had to talk loud because Mrs. Oshrin was a bit hard of hearing. She opened the door. She was a very stout woman, about sixty-five, a retired teacher. We always went shopping together on Saturday mornings, to the farmers' market at Union Square Park. For some reason she called me Alice and I called her Mrs. Oshrin. Maybe she intimidated me a bit. She used to be a minor Democratic-party official and she still talked incessantly about city politics when given the chance.

"What is the matter?" she asked, frightened. She always thought something was the matter. I pointed down the hall-way, where the white cat still sat.

"Who is that?" Mrs. Oshrin asked. As if it were a distant relative who had suddenly arrived and was about to ask a fa-vor. She was right.

"Her name is Clara," I said.

"Clara," Mrs. Oshrin repeated, as if the name rang a bell in her memory.

"Yes, Clara, and she needs a home for just a day or two."

My voice was pleading. Mrs. Oshrin could never with-stand my needs. She was a very nice lady. She stared out down the hallway again.

"But what do I do? I never had a cat."

That was all I needed. I rushed to my shopping bag, took out a can of cat food, ran into Mrs. Oshrin's apartment, opened it, strolled down the hallway to Clara so she could get a whiff, then carried the can back to Mrs. Oshrin's apartment. I left the door open and placed the can about ten feet inside.

Then Mrs. Oshrin and I sat down on her sofa. We waited. We waited. We chatted.

Then we saw one white ear. Then a black-and-white nose. Then a long lean body flitted through the doorway.

Clara was inside. We beamed at each other. Mrs. Oshrin watched Clara inspect the food and then walk regally away. The cat was beginning to explore.

"Why doesn't she eat the food?" Mrs. Oshrin asked.

"She will," I said.

We watched.

"My sister had a cat," Mrs. Oshrin noted.

I realized that Mrs. Oshrin and I were about to lapse into one of our constant Pinteresque dialogues that went on and on and nowhere at all. Usually I enjoyed them, but now I wanted to feed my poor cats.

"Everything will be all right, Mrs. Oshrin. Just talk to her once in a while. I'll call you tomorrow." And then I was gone, leaving the bewildered woman with a new companion.

∽

I called Mrs. Oshrin five times the next day to make sure she and Clara were getting along. Mrs. Oshrin did not seem to be enjoying the stranger but she was calm, stoic, and asked me only three or four times when I would get Clara out. Soon, I said, soon.

I discussed the problem with Bushy, my Maine coon cat. He was noncommittal. As for Pancho, he never stayed still long enough to listen.

As the hours passed and I came closer to my class, my anger toward that young man grew to truly monumental proportions. I envisioned an almost Elizabethan scene of vengeance and condemnation. Then I mellowed somewhat—after all, the young man was in love with a forty-one-year-old actress with long golden-gray hair and a reputation for dramatic innovation—me. I was, to be truthful, just a bit vain. And it had been a long time since I had elicited that kind of passion from anyone. Besides, that kind of crazy young man was what kept the theater alive. No wonder he had gone to Arkavy Reynolds' funeral. The young Arkavy had been a bohemian firebrand. Theater or death! It wasn't a game. It wasn't an art. It wasn't a pastime for speculators or dilettantes. The theater was life itself. Did *I* still have any of that commitment?

I arrived at the class earlier than usual and sat at my desk doodling. The students straggled in. The heavyset woman who had asked about Portobello smiled at me. I nodded to her, signifying that yes, indeed, I would deal with her inquiries in this class, this evening.

The young man never arrived. As I was giving my disjointed lecture, I kept anticipating the door opening and a lovesick young man with a ghastly sport shirt flitting in.

Thirty minutes before the class was about to end I abandoned the lecture, which they were all obviously finding boring, and asked point-blank if anyone in the class knew the missing young man who wore loud sport shirts and wisecracked all the time. Did anyone know his name?

The students looked at each other. They were perplexed. Curious. This was the New School. In Manhattan. No one asked or gave names in a formal sense. No one called the roll. At most, one student would say to another, "I'm Jo Anne. Hi." As for me, I had been given a list of the names of all the students who had signed up for the course—but I had discarded it immediately.

"He left something in the classroom," I told the class, a gentle half lie. No one in the seats in front of me uttered a word. I dismissed them early and angrily.

As I was gathering my things from off the desk, that ingenue in the tank top said: "He told me his name was Bruce. He asked me to have a cup of coffee with him after the first class. I said no."

I smiled my thanks. She waited to see if I was willing to talk theater with her. Then, seeing that my thoughts were elsewhere, she left. My thoughts were indeed elsewhere. The name Bruce didn't help me. What was I going to do with poor Mrs. Oshrin?

5

There was a new line on my face, on the left side, going from the edge of the mouth to the chin. It was ever so gentle and straight—but it was there.

"You are getting old, Alice Nestleton. And you are getting quirkier. And you are . . ."

I stopped speaking to myself in the mirror and concentrated on my brushing. Pancho was on the high bookcase, his rust-colored whiskers quivering just a bit, and his gaunt gray body with the scar on one side in a state of extreme alert for the unseen furies which were always chasing him. I raised the brush slowly and, in the mirror, watched his eyes follow the movement.

It was ten o'clock in the morning. I had overslept. Several times during the night I had awoken with a start from the same nightmare. In the dream I was lying in a coffin in the Frank E. Campbell Funeral Home on Madison Avenue and Arkavy Reynolds was paying his last respects to my body. But then my grandmother appeared and she and Arkavy got into a terrible row. And I kept waking up to stop their fighting. It was not just arguing—it was something horrible they were doing to each other. Each time I awoke, my heart was beating fast. But now the fear was gone. For the first time in days there was a cool breeze moving through my apartment; a promise of the autumn soon to come.

When I finished brushing, I made a cup of coffee and took it into the living room. Bushy was snoozing on the sofa, his head lying on a script. I removed the thin folder gently, but it woke him. He looked up at me, hurt, and then leapt to the floor to continue his nap on the carpet, groaning a bit at my incredible lapse of manners.

The script itself was only thirty pages long and bound into a strange-colored binder, a dull yellow. It had been sent to me by an old friend who taught at Boston University but who spent all his money and time on theatrical productions in the New England area. We had only one thing in common— we both craved, sought for, and aspired to theatrical pieces that were far outside the mainstream. We both wanted to explore the reality of the stage and the players and the relation of both to "what there is"—so we were both perpetually frustrated. I held the dull yellow binder in my hand with a kind of weariness. After all, I knew that the theater was so tyrannized by normalcy that even a Brecht play was not considered avant-garde.

My Medaglia d'Oro instant coffee, however, was black and sweet and bracing, and the breeze in the living room was truly delightful, so I opened the stiff front cover and began to read.

I burst out laughing when I read the title page: *Rats: An Alternative to Cats.*

The "Cats," of course, being the long-running Broadway musical of that name.

It wasn't really a script. It was a discussion of a performance. There are seven rats in the cast, part of an extended family which lives beneath the theater where *Cats* is playing.

The rats speak a kind of fractured Shakespearean English and they are hopelessly violent, oversexed, venal, and lunatic— a kind of murderous Marx Brothers.

A new litter is born, and this new litter, which lives offstage in large boxes among the audience, develops a decided taste for human flesh, particularly for the actors and actresses who play the cats in the musical of the same name.

It was a delicious, bizarre, very funny dramatic mess and I was just getting deep into the gory theatrics when I heard someone knocking.

At first I thought it was someone on the street. But no, someone was at my door. I approached cautiously and said hello through the wood.

"It's me, Alice," said the voice. Mrs. Oshrin.

I opened the door. She was standing there in a housedress, her arms folded, looking very clumsy and gloomy.

The sight of her unnerved me. I had forgotten all about Clara, the white cat, while reading the script.

Mrs. Oshrin marched in and sat down on the sofa. She

seemed to be very upset but trying to control herself. I knew there was trouble because she was wearing a very bright and new housedress. That was one of Mrs. Oshrin's sure signals that things were not going well with her. Another sure signal was the fact that she didn't look around my living room with her usual critical stare. Mrs. Oshrin didn't like my living room. The furniture didn't bother her. She liked the large French sofa I had bought at Pierre Deux in the Village when I was temporarily affluent. She liked the long, narrow oak dining room table. She liked my three cane chairs near the window and my beat-up coffee table. What she never liked was the clutter. But there was nothing I could do about that. My kitchen was small. My bedroom smaller. The long, very narrow hall which ran the length of my apartment had to be kept clear if it was to remain passable. So everything ended up in my living room. I truly lived in my living room, and the clutter was just too much for her. Oh, there was no question Mrs. Oshrin was out of sorts.

"Can I get you some coffee?" I asked.

"No, thank you."

I sat down on the sofa next to her.

"Is Clara giving you any trouble?" I asked.

There was no answer.

"I was going to bring you some more cat food this afternoon," I said.

There was no answer. I could see that she was glaring at poor Bushy.

"Alice," she finally said in a very peculiar voice, "I am going to visit my sister in Connecticut."

"Well, that's nice," I replied happily.

She reached into her housedress and retrieved a single key attached to a rather large piece of wood.

Now she was staring at the ceiling. Poor Mrs. Oshrin; by this time I had surmised the visit had to do with Clara. Once again I silently cursed that young man who had caused all these problems.

"And when I come back," she said firmly, "I would like very much if that cat was in its new home."

"Of course, Mrs. Oshrin," I said quickly. It was obvious that Clara was ruining our relationship.

"Has she been much bother?" I asked.

Mrs. Oshrin didn't answer. She stood up, smoothed her housedress, gave me the key, smiled kindly, and just walked out, not letting me know what kind of horrendous behavior Clara had exhibited.

That killed my day. If she would be back in a day or two, I had to find someplace else for Clara to reside, very quickly.

In the next ten hours I must have made about fifty phone calls. The range and variety of excuses why these people could not board orphan Clara were mind-boggling. But they all said no. No matter how endearingly I described Clara, the answer was the same: no.

It was around ten o'clock in the evening that I finally made an intelligent move. I called John Cerise. Now, John has absolutely nothing to do with the theater. He's a cat man, pure and simple. In fact, he was always a source of cat-sitting assignments for me. We met years ago when I first started cat-sitting for a rich lady on Central Park West whose passion was

English shorthairs. Cerise was a cat-show judge and breeder who lived somewhere in New Jersey. He is a gentle, knowledgeable man, now in his sixties, whose love for cats is proverbial. We rarely speak to each other more than two or three times a year, but there is a genuine affection between us, and he has a special spot in his heart for crazed Pancho, who, he once said, is a reincarnation of one of Napoleon's marshals.

What made me think of John Cerise was the fact that when I first saw Clara I had thought she was an Abyssinian, and Cerise, I knew, was breeding Abyssinians. He loved Abys, as he called them and, while normally a quiet man, would immediately discourse on them if given the chance. About how they are the true descendants of the sacred cats of ancient Egypt. About how they are the only breed with a close wild relative still extant—the North African desert cat, *Felis libyca*. About their wild looks but gentle affectionate nature. About how difficult they are to breed. About the strange fact that they produce predominantly male litters. About what excellent swimmers they are because they actually like water. And on and on.

I didn't lie to him when I called. But I didn't quite tell him the truth either. I concocted a gentle, imaginative story. There was this very strange-looking Abyssinian staying at a friend's apartment. Could he stop over and check it out, and if he didn't want it, recommend someone who would like it? I told him nothing about the deranged romanticism which had brought the cat to me and Mrs. Oshrin. He agreed. He laughingly asked for clarification of my phrase "a strange-looking Abyssinian." I got off the phone fast.

He arrived at seven thirty the next morning. It was very good to see him again. He was wearing one of those elegant white linen suits, a blue silk tie, and a lighter blue silk shirt. His still-black hair was slicked back. John Cerise always looked exotic—an ageless relic from another time and another place. It was fitting he was a cat man. He seemed to be perfectly and easily androgynous. He reeked of a kind of cool sensuality which was quite pleasing to watch, although one could rarely identify the object of his passion.

We walked down the hallway to Mrs. Oshrin's. I opened the door with her key and stepped inside, closing the door behind us.

"She's white," I whispered as we waited in the living room for Clara to appear. Why was I whispering?

"White?" John asked, astonished.

I nodded. Clara did not appear.

"Maybe she's in the bedroom," I said. We walked into Mrs. Oshrin's bedroom. Clara wasn't there either.

She wasn't in the kitchen. She wasn't in the closets. She wasn't under anything.

We were puzzled.

"Make some noise," John suggested.

I banged one of Mrs. Oshrin's bronze bric-a-brac against a table leg. It made a dull thudding noise. Clara was not interested.

"The bathroom," John said.

We walked there quickly and found Clara in the bathtub, staring malevolently at a slow drip from the bath faucet. Our presence seemed to make absolutely no difference to her.

"Get acquainted," I said to John in an incredibly patronizing tone, and then ran off before he could say another word.

My plan was to leave them alone for two hours. I went back to my apartment, retrieved a shopping list, and went to the supermarket.

I lolled down the aisles. Now that John Cerise was on Clara's case I had a tremendous feeling of confidence that everything would be all right. In fact, I was so confident I bought a Sara Lee chocolate cake to serve John when I got back.

When I finished my shopping list I took a slow walk around the neighborhood, luxuriating in the suddenly pleasant weather.

Then I headed home, pulling my shopping cart lightly.

When I turned the corner of my block and could see the stoop of my building, I knew something was wrong.

Police cars and an ambulance choked the street. A crowd had gathered.

As I reached the building, pushing my way through the onlookers, I saw the stretcher coming down the steps.

A leg with a white linen covering stuck out from beneath the EMS sheet.

"John," I screamed, letting go of my shopping cart and rushing to the stretcher.

It was him. His face looked like hamburger meat streaked with red dye number nine. There was blood splattered all over his body and clothes.

He smiled at me weakly. He reached up and patted my hand.

"Who are you, lady?" a burly man in an open blue shirt asked.

"I live up there," I replied. "What happened?" My composure had returned but I really couldn't comprehend what I was seeing.

Then I saw the badge hanging around his neck like a charm.

"Someone broke in. Your friend on the stretcher got in the way. But he'll be all right. He looks worse than he is. The thief got away."

"What about Clara?"

"He was alone."

"No, Clara is a cat. A white cat." I held my hands out to show him the size; to show him that Clara was a small animal.

"There was no cat in the apartment, lady. Listen, you don't look so good. Why don't you sit down on the steps for a minute? Your friend is going to be all right."

I sat down and watched them load poor John into the ambulance.

6

John Cerise grinned when he saw me at the door of the hospital room. Once again he was dressed in white. The left side of his face was discolored and there was a bandage over his left eye. He looked smaller in bed, much, much smaller, like a kitten in a high chair. He made a motion with his hand and I approached.

"Did you find the cat?" he whispered. The discoloration was like a brilliantly painted bruise—red and black and purple.

I shook my head. The cat had vanished. The detective had surmised that the cat had run out of the apartment, down the steps, and onto the street.

An old man in evident pain lay on the other bed in the room. He made a valiant effort to wave at me. I patted him gently on the arm as I made my way between the beds. What else could I do?

"I'm sorry I got you into this mess," I said to John.

He shook his head with as much vigor as he could summon, to assure me he bore me no grudge. Then he seemed to gulp air. He finally said: "Alice, Clara is not an Abyssinian. But she is a lovely cat. She looks like an Abyssinian. She walks like an Abyssinian. She talks like an Abyssinian. . . ." He sat up with some effort, raising his hand for emphasis. "But there is no such thing as a white Abyssinian."

I pushed his arm down to his side and helped him back down.

"The police told me," I said, "that a thief must have known Mrs. Oshrin went away, and then broke in, not knowing anyone was there. It was just one of those odd coincidences; you being in the wrong place at the wrong time."

He nodded. He twisted in the bed. He started to get up again, thought the better of it, and said pathetically: "I never saw who it was, Alice. I was in the living room. Clara was on the rug. We were getting to know each other. I heard a noise. It sounded like someone was fumbling around near the door. But I thought it was you. I didn't even turn around. And then I felt a terrible pain here. . . ." He gestured to the side of his face. "And then everything went black."

"You were hit with one of Mrs. Oshrin's antique candleholders," I told him.

He closed his eyes.

"It could have been worse," I quipped. "You could have been hit with Mrs. Oshrin."

He grinned, his eyes still closed. The sun was streaming into the room.

"I'll be out of here tomorrow," he said.

"Do you want me to come here tomorrow to help you check out?" I asked.

"No need. I'll be fine."

I walked around his bed and sat down on the chair by the window. Cerise seemed to doze. A painkiller, I thought.

It was bizarre how things got out of hand. A stupid young man falls in love with a teacher. He gives her a cat. The teacher places the cat with a neighbor. The neighbor is unhappy. The teacher calls a friend to look the cat over. A thief breaks in and almost murders the friend, who has absolutely nothing to do with anyone or anything in that apartment.

The absurd chain of events horrified me. But something else about the whole mess was just plain peculiar. The detective had said that the thief panicked when he saw Cerise, hit him, and fled. That's why nothing had been taken from the apartment.

I had the nagging doubt, suspicion, feeling—call it what you will—that the thief had broken in to steal Clara. That is what I felt; but the logic escaped me.

Sitting on the hospital chair, thinking those thoughts, I did feel stupid. Clara was a lovely cat, but why would anyone break into an apartment to steal her? No, the detective was right: it was simply an aborted breaking and entering, aborted by an unexpected guest in the apartment. So then why did I have that feeling? Oh, glorious, delicious, irrelevant paranoia. Alice Nestleton, the quirky out-of-work actress, the New School lecturer, the well-known cat-sitter, the obscure crime solver—getting delusional once again over a rather dim-witted feline.

Cerise was talking to me. I had been so lost in my thoughts that I hadn't heard a word he said. Then I realized he was asking me where I really got the cat. He had known all the time I wasn't telling him the unvarnished truth.

"From a lovesick student," I admitted.

"Still breaking hearts?" he asked.

"The young man isn't old enough to be my nephew. I'm teaching a class at the New School. And there he was, an obnoxious young man of about twenty-odd years with a very bad case of arrested adolescence."

"You didn't want the cat?"

"John," I explained, "he dumped it on my landing in a box—his conception of a love offering, I suppose. I didn't even know it was a cat. I thought it was just a large box with a muffler or something like that inside, or maybe an extended love poem."

"Cat in a box," he mused, and then winced. Too much talking obviously hurt the side of his face.

"John," I said, "stop talking. Anyway, what is there to talk about? I don't even know if it was his cat. Maybe he found it on the street."

"Poor Clara," he whispered.

I leaned back in my chair. The next class at the New School was in forty-eight hours. If that young fool Bruce Whateverhisnameis didn't show up, I was determined to find out his last name even if I had to pester the New School's administrative staff. He had already caused the pain of a dear friend, the alienation of a treasured neighbor, and the disappearance or even worse of a lovely white cat with black spots on its face and rump. His only redeeming trait seemed to be that he had taken the time to pay his last respects to a pathetic New York theatrical legend named Arkavy Reynolds.

7

The lovesick troublemaker, again, didn't show up in class. I waited twenty minutes, then told the class to keep itself busy, and walked resolutely to the administrative office. Only a clerk was at the desk, usual in the evenings.

I asked to see my class roster. She refused. I demanded. She waffled. I cajoled. She averted her eyes. I begged, hinting that I was only asking because of a health emergency. She didn't ask me to elaborate. That was sufficient. She showed it to me.

His name was Bruce Chessler. He lived at an address on East Fifth Street between First Avenue and Avenue A.

Then, armed with this information, I went back to the class and gave one of the most boring and irrelevant lectures in the entire history of adult education. At the end of the class I felt ashamed of myself, cursing Bruce Chessler again because it was his fault . . . everything was becoming his fault.

I went home and conversed with my cats. Bushy seemed

quite understanding, even favoring me with four or five paw swipes.

There was no Bruce Chessler listed in the Manhattan phone book at that address. I called information. There was no phone of any kind listed to any individual with that name.

Was I being obsessive? The thought occurred to me. Why didn't I just leave it alone? The cat was gone, God knows where. John Cerise would be okay. Mrs. Oshrin would forgive me. Yes, indeed—why didn't I leave it alone!

I began to pace. Then I walked to the hall mirror and stared at myself. Still thin, still lovely, still more golden than gray. Was that it? A middle-aged woman really fascinated by a young man who had fallen in love with her. No, I wasn't that stupid.

My antennae told me a crime had been committed. What was the crime? Simple. Someone had stolen Clara. That was what I believed from the first moment the detective had recounted his version of the events. There was no real proof . . . there was no real evidence.

But the logic of my belief was becoming more and more apparent as I thought about it.

Mrs. Oshrin had left on the trip very suddenly.

If her apartment had been targeted, she would have had to be under twenty-four-hour surveillance.

Why would someone be waiting for her to leave? She had absolutely nothing of value in her apartment.

It didn't make sense.

No, it was either a random break-in or a theft of the cat. One or the other. If it was a random break-in, any one of seven hundred individuals in my neighborhood could have been guilty. If it was a cat theft—who? The young man stealing his cat back? Absurd. A ring of cat thieves? But how would they know a cat was living with Mrs. Oshrin—in fact, had just arrived in her apartment? And why would they want Clara?

The whole thing was very strange, very perplexing, very engaging.

There was no doubt about it. I was going to pay a visit to young lovesick Bruce Chessler and find out all about vanished Clara. But I didn't want to go there by myself. I wanted company.

The next morning I called Anthony Basillio at his place of business—the Mother Courage Copying Shop.

Basillio was an old acting-school friend of mine who had long ago given up the theater in his head—but not in his heart. He had helped me out with the Long Island murders, and even though he sometimes got carried away . . . even though he still called me Swede . . . even though he still propositioned me ever so subtly . . . even though he still looked like a long-lost refugee from a long-haired ashram—I trusted him very much and I appreciated his kind of manic intelligence. To him, two and two were rarely four—but they were rarely five either. More important, he had that intense free-floating anxiety that made him long to do something, anything, which is, I suppose, why he gambled too much and probably did a lot of other things too much.

We agreed to meet at a coffee shop on East Eighth Street just before noon.

I got there about eleven thirty. He was waiting and

very happy to see me again, blowing into his hands as if he was about to embark on something extremely pleasurable—almost juicy. He looked exactly the same. His hair was getting longer. His face was breaking out again. How could a forty-year-old man continue to look so unfinished? Actually, I found it charming.

"Swede, Swede, Swede," he said as we sipped our Mexican coffees. I had long since given up any hope of him discarding that traditional nickname. No matter how many times I told him I was not of Swedish descent, he never believed me. But then again, Basillio probably calls all people who come from Minnesota originally Swede.

"I have been longing, Swede, to hook up with you again. You're the only lady who brings me back."

"Back where, Tony?"

"Who the hell knows?"

We laughed.

"Who do you have to find?"

"A young man who was in my class at the New School. It's a long story," I replied.

"Tell it to me."

I told him.

"Are you afraid of this character?" he asked. I didn't answer for a while. He had a point. Why, in fact, was I afraid to find him alone? I knew the neighborhood. He hadn't been violent—only crazy.

"I'm very nervous around young men who are passionately in love with me," I replied. But that really wasn't the reason. I simply couldn't articulate the threat.

"Then you should be afraid of me, Swede."

"A married man with children?" I replied.

He grinned and changed the subject. "What's new with you? Any parts? Anything happening in the great beast?"

"I'm reading a crazy script—about a family of rats."

"Why not?" He laughed.

We finished our coffee and left. Five minutes later we stood in front of Chessler's four-story tenement building. It was like a hundred thousand others in the East Village.

The day had become very hot and very muggy. It was the kind of August day in New York when you want to think only about distant galaxies. Nothing will ease your torment other than the vision of enormous explosions and implosions on a cosmic scale.

The building had two step-down stores on either side of the entrance. One was boarded up. The other was a shoemaker.

"Do you remember that fat woman who used to live down here?" Basillio asked. "The one who was in the Dramatic Workshop with us. I think it was in seventy-four. She was from North Carolina. She used to give parties. I think it was on Fourth Street."

I didn't remember. That was a long time ago. And if I did remember, it would probably be very depressing. There is nothing as sad as doomed theatrical careers. They are so predictable.

We walked into the small lobby. There was a panel of bells but the names next to them were so faded or mutilated that they couldn't be made out. No matter how intensely I stared at all those letters, none of them seemed to combine into "Chessler."

"We can wait until someone comes down and ask," Basillio said.

Suddenly the outer door opened and a Hispanic woman with an enormous bizarre wig moved inside the small lobby with us.

"Who you? What you want?" she demanded. Her tone was very aggressive. She was carrying a large pail with sponges floating around on top.

"I'm looking for Bruce Chessler's apartment," I said.

She crossed herself.

"All his stuff now in cellar. I couldn't wait longer. No longer. Very sorry. It all downstairs. Owner told me to put it there. I put it there."

"But where is he?" I asked, confused by her comments.

She crossed herself again.

"I thought you his family. Young man dead. Murdered in bar on Eighth Street. Few days ago. You not his family?"

"Murdered?" My chest felt like a bellows.

"Boom! Boom!" she said. "Shot in head. Dead."

I leaned against the wall, suddenly dizzy. Basillio pulled me away because my shoulders were pushing five bells at once.

8

Next to Chessler's building was a building with an orange stoop and on that stoop Basillio and I sat for a very long time in the humid air. The breeze was fetid.

I had gotten over the initial shock. After all, I hardly knew the young man. I could barely remember his face. But there was a lingering disturbance . . . a kind of blanket over the head, very light, very well-knit, very hard to shake. What had he said to me in the funeral parlor? Something from Ben Jonson: "Beneath this rock there doth lie all the beauty that could ever die." Or was it "stone" rather than "rock"?

"We should look over his stuff," Basillio said.

"Why? We didn't even know him." The bitterness in my own voice astonished me.

"Because," Basillio explained, "if he's been dead a few days and nobody came for his stuff, it may mean his family doesn't know . . . that the cops couldn't locate next of kin. So we should look through his stuff, find out who he is . . . I mean who he was . . . and contact his people."

Basillio was absolutely right. It was the proper thing to do. But I wasn't able to move. It was suddenly nice sitting there. There was all kinds of activity on the street to take my mind elsewhere. It was, in fact, what I had come to New York for, originally, from Minnesota, many years ago—for action, for all kinds of action if I may use that very ugly but very descriptive word: action in life, action in love, action in theater.

I was wearing one of my long country dresses, the kind that accentuates my already excessive height, the kind that my ex-husband used to say made me look like an erotic fantasy out of Virginia Woolf. I realized that I fit quite well in the East Village.

"There she is," Basillio said.

The woman with the wig was standing in front of the house staring at the door as if deciding whether or not it had to be cleaned.

We got up. We walked toward her. She knew what we were doing. She pulled a large key ring from her pocket, shook the keys at us, and we followed her through the door into the lobby, through the hallway, and down a very steep staircase that led to a cellar filled with more junk than I had ever seen in my life.

We heard scurrying among the objects. Cats? Rats? Derelicts? Junkies? Ghosts?

"Pigeons," said the woman leading us, with a broad grin. I couldn't tell whether she was being sarcastic or truthful. I realized also that she was not Hispanic, that the accent was something like Lebanese.

We walked through another door to a less-cluttered and better-lit space which had obviously once been the coal room and still had the partitions. She led us to one partition, piled with cartons and clothes and posters and toasters. She crossed herself and held out a hand in explanation—that this was what was left of Bruce Chessler. Then she was gone.

Anthony Basillio shook his head slowly as he stared at the stuff.

"We should, I suppose, be looking for something that identifies his family," he said.

I nodded. It seemed the intelligent way to proceed. A single overhead uncovered bulb burned ferociously down on the remains.

We started on the first large carton—Tony on one side and me on the other, emptying the contents carefully, almost religiously. About thirty seconds into the emptying, I was overwhelmed with such a sense of sadness, of futility, of hatred of whatever had extirpated him, that I just sat down on a low carton and started to cry. Above all, I couldn't deal with the memory of what the landlady or janitress had said. She had said: "Boom! Boom!" The young man had been shot to death. It was like an earthquake had been telescoped into one inconceivable splatter of violence. Steel. Noise. Blood. Pulp.

Basillio kept on, happily leaving me alone. I had the absurd notion, sitting there as I wept, that Clara, the white cat Bruce had given me to express his infatuation with an older woman—wherever Clara was now, she knew and was weeping also, as cats weep, from the stomach.

I could see Basillio removing book after book and flipping

pages—waiting for that telltale postcard or check stub used as a page marker which would identify him further. Then the magazines and the records and the pieces of a life on paper— menus, clippings, God knows what.

I wanted to help but I couldn't. Now I was beginning to see his face . . . and that sport shirt . . . and hear his caustic classroom mode . . . but now it was not threatening . . . death had given him a certain élan in my mind . . . the tragedy was becoming personally more intense, more intimate.

There were clothes and hats and beat-up sneakers. There were old check stubs and some canceled checks from the Chemical Bank branch on Eighth Street and Broadway.

Then Basillio pulled out a very fat white envelope, sealed with a thick ugly rubber band. He pulled the rubber band off, opened the envelope, and peered inside.

"Here," he said, bringing it over to me, "this is very sad."

Indeed it was. There were dozens of photographs in the envelope. Some of Bruce Chessler. Some of unidentified people. Some of Bruce in a group. It was his photo album of sorts.

In some of them he posed, wearing that chip-on-the-shoulder smile . . . the kind that said: I'm smarter and tougher and hipper than you and you'd better know it. Some of them showed a more pensive side, particularly when he was photographed with someone else. And sometimes, in the younger photos, he looked just plain desperate.

I came to the photo of an old woman.

I stared at it—the woman wore braids wrapped around her head. She wore a high-necked, very old-fashioned dress with a large ornament around her neck on a thick chain.

I moved on. Then suddenly I shuffled back to the old woman. The woman was old, but the photo was not. Maybe five years old at the most—the sides were still white and crisp.

The more I looked at the photo, the more I realized that I knew the old woman.

The hair, the ornament, the dress—they were all familiar. Then I remembered.

"Tony," I said, "come here for a minute."

He came back over. I showed him the photo.

"Do you know who this is?" I asked.

"No."

"Look hard!"

"I'm looking. But I don't know."

"Does the name Maria Swoboda mean anything to you?"

He cocked his head and screwed up his face. He was going through his thinking contortions.

Then he snapped his fingers: "The old acting teacher."

"Right," I confirmed, "the Method-acting teacher from the Moscow Art Theatre. She had a studio in New York in the fifties, sixties, and early seventies—on Grove Street. For a time she was the rage. I remember when I first came to New York I was able to get a few lessons from her, and I considered myself in the presence of a high priestess."

Yes, I remembered that crazy, wonderful old lady very well. But Method acting had long since gone out of vogue and I had no idea whether she was still alive, much less still teaching. She had not been a young woman when I went to her.

"Was Chessler an actor?" Basillio asked.

"Well, he was taking my class; he obviously had some interest in the theater. But he didn't talk like an actor. He talked like a political radical. You know . . . a lot of passion . . . a lot of hate . . . a lot of Brecht—like you used to talk, Tony. And he did show up at Arkavy Reynolds's funeral. You knew he died, didn't you? He got into a fight with a homeless man who murdered him on Jane Street. Two fools. Do you remember that fat man?"

Basillio nodded and went back to his work. I kept staring at the picture. God, how the memories surfaced . . . of Madame Swoboda, which was what she was called . . . speaking about Stanislavski and the vision they all had . . . speaking about the character being inside of the actor . . . speaking of how the character can only emerge authentically if the actor utilizes his own creativity, his own beauty, his own suffering to project the character from within to without. It was heady stuff. It was glorious.

Basillio interrupted my memories. He handed me a sheaf of papers that had been rolled and fastened with another rubber band.

"This is even sadder," he said.

I held the top and bottom of one sheet so it wouldn't fold. It was a handwritten letter.

It was addressed to me.

> Dear Alice Nestleton:
> You think I'm an idiot, don't you? You think I torment you in class to cause you grief. Don't you realize I must differentiate myself from all the others in any and every

way possible? Don't you understand that I am the only one in this stupid class who knows you are a great actress? I love you very much and I am afraid to tell you. I have a fantasy about you . . . a sexual fantasy . . . all the time . . . we are in a house built of reeds . . . it is high above some body of blue water . . . the house is on stilts and we are making love and you are wearing a beautiful . . .

I didn't want to read any further. I crumpled the sheaf of papers and thrust it into my bag. Basillio was right. Was there anything sadder than unsent love letters from a dead boy?

9

It was like a scene from an Edwardian melodrama. I sat on the edge of the bed. The love letters were scattered over the sheet in disarray. I was literally unable to read them except for very tiny snatches. It was too painful. He obviously hadn't known me at all. He was fantasizing. The saddest parts of all were his erotic fantasies, which he described in painful detail. There were twenty-two letters in all.

The first one was obviously written immediately after he attended the first class in the New School. He described what I wore and what I said during that first class. Bruce Chessler was older than I had thought—about twenty-five. And it was obvious to me now that his bizarre behavior in class was a function of his condition. He was unable to make contact with the object of his deranged love—me—so he could only attack me. He understood that he was causing me distress, and his letters were full of apologies.

I wanted to read them thoroughly and carefully but I couldn't.

Basillio called me about twenty minutes before midnight. He told me that he had checked out Swoboda, my old teacher, whose picture was inexplicably in Bruce Chessler's belongings. She had died four years ago in Lakewood, New Jersey. When he hung up I gathered the love letters in a fury of frustration and literally stuffed them into one of my chests. The young man was dead. He had no family or friends. His cat, given to me out of disjointed love, was gone. At least John Cerise was fine.

I couldn't fall asleep until two, and when I did fall asleep I had a whole series of dreams about my first boyfriend in Minnesota and necking in one of the dairy barns while my grandmother was twenty feet away behind the partition and didn't know a thing was going on.

The first thing I thought of when I woke up was retrieving the love letters and reading them carefully. I fought back the impulse. It obviously had something to do with the dream.

I spent a great deal of the next hour staring out of my living-room window onto the street, hoping for a glimpse of Clara. Perhaps she had just run out onto the street and was living from garbage can to garbage can. Perhaps she was now living feral in one of the overgrown backyards that run like a scar between the two rows of houses that front the street—and can be reached and seen only through the basement apartments or the interior hallways on the ground floors or by fire escapes from the roofs. Why not? Maybe she was there. But I saw no beast that resembled the strange white cat Chessler had delivered to me.

When I finally pulled myself away from my obsessive nonsense of staring out the window to find Clara, I slipped into a very agitated depression. I started to pace back and forth across the living room, stepping over Bushy each time. I was pacing so quickly in my agitation that Pancho even aborted one of his rushes to stare at me reflectively. Maybe he was thinking: Ah, the fool now knows what I go through twenty-four hours a day. She finally realizes they are after her as well.

In fact, the last time I was feeling so bad in the head was when I started *Romeo and Juliet* rehearsals in Montreal and I was frightened that the director, Portobello, would nip my interpretation of the Nurse in the bud.

I ceased my pacing when it dawned on me that if no one of Bruce Chessler's family had been found to claim his belongings or identify his body—it was the landlady who had done that—then there had to be no one to claim the body. And that meant that the young man, sport shirt and all, had been buried in one of those horrible derelict graves on small islands in the East River. I had once read about them—about how convicts from Rikers Island dig the graves, and the anonymous bodies, mostly from the Bowery and its environs, are slipped into them . . . like omelets.

I found that unbearable. But it was too late. The young man was already interred.

Things in my head were starting to get out of hand. I remembered part of one of the young man's fantasies—a house made of reeds. For the first time the imagery seemed familiar. From Yeats? I couldn't recall. From Euripides?

"Boom! Boom!" the landlady had said. Shot in a bar.

Why did Bruce Chessler die? That was the stupid question that aborted it all—that aborted my agitated depression; it was like a Zen koan, focusing all my energies. Why was it important to know? Because he loved me? Because I didn't reciprocate? Was it guilt? Old-fashioned corrosive guilt?

Why did Bruce Chessler die? Forget the white cat. Forget the beating of John Cerise. Forget the photo of my old drama teacher. Forget the love letters. Forget the funeral of Arkavy Reynolds. Forget Bruce's obnoxious behavior in my class. Forget everything.

Why had he died? Boom! Boom! Why?

No one asked me to inquire. No one paid me to inquire. There was no quid pro quo.

I just picked up the phone and called various numbers within the New York Police Department as listed in the telephone book. I was switched to an information officer and then to an assistant to a precinct commander and then to the civilian review board and then to a divisional spokesperson (whatever that meant), until finally, hours later, numb and dumb, I found myself talking to a detective named Harold Hanks. He was in a hurry.

He asked me if I was a relative of Bruce Chessler's.

I said no.

Then he asked me if I had any information concerning the murder.

I said no.

Now he really was in a hurry to get rid of me. I went into one of my acting modes: a woman who has lost a "son" . . .

a "child" . . . a student . . . a brilliant young mind cut off, et cetera, et cetera.

To get me off the phone he said that he had to be at the Gramercy Park Hotel at about two—and I should meet him on the corner, where Lexington ends at the park, right across from the hotel.

So that's how I met Harry Hanks, a thin, nervous black man. He was waiting there for me when I arrived, with a scowl on his face as if I were late—which I wasn't.

"So Bruce Chessler was a student of yours?" he asked.

"Yes."

"And he was a brilliant student . . . a kid with a real academic career ahead of him . . . isn't that what you said on the phone?"

"Yes."

"Don't lie to me, lady, I'm tired. Okay. Here's what I know. What *we* know. The kid was a small-time 'speed' merchant— pills mostly, all kinds of meth and dex. He was shot to death in some kind of drug-related dispute. The kid was sitting at a back table in a bar called Halliday's on Eighth and First. About three in the morning a character with a beard, about fifty, walks in and sits down next to him. He and Chessler talk. Then they argue. The guy shoots the kid in the head and walks out. The weapon used was a twenty-five-caliber semiautomatic pistol. We found four hundred 'greens' on the kid and six hundred dollars in cash."

A twenty-five-caliber semiautomatic pistol? My forehead broke into a cool sweat.

He opened a stick of gum, folded it, and placed it into his mouth, signaling that he was finished with his information briefing; that it was all he knew and he really wasn't exorcised over the whole matter.

Then he grinned and said: "Oh, yeah, I forgot. The kid was also an out-of-work actor."

"Yes, I'm aware of that." My voice was abstract.

"Well, what else do we got to say to each other?"

"Was the weapon a Beretta?" I asked quietly.

"Yes. How did you know?"

"I guessed." His mention of a twenty-five-caliber semiautomatic handgun had jolted me into a connection. It was suddenly very odd to me that Arkavy Reynolds and Bruce Chessler had both been murdered by the same kind of weapon. And one had showed up at the other's funeral.

"These kinds of cases," Hanks said in a patronizing way, "get solved eight years later by mistake, or they don't get solved at all. Speed kills, lady, like the man says." He walked away. It was very hot. I looked across the street into the posh park through the railings. Two white-coated nannies were pushing carriages, around and around and around. Why did Bruce Chessler die?

10

It took me six hours to locate and meet with Detective Felix of Manhattan South Homicide. He was one of the two police officers who had visited me in the New School after class and asked me to identify photographs of people who attended Arkavy Reynolds's wake on Madison Avenue. Felix agreed to come to my apartment only after I told him I had important evidence concerning Arkavy's murder.

He seemed nervous when he entered my apartment, staring at Bushy with a hint of fear in his eyes. "He doesn't bite or scratch," I said. Detective Felix was wearing a spanking-clean button-down blue shirt and a lovely soft gray suit. How different he was from Detective Hanks! He made a few inquiries about the current state of my theatrical career and then sat down gingerly on my sofa, very gingerly, as if the cats could give him some sort of communicable disease.

Once he had seated himself and demurely opened the

buttons of his jacket, he asked: "Do you remember a play about Joan of Arc starring Julie Harris?"

"I do," I replied, "but I forget the name of the play. Anyway, I think it was before your time. Did you see it?"

"No," he admitted. Then there was an awkward silence. He was looking at me very intently.

"Well, what do you have for me?" he finally asked.

Have? Did he want coffee? Chocolate milk? A beer? Then I remembered that it was simply a police expression.

"That young man, that student of mine, who went to the funeral home for Arkavy's wake . . . he was murdered by a twenty-five-caliber semiautomatic Beretta a short time later. The same kind that killed your informer."

Felix guffawed. "It's a very common street weapon now. These things go in cycles. One year the fad is twenty-two-caliber Longs . . . the next year all the bad guys are using .357 Magnums. This year it's twenty-five-caliber Berettas. So what?"

"Did you do a ballistic check on the bullets?" I asked, trying to sound knowledgeable but not accusatory.

"No! Why should we have done that? There was no connection at the time. The murders were in different places and different jurisdictions. And it can't be done now. It would require too much paperwork and too many goddamn signatures without enough jurisdiction."

I finally sat down at the other end of the sofa. Detective Felix looked even more uncomfortable now. He ran one hand through his brilliantly cut short haircut. One could still see the scissor marks.

"You told me at the New School that Arkavy had become a police informant. I suppose you mean that he had been arrested on some charge and you let the charges drop in exchange for his continuing cooperation."

"Right."

"What was his crime?"

"Possession of amphetamines with intent to sell."

I exhaled. "Well," I noted, "that young man, Bruce Chessler, was an amphetamine pusher. When he was murdered he had a few hundred pills on him."

"Do you mean the fat man and this student of yours were business associates?"

"Why else would he go to the funeral?"

Detective Felix grinned wickedly at me, as if I were some kind of bumbling idiot, and then said: "You mean there was speed stashed in the coffin? Or do you mean pushers like to pay their last respects because they're so filled with compassion?"

I did feel like an idiot. Because I believed Bruce Chessler had gone to the funeral home for some nostalgic tribute to a lost tradition personified by the fat man. But the speed connection had seemed to me to be the right one for the detective— the one he would find logical, palatable. Wrong again.

"Besides," Felix continued, showing a trace of alarm as big bad Bushy began to walk stiff-legged around the sofa, "Arkavy hadn't touched or dealt that stuff for two years."

"Are you sure?"

"Of course I'm sure," he said contemptuously, "because I even tried to give him some stuff to keep him happy, but he said he was getting his kicks from other things now."

"What things?"

"Maybe boys," he said, "or maybe older actresses."

I flushed. His comment infuriated me, but it may have been unintentional. He was beginning to act a little like Bruce Chessler. I hoped he wasn't getting amorous.

I left the sofa and sat at the large dining-room table, along the wall, leafing through some papers.

"Well," I finally said, "I'm sorry to have wasted your time."

He stood up quickly. "Look . . . thanks for the information. If you hear anything else, let me or my partner know. Maybe they did know each other in the past. Maybe they did business together when the fat man was into speed. Why not? But as for the twenty-five-caliber Beretta . . . it's meaningless. There are thousands of them on the street. If you're going to get blown away—why not with one of those? And pushers and crazies always get blown away sooner or later."

"But I thought you told me you wanted very much to get his killer."

"We do."

"Well, if there's a good chance that the same man who murdered Reynolds murdered Chessler . . . or even a slim chance . . . shouldn't you start looking into Chessler's murder? I know the detective working on his case. His name is—"

Felix held up his hand, stopping me. "We'll get the one who killed the fat man. Believe me."

He carefully buttoned his suit jacket, signaling me that the interview was over. I let him out and heard him skip down the stairs as if he had been released from a mental ward.

The meeting with him had exhausted me. Once again I had discovered—a lesson I seemed to have to learn again and again—that police departments cannot handle obscurity. They flee from it. They need defined objects. They flee from obscure people and obscure deaths and obscure connections. Like a cat approaching a rosebush. It was I, not the NYPD, who was going to have to unravel these obscurities.

11

"Listen, Swede, you're not acting rationally. This is not a rational decision," Basillio said, nudging Bushy's tail with his foot. Bushy ignored him. Pancho was staring at the stranger from beneath the long table, crouched, ready to flee.

I had called Basillio and asked him to come over even though it was a long drive from Fort Lee and his wife might go crazy. I had told him what I planned to do . . . to pursue the question: Why did the young man die? I told him that I wanted to start hanging out for a while at the bar in which Bruce Chessler was murdered. I had told him that I needed his help. I needed him to accompany me—to provide, as you will, the cover.

"Swede, listen. This isn't like those murders out on Long Island. The cops there were baffled, and every conclusion they came to was stupid. You had to intercede. It was a question of . . ." He hesitated, searching for a word, then said: ". . . justice. If you hadn't gotten involved, they never would have caught the murderers. Because the whole thing was bizarre and out of the cops' comprehension. But here we have a pill-pushing kid murdered. This, the cops deal with every day. They aren't obligated to understand what you're talking about."

"Do you want to help me or not?" I persisted.

"This kid, this Chessler. I don't care if he was in love with you. I don't care if he was an out-of-work actor who had a picture of your old acting teacher. He was a druggie, Swede, a hustler. There's no confusion. There's no puzzle. It was a goddamn drug deal gone wrong. The kid had hundreds of pills and plenty of bucks in his pocket. He was a dealer. You *know* why he died and how he died. Like the cop told you, it's that old slogan: speed kills. God, I haven't heard that slogan in years."

He was getting agitated, almost yelling at me.

"Calm down, Tony."

"Okay. I'm calm. Can we talk about this? Do you really think they snuffed him out because of a crazy white cat?"

"I don't know," I said, and I really didn't. The Arkavy Reynolds connection, real or imagined, had tempered a lot of my flights of fancy and intuition.

He started to walk about the apartment, shaking his head.

"Tony, do you remember Theresa Lombardo?"

"No. Should I?"

"Think back. Remember the Dramatic Workshop. Remember her?"

He stopped and stared at me. "That small dark girl. A very good actress. Right?"

"Right. You remember her."

"So what?"

"Remember how crazy she was about being an actress . . . about how nothing on earth—and I mean nothing—meant a goddamn thing to her except the theater?"

"A lot of us thought like that then."

"Sure. But Theresa was a very poor girl. Do you remember how she supported herself?"

"No."

"She turned tricks."

"Oh, here we go . . . hearts and flowers. Are you telling me this kid sold speed because of his great love for the theater?"

"I don't know. I know nothing about him. Neither do the police. I'm just making a point."

"About what?"

"About theater people. About actors and actresses and directors. About their heads and hearts."

He sat down on the sofa. Our conversation had obviously exhausted him.

Then he said: "I'll make a point. Here I am, a forty-two-year-old failed theatrical designer who makes more money than he knows what to do with, simply by making xerox copies of company reports—talking to a forty-one-year-old actress with enormous talent who is forced to cat-sit for a living because she can't stand either Broadway or Hollywood and all they represent and she's determined to blaze her own avant-garde path when she's not solving bizarre crimes. . . . Here we both are, discussing a young pill pusher who gets blown away. . . . Don't you see, Swede? The whole thing is crazy."

He leaned forward and stared at Bushy, who was sitting up like an oversize Egyptian cat, perhaps startled by Tony's rhetoric. Bushy didn't like excessive chatter. It interfered with his naps.

"I hope, Swede," he continued, "that when a disgruntled customer blows me away you'll start an investigation as to why I died. After all, I loved you also."

"But you never wrote me letters that you didn't send," I quipped.

"You should know," he said, and I suddenly felt very uncomfortable.

There was a long awkward silence. Basillio started to play with his car keys.

"Okay, Swede, I'll take the part."

"Thanks, Tony."

"But remember, my limit is two drinks. So if I'm sitting with you in that bar and you let me go over that limit and I start getting wild—it'll be on your lovely head."

He left without another word to me or to Bushy or to Pancho.

12

When one walked into Halliday's, one first saw a cigarette machine on the left. To the right was a small horseshoe bar with a mirror and a TV set behind it. The walls had innocuous beer emblems pasted or fastened on. An eclectic new jukebox was against the left wall. Walk through the partition, and there's a pay phone and the "dining area"—tables, two booths, pinball machines, video games. But in fact, no food is served. And only three bottled beers. During the day it's a local bar— Ukrainians, lost souls, and passersby. Between seven and eight in the evening the younger set starts coming in—black leather, musicians, young shirt-and-ties on a night out, students, architects, urban planners, poets, and an assortment of bizarre persons at the many fringes of the art world.

The bartenders are old Eastern European men—all short. No waiters or waitresses. You buy your drink at the bar and take it to the tables if you wish, or just stand around and drink. Two bouncers are visible: one, an enormous, silent, lazy

Slav; and a thin one who doubles as a cleanup man and bus-boy. The front of the establishment is fairly well lit; the "dining area" is very dark.

It was seven thirty on a Tuesday evening when Basillio and I walked in. We bought two mixed drinks at the bar—Bloody Marys—and went to one of the tables in the rear.

The place was beginning to fill. Basillio had constructed our cover theatrically: a married couple from New Jersey, dressed absurdly, seeking an authentic East Village milieu, desiring to see the denizens, to soak in what the East Village still promised—a heady whiff of undiluted bohemianism. Basillio wore a banker suit topped with an outlandish tie. I wore a lot of jewelry on a very flimsy, very sexy, and very gauche silk blouse and silk pants. I wore high heels, raising my normal tallness to Amazonian levels. It was all a bit much, but Basillio relished his new directorial and costume assignments.

"Jesus," Basillio whispered to me, "it looks like a set for *Lost Weekend*, designed by a guy who can only use crayons. I may have read the scene wrong."

An hour went by. The tables and booths filled. The crowd at the bar was three deep. The noise went from a soft hum to a soft roar. We could hear snatches of conversation—about paintings, about plays, about sports, about the subways, about books, about who was in the bar and why.

"I don't want to be aggressive, Swede, but what the hell are we looking for?"

"Regulars," I said. "I want to identify regulars who might have known Bruce Chessler."

He nodded and grinned. "Remember that bar on the West Side we used to go to after class?"

"Very well," I replied. "That was in one of your earlier reincarnations, Tony, as a theatrical barfly."

We reminisced about the old times, about the cat he used to bring to class in a shopping bag, about our teachers, about old acquaintances whom we both had lost contact with. This undercover work was becoming enjoyable.

By the time ten o'clock rolled around we had identified three possibles: a young couple dressed all in black who sat in the adjoining booth and who had their hands clasped tightly across the table and were speaking low and passionately to each other; a slim, small black woman with a close-cropped haircut who sat doodling with a pencil in the near-darkness at one of the tables; and a very old man who had a breathing problem and carried a canvas bag with a New York Mets logo.

We left the bar at eleven thirty and came back the next two nights.

On the third night I thanked Basillio and dispensed with his services because I knew that the black woman was the one I had to contact—she was there every night in the same spot with the same doodling pencil and with the same bottle of virtually untouched Rolling Rock beer in front of her.

Her name was Elizabeth and she smiled when I asked if I could join her. She gave her name freely, as if she were waiting and happy for some company.

A poet, she said she was. And what was I? An actress, I

said. She nodded compassionately, as if I had tuberculosis or some other chronic disorder.

"I notice," I said, "that you never drink your beer."

"I don't drink alcohol."

I didn't know what to say except to ask her why she didn't, then, sit in a coffee shop rather than a bar, but I decided against saying anything.

"And I only eat one meal a day," she added, "because I consider myself a disciple of Patanjali, and the appetite is just another vehicle that must be discarded."

"Who is Patanjali?" I asked.

She smiled sadly at me, as if my ignorance was not really my fault, but a function of my age and height and bad taste in clothes. She was wearing a beautifully simple sheath with sun-flowers.

"Patanjali was the founder of yogic philosophy."

"Ah," I replied, trying to sound properly apologetic.

"'It was Patanjali who first understood that the source of the great cosmic tragedy was when consciousness became entwined with matter."

Elizabeth spoke very precisely, with a very odd accent— the origins of which I couldn't place. It was probably an affectation, because she was an obvious kook—but it was very charming and her voice was low and resonant and one wanted to hear her speak more.

However, it was time to get down to business.

"Were you here when that young man was shot to death a few days ago?"

"Of course," she said. "Of course I was here. Right here."

We were silent for a while.

"Did you know him?"

"We had talked."

"I want to find out more about him," I said.

"Why?"

I didn't lie to her. I told her the truth to the best of my knowledge. I told her that he had been a student of mine at the New School. He had fallen in love with me. I simply wanted to know *why* he had died.

"Why?" she asked with a lilting inflection. "He died because the karmic forces are totally disjointed. Can't you see it all around you?"

I ignored her philosophy.

"The police," I said, "told me he got into an argument with an older man and the older man shot him to death."

"That is what happened," she affirmed.

"And you were there?"

"Here," she corrected, "right here. And he was shot here, right where I'm pointing."

"What did you do?"

"Nothing."

"Then what happened?"

"They came. The police and the ambulances. But he was dead. He didn't even slump over. There was a hole in his forehead. He was dead."

She reached over and patted my hand as if I were a child.

"Did he have any friends? Did he always come in here alone?"

"He came in with a woman sometimes."

"Who?"

"Her name is Risa."

"Is she here now?"

"No. I haven't seen her for some time. She wasn't here when he was shot."

"Do you know her last name?"

"Macros have no last names."

I didn't understand what she meant.

"What is 'macro'?"

"She's macrobiotic. She eats at that restaurant all the time, near Second Avenue. Sarah's—the macrobiotic restaurant."

Then she started to tell me how foolish it was to persist in my inquiry; that even if the young man loved me, love itself was absurd. It had no content. It was egoless and ownerless. It was an echo, for it resulted only from cause and condition. It was like a fire that consumed itself.

"Can you tell me what she looks like?" I asked, interrupting her philosophical flight, which was accompanied by a frenetic doodling of her pencil.

"Risa is short and heavy and her hair is red," Elizabeth said—then made a motion with her hand to show me it was cut in neopunk style, half of the head straight up.

I sat back. Now finally I had a name and a body and a lead. I had someone who knew him well. I wanted to rush out of the bar to the macrobiotic restaurant, but I knew it was too late . . . the restaurant was closed by then. Tomorrow would be time. And I didn't want to leave Elizabeth. She had endeared herself to me. There was something so fey about her, so ephemeral . . . like a cat circling a dish of strange-smelling food. And she might know even more.

"Did you ever see him with a strange-looking fat man? A man who wore coveralls and a shirt and tie and a cabdriver's hat?"

She looked up intensely, as if trying to re-create in her mind my description of Arkavy Reynolds.

"Black or white?" she suddenly asked.

"White," I replied.

"No." Then she laughed. "If he was black, he might well be one of my uncles." She giggled nervously and fell silent. We sat together, oddly at ease with each other.

"Oh, look there," she said suddenly, pointing toward the bar.

I followed her point, found nothing, turned back to her for information, but she was already thinking of something else.

Yes, like a cat approaching strange food. I stayed there another two hours or so, listening to her intermittent lectures on food and the cosmos and karma, in fits and starts, with large doses of silence in between.

Then I thanked her profusely and went home. Risa was the next stop.

13

When I saw her through the window—I was standing on the street peering in—the first thought that came to me was the incongruity of Bruce Chessler having this young woman as a lover and falling in love with me.

She was indeed stout and very young and very punk and her hair was very red.

From the window I could not identify what was on her plate—it looked like kelp and brown rice and sprouts. She was eating slowly, reflectively, chewing thoroughly.

I like people on macrobiotic diets even though I haven't the foggiest idea what they're doing—spiritually or nutritionally. After all, if you're not what you eat, what are you? Of course, I didn't believe the whole thing for a minute. A producer once asked me if I was macrobiotic. When I said no, he replied that I had that extreme slimness which often is symptomatic of either anorexia or a macrobiotic diet. I told him it came from poverty. He didn't think that was funny. But what would he make of Risa—a chunky macrobiotic? It would knock his theory to hell.

Anyway, Sarah's was packed. I waited outside. It was a full forty-five minutes before the young woman finished chewing all her food properly. Then she came out.

I waited until she had turned west on Eighth Street and started walking resolutely before I caught up to her.

"Excuse me. Did you know Bruce Chessler?" I thought the direct approach would be the best.

She stopped suddenly, as if she had been hit with a blunt object. She turned and stared at me.

"No, I didn't know him. I slept with him but I didn't know him. Who the hell are you?"

"Alice Nestleton. His teacher from the New School."

"Oh," she said sardonically, "his great unrequited love."

"Can I talk to you a minute?"

"About what? What is there to talk about now? He's dead. He was murdered."

"Yes, I know that."

She started to walk again, faster. I caught up with her and kept pace, not saying anything. She was mumbling to herself.

Finally, as we walked past Cooper Union, she stopped and whirled toward me, and this time she was crying.

She said: "What do you really want? What can I tell you? He's dead. For no reason."

I took her arm and guided her close to the building line. She didn't resist. She fumbled for a cigarette from her purse. She lit it and inhaled mightily.

"Tell me about him, please. It was all so strange. He

showed up one evening, told me he loved me, and left a white cat—"

Risa held up one hand suddenly, interrupting. "A white cat?" she asked, incredulous.

"And the next day it was stolen," I said.

She laughed like a lunatic and threw her cigarette away.

"Don't feel bad," she said, "he left me *two* white cats and both of them vanished from my apartment during a robbery."

"Two white cats?"

"Two white cats."

"Tell me about him, Risa," I said, and my voice was kindly because I suddenly felt an enormous white-cat camaraderie with her.

"What can I say? He was a lunatic . . . a lovable junkie lunatic speed-freak alcoholic who wanted to be a great actor. But he hated theater people . . . he had only contempt for them . . . for all of them . . . and especially for his grand-mother and her friends."

"Did he ever mention a man to you named Arkavy Rey-nolds?"

"You mean that crazy one with the hat . . . the one who was shot to death? I met him once. Bruce used to sell him speed. And sometimes they got into arguments about plays and scenes and directors. And once they got into a rough ar-gument about his grandmother."

So that was the connection. Speed. Bruce sold Arkavy drugs. It was logical. I figured that was the case. But Detective Felix had thought the connection unimportant. And this thing with the grandmother was bizarre.

"Who was his grandmother, Risa? And what did she have to do with all this? With the theater?"

"His grandmother was Maria Swoboda."

The astonishment on my face was quite noticeable.

"Then you know of her," Risa said. "Yes, Maria Swoboda, the old Russian lady from the Moscow Art Theatre . . . the one who knew Stanislavski. Bruce hated her. And her friends—Bukai, Chederov, Mallinova—I think those are their names. Sometimes when he got high he used to rant for hours about them. That they were fakes, hustlers, idiots . . . on and on he went."

"Where did he get the white cats?"

"I never knew. He never told me. But then again, he never told me a lot of things. I knew he took speed and sold the stuff. I knew he had devils in his head."

She choked back some tears, then continued in a strange, sad, husky voice, "Do you know how sad the city is? There are thousands of Bruce Chesslers wandering around. They don't even recognize each other. I'm a songwriter. I once wrote a piece called 'Soft Dreams in Hell.' But no one would buy it because it was about them. Do you understand? All these sad people wandering from street to street and they can't even recognize their own truth."

She seemed to be drifting. I brought her back to reality.

"You know, Maria Swoboda used to be a teacher of mine—years ago. In fact, I found a picture of her in Bruce's belongings, but it never dawned on me they were related."

She straightened her back as if determined not to make

any more personal revelations. "Yep, a real old-fashioned grandma. That is, until she died."

"You mean he still ranted against her after she was dead?"

"Well, when I met him she was already dead. He talked about her as if she were alive."

She started to walk again, turning north on Fourth Avenue. She said: "I have to go . . . I have to go to the post office."

I stayed with her. We were a strange couple walking. No doubt the passersby constructed their own scenario—mother and child. Mother unhappy with punk antics of daughter. Mother and daughter going to a physician. How many scenarios were there? None of them remotely correct.

"There's the post office," she said, and I could tell by the way she stood that she was determined I should be gone.

"Can I talk to you again sometime?" I asked.

"About Bruce?"

"Yes. And other things."

"Other things," she repeated bitterly, and then wrote her phone number down on my wrist with a Magic Marker— right on the flesh. I was so shocked I didn't even protest. It was a subtle form of revenge perhaps . . . for Bruce falling in love with an older woman. I snatched the Magic Marker from her hand and wrote my number on her wrist.

She ran into the post office. I started to walk home, trying somehow to cover the script on my flesh but not wanting it to be blurred until I could transcribe it.

As I walked I found myself enjoying the gathering heat.

The young man had turned out to be much more perplexing dead than alive.

And the idea that now I knew of three white cats taken—three white cats placed by Bruce Chessler in inappropriate "foster" homes from which they were abducted—all that made me kind of inebriated with the absurdity of it. I realized, to my chagrin, that I had forgotten to ask the young girl whether her two white cats had the same black spots on face and rump as Clara—poor Clara.

As for Grandma Maria Swoboda—that was very difficult to believe. That they were related. Or was it more difficult to believe that he would hate his grandma? How could anyone hate Madame Maria Swoboda? Alive or dead? And why was it difficult to believe? Did I expect a twenty-five-year-old man living on the Lower East Side, who had been born in this country and never spoken anything other than English, to behave like a Russian theatrical personage? Did I bear any cultural resemblance to my dairy-farmer grandmother? I realized in fact that I did have such a resemblance. I walked like her. I looked like her. I was still a farm girl at heart—well-read but unable to be sophisticated; cynical but unable to act in that mode; passionate but forced by circumstance into a kind of suspended celibacy.

It was odd how Bruce Chessler's strange relationship with his grandmother had started me thinking about mine. I rarely thought about her, for some reason, in hot weather. And when I did think about her, there was always one image that came to mind: whenever my grandmother had entered the dairy barn to check on the cows, she would, somehow, without saying a word, set all the barn cats into motion. As she walked down the sheds the cats would leap about—overhead, below, from side to side—as if my grandmother had choreographed them into a complex dance through some psychic power. And the moment my grandmother left the barn, they would cease.

I reached Twenty-third Street. The bank on the corner said it was ninety-one degrees at two twenty-one in the afternoon.

I was getting weary. Only a few blocks more. It had been a long few days—bars, health-food restaurants, macrobiotics, Yoga, black woman poet, punk girl songwriter—yes, it had been exhausting.

And what I had found out about Bruce Chessler really didn't give me any good clue to the philosophical problem: Why did he die? Nor did anything I had learned really contradict the police story that he was shot to death in a drug-related incident.

What I had found was a completely new and related crime—the kidnapping of three white cats who had been delivered to Risa and me by Bruce Chessler. What was going on?

14

Basillio laughed so hard that he almost fell off his swivel chair.

"You mean all our undercover work has revealed the astonishing fact that three goddamn white cats are missing?"

We were in his office in the back of the copying store. We could hear the copy machines whirring. We could see the customers clutching their papers.

I let him laugh. Until that very morning I had thought it funny also, from time to time. Well, not really funny, but like something from Mother Goose. But then I had begun to think carefully . . . to think about Bruce Chessler.

"No, we found out a bit more," I said.

"What?" he retorted. "That he hated his grandmother and in fact all Russian émigrés from the Moscow Art Theatre? That the kid had an arrested adolescence? That he was another pathetic out-of-work actor living on egotistical fantasies? That he was a speed freak? Yeah, I guess you did find out a lot."

His last line was thrown away with excruciating sarcasm.

"Everything you're saying now, Tony, I thought yesterday when I got back. But there is another way to look at it, a way that could very well mean the NYPD doesn't know what it is talking about."

He leaned forward, the sarcasm gone. He began to tap a staccato beat on the desk. He was very interested but he wanted to retain his cool. That was Tony. I found myself looking at him suddenly with enormous affection. Why hadn't Tony and I ever slept together? Why hadn't we become lovers? He was a dear, sad, crazy, talented man. So what if he was married? Why hadn't I taken that final step? I was very lonely. I knew there was no promise of love unless one initiated it . . . unless one fought for it. Was I happy with my career as a priestess of avant-garde theater? It was profoundly fake. There were few plays and fewer parts that interested me. My cats indeed were beloved by me, but even they could not fill the widening hole in my life. What was the matter with me? He was there . . . willing . . . eager . . . waiting. To him I was always beautiful, cryptic, intelligent—his erotic theatrical fantasy. Why not?

Then I pushed all that nonsense out of my head. I could think about it later. Now there was work to do.

"I now think, Tony, that Bruce Chessler knew he was going to die."

"That's bizarre."

"Not really. Follow me carefully on this. Try to look at it the way his grandmother used to look at character development in a role. Remember? The part is within you, no matter how different the role is from yourself. It will come out real only if your emotions are real."

"Shit, Swede, is this a Method class in how to play Bruce Chessler?"

"Sort of, Tony. Bear with me. Suppose you had a dog . . . a much-loved dog."

"Okay."

"Now, under what circumstances would you give your dog away?"

"None."

"What about if you lost your job?"

"No."

"If you got kicked out of your apartment?"

"No."

"If you were sick?"

"No, Swede, under no circumstances."

"Except one."

"Which is?"

"If you knew you were going to die."

"Well, that's about the only one."

"Right. So I think, Tony, that Bruce Chessler knew he was going to die, so he gave his cats away."

Basillio got off his chair and began to pace, peering out toward the machines from time to time as if to let his employees know that while he was indeed entertaining a tall handsome woman in his office, he, the entrepreneurial genius behind Mother Courage Copying Shop, was on the case.

Then he patted me on the head in a humorously patronizing manner, as if I were a gifted child who was also a disciplinary problem. Then he sat back down in his swivel chair.

"So what else is new, Swede?"

"There's more, Tony. It is because he felt he was going to die that he was able to confess his love for me. Before then, he could only write letters that he could not mail."

"Look, Swede, what you're saying is possible. But only barely possible. And, if so, so what? Maybe he had screwed some drug supplier and knew he was going to get shot."

"Then why would he show up for the meeting? No, Tony, that doesn't wash. From all accounts of the murder, there was an amicable meeting in the bar, then a sudden argument, and then shots fired. He didn't go to the bar that night thinking a drug supplier was going to murder him."

"Then who did he think was going to abort his short, glorious life, Swede?"

"I haven't the slightest idea," I admitted.

"So what do we do?"

"Well, first of all, we have to track down or understand his pet hates . . . or at least the hates his girlfriend identified."

"Which are?"

"His grandmother."

"Who's dead."

"Right. And three of her émigré colleagues. The girl Risa mentioned Bukai, Chederov, and Mallinova."

He repeated the names like they were lyrics of a song.

"I thought maybe, Tony, you could take the afternoon off tomorrow and come with me to the Lincoln Center Library of the Performing Arts."

"Why not, Swede? What else do successful businessmen have to do on afternoons other than manufacture erotic fantasies?"

"Bless you, Tony," I said, kissing him lightly on the cheek before I walked out. My legs were trembling and I had a ferocious desire to brush my long hair.

⁂

We met by the pool with the Henry Moore sculpture—in front of the Vivian Beaumont Theatre at Lincoln Center. Basillio stretched out languorously on one of the stone benches.

"I think we should go in and get to work," I said.

"There's time," he replied.

He kept refusing to go in and I kept getting more and more impatient, more and more nudging.

"Well, you might as well know the truth, Swede; I am enjoying sitting here because it is on this very bench that yours truly, Anthony Basillio, stage designer par excellence, theatrical philosopher, Brechtian scholar—it was right here in either 1976 or 1977 that I gave up theater and became a goddamn capitalist."

"I thought people gave up the theater in bars."

"How would you know, Swede? You never gave it up," he retorted happily; then he swung his feet over the side and we walked into the library, which specializes in theater, film, dance, music, and allied fields.

Within a half hour after entering, we had requisitioned an entire table and piled it high with sources—collections of theatrical reviews bound and unbound . . . biographical directories of theater people . . . histories of the New York theater and the Russian theater and the world theater.

What we found was this. Lev Bukai, Nikolai Chederov, and Pyotr Mallinova were all members of the Moscow Art Theatre up to the 1920s, when they all, at one time or another, left Moscow and went into exile. They all ended up eventually in New York by the late 1940s, where their colleague Maria Swoboda was living and was about to become a respected drama coach because of her association with Stanislavski and his Method.

In the late 1950s they all banded together to form a repertory company—the Nikolai Group—which would continue the tradition of the Moscow Art Theatre. Bukai and Chederov were the directors. Mallinova, the producer. Maria Swoboda was on the board and played many character roles. The group traveled throughout the world and was much acclaimed. Its last production in New York was in 1967—Gogol's *The Inspector General*—and then it disbanded.

So there it was for what it was worth. We gathered the books and directories and clippings and brought them back to their respective shelves and desks.

Then Basillio and I walked across the street to O'Neal's Balloon and had drinks.

"So what happens now?" he asked as he played with the large, almost grotesque piece of celery jutting out of his Bloody Mary.

I didn't really know "what happens now," as Basillio put it. The visit to the library had obviously been successful—information-wise. But it had opened up a whole other can of heuristic worms. The oddity of the situation became acute. How and why would a young actor like Bruce Chessler have a contempt for and hatred of people like Bukai, Chederov, Mallinova? It didn't figure. Young actors always hate people who "sell out," who go Hollywood—they hate the hustlers and liars and frauds who seem to infest the theater in all cultures and at all times.

But they rarely hate people like the Russian émigrés from the Moscow Art Theatre. These people were truly dedicated, truly important, truly persecuted. These people have always been considered the very best of what the theater had to offer in modern times.

They had been through the whirlwind. They had studied and worked and suffered and triumphed with the great Stanislavski. They were theater people par excellence.

"I think," I said to Basillio, "I'm going to pay a visit to Lev Bukai."

"Why him?"

"Why not?"

"I mean, why not the others?"

"Them too. But first I think I'll pay a visit to Bukai. After all, he was probably the most famous of the émigrés and he was a director of the Nikolai Group—whatever that was."

"Do you want me along?"

"No. Not for the first one. Maybe later."

He pulled the celery stalk out of his Bloody Mary and made as if to fling it across the bar.

"Tony!" I censored him quickly and strongly, then realized he was not going to do it—only faking the throw.

"Still a middle-class schoolmarm at heart, huh, Swede?" he taunted, and I felt stupid.

"That's because no matter how old you get, Tony, you still

don't know how to be around women . . . you still must act the difficult child."

"But not as difficult as Bruce Chessler," he noted in response, and suddenly a gloom seemed to descend from the walls and the ceiling and wrap me in despondence. Tony placed a gentle brotherly arm around my shoulder and I let him keep it there.

15

It was very difficult to believe that Lev Bukai lived here. I was standing in front of a magnificent old white-stone building on Ninety-fourth Street just east of Fifth Avenue—the Carnegie Hill section of Manhattan. Where had he gotten all the money to obtain it? The original front had been demolished and replaced with a brick wall and a large burnished oak door that opened directly onto the street. It was as if the new owner had decided to build a monastery and then thought better of it. Or maybe after he had moved into the posh neighborhood he realized a monastery wasn't necessary because two blocks away was the main headquarters of the Russian Orthodox persuasion in North America, which housed, among others, the exiled patriarch. Even I knew that, and I'm not Russian Orthodox.

A young woman in a smock answered the door quickly when I twisted the elaborate ringer.

"May I see Lev Bukai?" I asked.

"Who are you?" she countered, obviously not used to having people show up at the front door. She looked like an art-school teacher. Her hair was pulled back severely.

"An old student of Madame Swoboda's," I answered, thinking that it was my connection with the old teacher that would guarantee me an audience. I also made a point of lapsing into the deferential dialect that all the émigrés seemed to require in the student-teacher relationship. One should always, at least metaphorically, bow one's head to one's teacher.

I was right. The name Maria Swoboda was the key. The woman left me at the door with a hushed gesture and returned a minute later, ushering me in.

The place was like a vengeful mausoleum. Huge pieces of old dark furniture soaked up the summer light and seemed to convert it immediately to heat. It felt like it was about two hundred degrees.

Lev Bukai was sitting in what appeared to be a study, although there were no bookcases and the literally thousands of books in the room were piled up on what seemed to be folding tables. Many paintings hung without any sense of balance or composition on the wall. They were portraits of people I didn't know or didn't recognize, done in a heroic style—arms crossed, legs thrust out and apart, jaws jutting, tunics only half buttoned. And the women were all in languorous poses with enormous heads of brilliant hair.

Lev Bukai looked me up and down. I smiled. He still had that director's eye. He was a tiny, twisted gnome of a man, hidden in a terry-cloth robe. A glass of tea was in his lap. There was no fan or air conditioner in the room.

His nose and ears were bulbous and one eye was partially closed. His blotch-marked skin seemed to have been stretched tight against the bones as if by a machine.

"So, you knew Maria Swoboda."

"Years ago," I said. I wasn't nervous. But I was frightened by him . . . by the tradition he incarnated. It was, in a sense, like being about to interrogate a Buddha. I realized that I should have brought Basillio. And for the first time in a long while I was very conscious of my dress. I had put on a long skirt with a long-sleeved black cotton jersey. Like a drama student, I realized shamefacedly.

"You were student of hers?"

"Yes."

He grinned, one of those arrogant Russian-émigré grins that say no one from Minnesota will ever understand what they are all talking about.

"She is dead," he noted, running an arthritic hand through what remained of his brushed-back white hair.

"Yes, I know, and I appreciate your seeing me—but it's not about her that I came to see you."

"A part? You want a part?" He laughed uproariously at his own joke.

Then he added: "But I am no longer in theater. I'm country gentleman now. Like Oblomov." And he laughed again and then began to cough and choke and wheeze.

Did he really believe that he was in the country? It was a possibility, I thought.

"I want to talk with you, Mr. Bukai, about her grandson."

"Whose grandson?"

"Maria Swoboda's grandson."

He stared at me from beneath a lowered head and sipped the tea in his glass. For the first time since I had entered his home I really felt the power of the old guard—tea from a samovar, dark and pungent, not from a tea bag. This tiny arthritic eighty-five-year-old man in front of me had more theater in one toe than I had in my whole body. And above all, he was European theater in all of its glory and excesses and wanderings and abortions. I remembered how I was literally speechless the first time I met Maria Swoboda—so many years ago. The towering ghost of Stanislavski covered them all like a mantle.

"I don't know that she had grandson," Bukai said. It was obvious he was not going to ask me to sit.

"But surely she must have told you . . . or showed you a picture of him. His name was Bruce Chessler."

"No."

"Did she never speak about him?"

"No. Never."

"And no one else spoke of him?"

"No."

"But she had a grandson," I said to him, frustrated. The back of my jersey was now clinging wetly to my skin.

He nodded his head as if everything were possible and then went back to his tea. I waited. He said nothing. He stopped looking at me. "Please!" I suddenly blurted out. My plea seemed to infuriate him. He lifted a small table with one straining hand and let it smack into the floor. The young woman was instantly in the room. She stared at me threateningly. Then she ushered me out without another word. The door was slammed behind me.

It was eleven thirty in the morning. My next stop was Nikolai Chederov. He lived on Seventh Avenue and Fifty-fifth Street in a magnificent landmark apartment house. The doorman wouldn't let me in. He called Chederov on the lobby phone. I shouted into the receiver that I wanted to talk to him about Maria Swoboda's grandson—Bruce Chessler. He said in a very loud voice: "Who?" I repeated myself. "Don't know," he yelled. Then: "You crazy! Go away!" And he hung up. The doorman escorted me out.

Pyotr Mallinova, unlike Bukai and Chederov, had only his phone listed in the phone book—no address. This was odd, because émigrés are always obsessive about listing their full and correct and current names, addresses, and phone numbers in any and every source they can, because one never knows when old friends will suddenly pop up and look for them.

Anyway, I called him from a phone booth on Seventh Avenue and Fifty-seventh Street, right in front of Carnegie Hall. I let the phone ring a long, long time. No one answered. I called a half hour later. Then another half hour later. I then began to call every fifteen minutes until I met Basillio, as planned, in a coffee shop in the Village.

Once, during the calls, someone picked up the phone, listened, then hung up.

"I contacted Bukai and Chederov," I told Basillio when we were seated and served, "and neither of them claimed to know anything about Bruce Chessler, much less confirm his existence. Mallinova, I couldn't contact."

"Do you believe them?"

"I don't know. I really don't know."

"Where does this all leave you now? I mean, your theory that Chessler knew he was going to die and that it was something involved with his hatred for those people that did him in rather than a bad drug deal."

"I don't know. I don't know what to think. It was just something to follow up. Like his connection with Arkavy Reynolds. It was just something unique—a young man's bitter hatred for some old people. Don't you think it should have been followed up?" I asked him somewhat tartly.

He grinned and bent over his cup and blew some foam from the top of his cappuccino by way of an answer.

"And I'm glad I followed up, because there is something very strange about these Russians."

"What? That they're still alive?"

"Their wealth, I mean. Where did they get the money to live the way they do? They were émigré actors, directors, producers. They were starving like all the others. They never made it to Hollywood like the Germans. Maria Swoboda never seemed to have a dime."

"Swede, that kind of stuff is very hard to find out."

"Why?"

"Remember when we were in the library? The biographical directories don't give information on finances. They tell you about their careers . . . where born . . . where educated . . . who married. That's it."

"What do you suggest?"

"Call their accountants."

"Very funny."

"There probably is a way."

"How?"

"Get someone who really knows these people."

"These people are in their eighties and nineties."

"I mean someone who knows their history, their ties to Stanislavski. I mean someone who knows how they grew and splintered and scattered."

"Fine in theory, Tony, but I don't know anyone like that."

He cocked his head in his infuriating fashion and said slyly: "Oh, yes you do, Swede."

"Don't tell me who I know," I replied angrily. He was beginning to annoy me again. How had I ever contemplated sleeping with him?

"Joseph Grablewski," he said slyly.

I don't know what I looked like at that moment, but I do know that I felt like the blood had drained from my body.

It was a very special, very fearful name from the past.

Grablewski had been one of the bright-shining stars of theatrical criticism in the early 1970s. He used to lecture at the Dramatic Workshop when Basillio and I attended, and I had fallen wildly, crazily in love with him.

And I had done about everything I could think of to get him interested—from the subtle to the exhibitionistic—but he wasn't. It didn't happen.

I could visualize him easily—corduroy jacket, ridiculous tie, face like a large bird's—a hawk or a falcon—and that enormous shock of black-gray hair.

And I could remember that intense, quiet, enfolding,

mind-bending way of talking that swept you up into his way of thinking . . . that made you want to think. . . .

He had been a mesmerizing intellectual. He talked about the theater like no one I had ever heard talk about it before. He, above all, had been the reason I decided to cast my lot with the concept of an avant-garde . . . with a concept that no longer existed. He, above all, was the reason I was still supporting myself by cat-sitting at age forty-one—because I simply could not put my art and craft, my brain and heart, at the service of a popular culture I loathed. Or, to put it another way, he had activated my intellectual and theatrical arrogance. I wanted to be immortal—not a movie actress. Grablewski had loved the Russians and their Moscow Art Theatre and all theaters caught up in revolutions—real and imagined—and he taught us to love them.

I had been desperately in love with him, and his ignoring me was, at the time, an enormous tragedy . . . it made me fearful for my life . . . it shattered my sexual self-confidence. Men had always desired me. Why not him?

All I could say in response to Basillio was: "Is he still alive?"

"Alive and crazy and still holding court in that bar on Forty-fourth Street."

"He must be an old man by now," I said.

Basillio grinned at me in response. "Not all that old. And even if he's ninety—so what? If anyone can tell you about secret things in the lives of Bukai, Chederov, and Mallinova, it's him. Right?"

It was nine o'clock that evening. I was standing, believe it or not, in the Forty-fourth Street bar, west of Eighth Avenue, staring through the dim light at the man who sat in a far booth—Joseph Grablewski.

He didn't look much different. His hair was still thick and wild, although all white. He wore the same kind of clothes. He emanated the same kind of nervous energy. And he was drinking the same thing—vodka.

But where were the young people? The actors, actresses, designers, students who used to throng about him? Was he talking to himself now? Was he still talking? What kind of hole had he been in all these years? Why had he become anonymous?

I started walking toward him.

Halfway there, he saw me and began to sing, sardonically: "There she is . . . Miss America."

Suddenly weak, I slid into the booth across from him. His stupid sarcastic song brought back a thousand conflicting memories. My head was like a deranged projector.

He smiled at me. His face, up close, had indeed changed— broken down and weary. But the form, the frame, was ageless.

"Do you remember me?" I asked very quickly. I was still shaking a bit.

"Oh, yes . . . oh, yes," he said, leaning back and clasping his hands behind his head as if he were about to make an academic point.

He described his remembering: "The Dramatic Workshop. Many years ago. There she is . . . Miss America. Vaguely beautiful. Vaguely committed. Vaguely talented. Vaguely, vaguely, vaguely."

"Well," I retorted bitterly, "it is better than always being vaguely drunk."

His eyes sparked anger. Then contempt. For whom? Himself? Me? Then he relaxed.

"And you have come to see me because you want to know what happened to the theatrical lion. What happened to my worldview. To my criticism. Where are the books? Where are the productions? Where are the insights which dazzle and dazzle?"

"Perhaps." The bar was like a tired, seedy cathedral.

"I became enlightened," he said.

I looked at his vodka glass and at the table in the booth, which seemed not to have been wiped in a decade. I was making a silent point.

"It was all nonsense," he continued, "the theater is all nonsense. Probably has been nonsense since the Greeks."

He sipped his vodka, then drank some Coca-Cola, then lit a cigarette.

"If I remember, also, you tried to get into bed with me. You tried real hard."

"Yes, I did."

"Sorry," he muttered. "I had other agendas at the time. And you probably would have caught a social disease from me. Anyway, in retrospect it was all a mistake. Look how well you've aged."

"Still vaguely beautiful?" I asked, laughing. The laugh seemed to defuse my awe and painful nostalgia.

"Decidedly so."

A waiter came over. I ordered a club soda. Joseph Grablewski ordered another Stolichnaya.

He stared hard at me.

"So, you sought me out once again to verify your original desires. You want to sleep with me. You want to confirm a desire—how long?—fifteen years old. You want a ripe old alkie like myself to share your bed to confirm that at one time in the past you were right—that the theater is of great cosmic importance and that I am-slash-was one of its gurus. You are still in the theater, aren't you? Could you be anywhere else?"

"My name is Alice Nestleton," I said in response, "and the only reason I'm here is to ask you about some Russian-émigré theater people."

"Who?"

"Their names are Bukai, Chederov, and Mallinova."

He laughed hugely, sweeping his arms backward. "A third-rate gallery of Stanislavski clones. God, I haven't heard their names in years. I thought they were all dead."

"And I thought you were dead," I retorted.

"Lev Bukai . . . director of the ill-fated Nikolai Group . . . left the Soviet Union I don't know when . . . in Paris for a few years . . . debacle as dramatic consultant for the old Ballet Russe de Monte Carlo . . . brought to the United States by Hurok in the late forties . . . arrogant, retarded son of a bitch."

I was astonished by this alcoholic's almost total recall.

"What about the others?"

"What about them?" He sneered and drank his vodka.

Then he said: "Do you want me to tell you about the productions of the Nikolai Group? . . . Their repertoire? . . . Their special brand of fakery? All fake . . . all those émigrés were fake. They couldn't stand the revolution's heat and its poverty and its demand for real theater, so they left for the usual bullshit—artistic freedom."

He began to laugh so loud I thought he would fall over. Then he stopped suddenly and stared at me. He reached over and touched me on the side of the face. I pushed his hand away as if it were poisonous. He reached over and touched me again on the face. I let his hand stay there. I wanted it to stay there. It was astonishing, but my old feelings for him were beginning to resurrect themselves.

"How old are you?" I asked him, breaking the spell.

"Sixty-six chronologically . . . one hundred and sixty-one spiritually."

The bizarre thought came to me that I should take him home with me and take care of him and give him some soup and some coffee and then sit down and talk. How I wanted to really talk to him then . . . right then . . . about the theater . . . about the old times . . . about what he knew and why he kept it a secret . . . about why he had pulled into himself and the vodka. The thought frightened me. I was becoming very frightened.

I moved as far away from him as I could in the booth.

"I want to know where Lev Bukai got his money."

"How do you know he has money?"

"I know. I saw his home."

"Why should I tell you?"

"Do I have to give you a reason?"

"Not really. I just want one."

"Because something terrible happened and it may involve him."

"Everyone knows where Bukai got his money."

"Where."

"Diamonds. He's part owner of a diamond firm. Did you really think he got his town house by producing and directing ridiculous plays by Gogol?"

"What firm?"

"I don't know."

"Please think."

"It was some kind of funny-named firm . . . Syrian or Egyptian. No . . . Turkish. That's what I heard—a firm run by Turks . . . or Turkish Jews."

"Can't you remember?"

"Give me some Turkish names. I'll try."

"I don't know what a Turkish name is."

"Wait," he said, rubbing his nose lightly as if the gesture brought him recall. "It was the same name as a singer . . . an old pop singer. Wait . . . right. Sedaka . . . like the singer Neil Sedaka."

"Thank you," I whispered.

He had given me what I came for. Or had he? I didn't want to leave. I wanted to talk about something else, but words wouldn't come. A feeling of almost unbearable sadness seemed to envelop us. I had the feeling that if we had had an affair—

right then—everything about our lives would have been different. I would no longer be struggling. He would not be drinking himself to death on Forty-fourth Street. I would not have a history of broken affairs and a broken marriage. Everything would have been different. Even the theater . . . yes . . . even the theater . . . together we would have made a difference.

I was lapsing into megalomania. I couldn't afford it. Bruce Chessler's loud sport shirt seemed to be waving toward me. I had a murder to solve.

"Visit me again," he said softly. I nodded as I left.

16

"I really question the wisdom of this move. We're going over the line, Swede."

We were standing outside the building on Forty-seventh Street that housed Sedaka and Sons, Diamond Merchants. It was a street that had always fascinated me . . . and repelled me. It was so much like the theater. Glittering rocks passed hands for enormous sums. Rational people became obsessed with form and color.

I didn't answer.

"We really can't just walk in there and ask all kinds of questions. They'll kick us out. Listen, Swede. What does this have to do with anything? You have this crazy notion that the kid knew he was going to die. So he gave away his white cats. And now you know that this kid hated old Russian theater people and the ones he hated most turn out to be rich. What the hell does anything have to do with anything?"

"Nothing has to do with anything," I replied, "until you make it."

Basillio groaned. "Are you going to give me a goddamn lecture on the philosophical aspects of criminal investigation? Don't! It's ten thirty in the morning and already eighty-one degrees. Besides, I don't care anything about criminal investigation as a branch of philosophy."

"Are you coming?" I asked, making plain to him that I wouldn't be surprised if he didn't.

He followed me, grumbling, into the lobby and up in the elevator to the third floor.

A receptionist who was wearing a beautiful blue silk dress refused us admittance at first. What is your business? Personal, I replied. Not good enough, she said. Please leave or I'll call security. On and on it went like that. Back and forth. Predictable. Basillio was becoming very embarrassed. We were receiving ugly stares from other people in the reception area, several of them carrying those small strange leather cases under the arm. Diamonds, no doubt.

Finally I said: "Please tell Mr. Sedaka that we wish to speak with him privately—about Lev Bukai."

They were truly magic words. A minute later a heavyset man of about fifty, with a thick mustache and wearing a beautifully tailored silk suit, white shirt, and silk tie, stepped outside and beckoned for us to follow him into his office. Silk seemed to be the motif of this milieu. Diamonds and silk.

We followed. He pointed out the two chairs we should sit on and then slid himself behind a large, totally empty desk.

"What is this all about, now?" he asked, obviously annoyed and not hiding it, staring first at me and then at Basillio and then from one to the other as if he couldn't really decide who was the real culprit.

Basillio was squirming. He didn't understand . . . he could never understand that one must follow each strand back to the center no matter how absurd the strand seemed . . . or how far away the center appeared.

I jumped in. "I want to know what kind of relationship exists, if any, between Lev Bukai and your firm."

"That's none of your business."

"I would appreciate your cooperation in this matter."

"Who the hell are you, lady?" he exploded.

"The ghost of Christmas past," I replied. It was odd, but I felt no sense of being intrusive. I was where I was supposed to be.

"Oh, God," I heard Basillio moan.

The man across the desk stared at me for a long time, as if making an evaluation; as if trying to decide whether I was a cop or an insurance investigator or a bill collector or a plain lunatic.

He seemed to be evaluating the price of his silence. He seemed to be running through options. The longer he remained silent, the more he implicated himself.

Then he gave a great wrenching sigh and said: "Lev Bukai has been a silent partner in this firm's start, its development, and its success. And he was a very close friend of my late father, who founded the firm. I have met Mr. Bukai maybe twice in my life. I really have no contact with him whatsoever."

He waited for my response. I felt a sense of triumph. He

had told me what I wanted to know. What it meant didn't really matter. The knowledge was sufficient. Grablewski had been confirmed.

"I want to thank you for your help, Mr. Sedaka," I said. "I doubt if I will bother you again."

And then we were out of his office as quickly as we had entered, whisking ourselves out as if our bodies would leave telltale stains on the furniture. Basillio and I walked east on Forty-seventh Street until we reached Fifth Avenue.

"So," he said finally, bursting, "what the hell does it prove? Three Russian émigrés come to the promised land and parlay their hard-earned cash into what turns out to be a winner—the diamond merchant named Sedaka. It's the goddamn American dream. What does it all have to do with that poor dead fool named Bruce Chessler—who, by the way, hated them and his grandmother? Really, what does it have to do with anything?"

I put my fingers to my lips for a moment, to shut him up.

"Did anything seem strange about him, Tony?"

"Yeah, it was strange he didn't kick us out on our asses."

"I mean about his appearance . . . his face in particular."

"No."

"Didn't you notice that his jaw seemed to be lighter in color than the rest of his face?"

"No, I didn't. Maybe he forgot to turn over when he went to the Bahamas. Maybe his window is striped from dirt and the sun hits his face in stages."

"It was as if," I continued, ignoring his analysis, "he had

worn a beard for a long time and then recently shaved it. The skin under the beard, once exposed, would be lighter than the rest of his face."

"So what?"

"The detectives told me they have a description of the man who murdered Bruce Chessler—a heavyset man with a beard, about fifty."

"Sure," said Basillio sardonically, "and he also deals in speed when he's not cutting diamonds." He kissed me quickly and hailed a cab. He had to play the boss.

I walked home. It was a very strange walk. I kept thinking about Bruce Chessler and Clara and all the peculiar connections which continued to arise surrounding them. But something else kept intruding—Joseph Grablewski.

His—Grablewski's—contempt for the three émigrés had been total and relentless, in much the same way Bruce Chessler's had been, at least according to his girlfriend. And there was a wide gulf between what I and others I knew thought about the old émigrés and what Grablewski and Chessler thought of them. How could the émigrés have earned such widely varied judgments on their lives and time and art? Just because they invested in diamond companies? It was all very strange.

My thinking about Grablewski was becoming more and more intense. I was determined not to go to that bar again. Why should I? But I knew I would go there. I would go there again, I would talk to him again, I would sit in that booth again, directly across from him. I silently cursed Basillio for telling me where I could find him . . . for reminding me that he would have the information I needed.

I finally reached my block and house and began to climb the stairs. Bushy had been sulking lately because of my irregular hours, and I had planned to bring him a goody. I was at the third landing before I remembered, but I wasn't about to go back down and up. Next time, Bushy, I promised him silently.

"Thank God you're here," a voice suddenly yelled out at me as I reached the final landing.

I cringed at the sudden loud noise and shrank back when a figure seemed to materialize out of nowhere—just as Bruce Chessler had appeared that night.

"Don't you remember me?" the figure yelled again—her voice seemed on the cusp of lunacy.

When my sudden fear vanished I knew quite well who it was—Risa, the girl who had been Bruce Chessler's on-and-off lover.

"Calm down, calm down," I said to the obviously hysterical girl. Then she burst into tears and started to tremble so hard that I grabbed her shoulders.

With great difficulty I got her into the apartment, onto the sofa. She had trouble breathing . . . and then would be fine and speak a whole sentence or two . . . and then become incoherent again and gasp for breath.

Finally she calmed down and sat on the sofa like a rag doll, her punk hair sadly askew, her arms strangely dangling.

She started to explain in a singsong voice: "I was in my

apartment on East Fifth Street, listening to some music. I live on the ground floor. I don't know why, but I suddenly looked up and a man standing outside the window started to shoot. There was glass flying all over and my things were breaking and I was sure I was going to die."

She stopped and looked around as if she finally realized she was in a strange apartment.

"I think it has something to do with Bruce. I don't know why. But I know it. And I remembered you and thought you could help me . . . keep me safe . . . so I brought you some of Bruce's stuff . . . what he kept with him all the time . . . or that he kept at my apartment because when he was popping pills and drinking he used to get so paranoid."

I told her to relax, that she was safe with me, that she could stay as long as she wanted.

I made her some iced tea and showed her where to shower; her clothes were drenched with sweat and smelled of her fear.

After she had showered and drunk and eaten a little she was much calmer and she opened the creased envelope she had brought with her and laid the items out on my rug. Bushy investigated them, found them harmless, and walked away. Pancho flew by them so swiftly he didn't even notice them.

But I noticed them. They were fascinating.

It was a collection of old programs from the Nikolai Group . . . programs of their performances in Central and South America—Mexico City, Rio, Panama City, Managua, Maracaibo, Caracas, Concepción, Quito, and dozens of others, large and small.

"He always studied them," she said, "always, and wrote all over them and . . ."

I knelt on the floor to study them more closely, and she stopped talking.

Bruce Chessler had written obscenities all over the programs in black and red and purple Magic Markers.

There was something about the Nikolai Group that had obviously engaged and infuriated him even more than the individual émigrés.

I stood up and sat down on the sofa alongside Risa, staring at the strange assemblage of old programs.

"What do you think it means?" Risa asked, now obviously convinced by the bullets fired into her apartment that there was something more to her boyfriend's murder than little green pills . . . now ready to reexamine even the most trivial objects.

"I don't know," I replied.

We sat in silence for some time.

"Did you love him?" I asked.

"Who knows? I think so. But he was hard to be with. It was not warm or close with him. Do you know what I mean— it wasn't warm?"

I nodded, reached down and picked Bushy up. Holding him right then, for some reason, made me think of Joseph Grablewski again, and I dropped poor Bushy onto the rug as if he were diseased. He was very insulted.

When I looked at Risa again, she was fast asleep. I knew what I had to do next—pay closer attention to Bukai, Chederov, and Mallinova.

As for her, she was one of those child-woman enigmas who seem to haunt the city from generation to generation. She was a cipher. No matter what she told me about herself, I knew nothing. Her sands were always shifting. This year punk . . . next year wholesome . . . the following year demi-punk. Doomed to insubstantial change.

17

Lev Bukai exited from his magnificent dwelling at about ten thirty in the morning. I had been waiting since nine, having decided that surveillance was my only logical move. There was nothing else I could think of. My wait was eased by the knowledge that Basillio was also waiting—for Chederov. Risa had agreed to follow Mallinova, but we could never find out where he lived.

Bukai moved very slowly toward Fifth Avenue, so slowly it seemed the sidewalk was moving instead of him. He carried a yellow cane and he was dressed much too warmly for the late-August weather—a jacket and tie. He crossed over to the park side and entered Central Park at Ninetieth Street, where the horse path meets the reservoir.

Then he began a painfully slow walk down the east side of the park to the sailboat pond, where he finally settled himself down on a bench and watched.

I seated myself on a small grass-covered hill about fifty yards from the beach. I could see him but he could not see me.

He dozed and woke and dozed and woke again. He shifted the cane from one hand to the other. He smiled at the small boats in the water, at passing nannies with their baby carriages, at dog walkers. He seemed totally at peace with the world.

I should have brought a book along, I realized. The sun and the heat and the bucolic milieu were making me sleepy.

He sat on that bloody bench for three and a half hours. Then he stood up, stretched, and began the laborious walk back to his house. I followed. By the time he reached his door he seemed totally exhausted and the young woman whom I had met earlier had to come outside and help him in. It was obvious Lev Bukai was not going out again this day. I went back to my apartment.

When I opened the door I was startled to see Risa on the carpet, poring over one of my old scrapbooks.

She looked up, embarrassed, and explained: "I got the chills, so I looked in your closet for a wrap and found this. I hope you don't mind." She looked very cute and vulnerable and apologetic and I didn't mind at all. I had invited her to stay with me as long as she was frightened and she could do what she liked.

"I didn't know you were so famous," she said.

I laughed. "That was in Minnesota," I explained. "I was the Minnesota actress who was going to come to New York and rock it on its heels with my interpretations of deep parts . . . big parts . . . significant parts. It didn't happen. I basically have become a star in the cat-sitting world."

She went back to the scrapbook. I made myself a small salad with cottage cheese and took it into the living room to eat.

"Did you find out anything?" she asked.

"Well, I found out that Mr. Bukai likes to watch toy boats for hours."

"You know, this is really very exciting. I once saw a movie about Murder Incorporated. Do you think these old men have a gang? A murder gang? Is that why you are following them? Do you think they murdered Bruce?"

Her kind of buoyant, naive enthusiasm startled me.

"Where are you from originally, Risa?"

"Maplewood, New Jersey."

"Where is that?" I asked. The name of the town seemed vaguely familiar. But maybe there had been a town called Maplewood in Minnesota.

"Oh, out there," she said, obviously not interested in pursuing her geography any further. She went back to the scrapbook. I could see her staring at a large picture of me in *The Trojan Women* during my first season with the Guthrie Theater. Ah, what a star I was!

"Did Basillio call?" I asked.

"The phone didn't ring at all when you were gone."

"You sure? I was also expecting a call from a Mrs. Gordon about a weekend cat-sitting assignment."

"Wait," she admitted, "the phone did ring but I couldn't

get to it in time . . . I had fallen asleep . . . so I thought I would put on the answering machine, but I didn't know how to work it . . . and so—"

I stopped her with my hand. It was okay. Did she want anything to eat? She jumped up, flew to the kitchen, and came back with what was left of the cottage cheese in its container and a soup spoon. We ate together and stared at Bushy, who was staring at us because he liked cottage cheese. Pancho flew by only once and flicked his half-tail at us as if we were flies.

"Doesn't he ever stop running?" Risa asked incredulously.

" 'Stop and die' is Pancho's motto," I explained. She shook her head sadly.

By five Basillio still hadn't called. Risa had fallen asleep over the scrapbook.

I felt a sudden need to walk quickly, to stretch my legs, to get out of confinement. I went out of the apartment, down the steps, and onto the street. I began to walk uptown.

At Thirty-fourth Street I stopped. The streets were black with people leaving work. Only there and then could I admit to myself where I was going—to that bar on Forty-fourth Street.

I wanted to see Joseph Grablewski. The realization shocked me at first but then made good clear sense. It seemed the logical thing to do. Like the surveillance. The thought came to me that I was beginning to confuse desire and logic. If so, it was pathetic. I pushed the problem out of my mind.

The bar was crowded. Once inside the coolness and the dimness, I wondered if the long day in the sun watching Lev Bukai had given me a sunstroke. Was that why I was in the bar?

Joseph Grablewski was sitting in the same booth, wearing the same clothes, drinking the same drink. He stared dimly, as if someone was seated opposite him. I walked quickly to the booth and slid in beside him—not across from him like the last time, but beside him. My shoulder was touching his. I could smell him—a mixture of vodka and sweat and anxiety . . . a desperate smell.

"What is the matter?" he asked. His fake solicitousness enraged me for some reason or another.

"The matter? Nothing's the matter with me. It's with you," I yelled, and my hand hit his vodka glass so that it slid across the table and upended.

Then I started to cry. And I started to babble. About Bushy and Pancho. About my class in the New School. About the old scrapbook that Risa was looking over. About my desperate need for a part, a real part. I was talking about theater . . . about what I loved . . . and I talked about my last lover, the horse trainer . . . and the last murder I had solved, of that wonderful demonic old man Harry Starobin . . . and I talked about curtain calls and scripts and makeup . . . back and forth I babbled and then, exhausted, turned to face him as I pressed myself against his chest, fiercely, as if we were lovers, as if by doing that I could erase the past fifteen years . . . or bring him back his mind.

Without looking at him, I let my hand run over his face. But it wasn't an old face my fingers felt; it was a young face; and it wasn't the face of Grablewski—it was the face of Bruce Chessler.

My God! I pushed myself away from the man and stood

up. People were beginning to stare at me. The waiter started to walk over. I ran out. I needed to rest. I needed to gather my forces and talk to my cats. The investigation of the three old men was beginning to unravel me, but nothing yet had happened to do so . . . not one single thing . . . not one solitary juncture. It was all objects in space: diamonds, theatrical programs, white cats, punk girls, wealthy émigrés. All, as Grablewski had said, lackluster clones of Stanislavski.

18

Basillio lasted seven days on surveillance before he resigned in disgust. He told me the old man he was watching went around the block twice a day and that was it, except on Saturday, when he walked to Bloomingdale's and bought a tie, and on Sunday, when he went to the D'Agostino on Fifty-seventh and Ninth to shop. Since we never found where Mallinova lived, that left me alone, doggedly waiting for Bukai to emerge each day. I began, in fact, to welcome the drudgery because it kept me from any further lunatic forms of behavior vis-à-vis Joseph Grablewski.

I kept on. I was dogged. I would follow the strands to the center just as Bruce Chessler had followed them to his death. That it kept me from Grablewski was no doubt important—I wanted to get control of that escalating danger . . . a pathetic attempt to escalate an old unrequited love. And the worst delusion of all—that there was some relationship between Bruce Chessler, the boy who loved me, and Joseph Grablewski, the man I had once loved as desperately and futilely. Oh, there were so many strands now—Arkavy Reynolds, diamonds, speed, white cats, theatrical contradictions. So many . . .

My doggedness paid off on the second Tuesday in September.

Bukai left the house, crossed Fifth Avenue, but did not enter the park. Instead he boarded a downtown bus, with me five passengers behind him. He rode all the way downtown, got off at Eighth Street, walked through Washington Square Park onto La Guardia Place, south on La Guardia Place to Bleecker, and then turned west on Bleecker.

It was a long, arduous walk for the old man, but he kept it up. Finally he turned off Bleecker and into a coffeehouse—Café Vivaldi—a wonderful place where I had been many times.

I waited across the street. He did not reemerge. So I crossed over and sat down in the sidewalk-café section of the coffeehouse. From where I sat I could see Bukai's head through the window.

But he was not alone. Two other old men sat with him. I knew who they were instantly: Chederov and Mallinova. The words of that punk girl, Risa, came chillingly back to me: a Murder Incorporated of old men. But who really knew what they were doing there?

They ordered coffee and exotic pastries and I could dimly hear that they were talking in what had to be Russian.

I ordered an espresso and sipped it, watching the street, listening to the sounds from inside.

A man passed, walking a dog. He smiled at me. I smiled back, broadly. I was happy. My speculations had been confirmed. I had postulated that the three old men were not random hates of Bruce Chessler's, that they were a unit, a set, that whatever existed in their group or in their relation to others could only be understood because they were acting or not acting in concert. There had been other members of the Nikolai Group, but only these three had garnered Bruce Chessler's almost lunatic hate—and only these three were relevant now. At least to the young man's death.

The man walking the dog crossed the street, holding the leash tightly. I started to speculate as to why dog people make good street cops, for example, but only cat people make good investigative detectives. It had to do with the interpretation of behavior. With dogs, everything was hands-on or paws-on. The dog wagged his tail, licked your face. You put him on a leash, hit him with a paper, soothed him with a bone, scratched his head.

With cats it was different. To know your cat's feelings or to interpret its behavior, you had to rely on clues, on interpretations of past facts and past complexes of facts, none of which were mathematically precise.

My musings were interrupted by the sound of scraping chairs. Why was the meeting being adjourned?

What had the émigrés agreed or disagreed about? What had they been discussing? Were they twisted assassins or were they lovable old men?

Mallinova left first; then Chederov. Bukai remained seated, but I could see he was paying the bill. I left my payment on the outside table and waited across the street.

After he exited, Bukai began to walk slowly through the

streets, finally ending up on Hudson Street. He walked two more blocks downtown and then vanished into a store.

It was a pet store. Maybe he's buying a turtle, I thought, to accompany him on his walks.

I peered into the window. The front part of the store carried specialty dog bones, exotic cans of cat food, leashes and mufflers and all kinds of pet paraphernalia, ranging from the practical to the absurd.

Deeper into the store were the cages. It was obviously a place that boarded dogs and cats as well as sold them.

I could see Bukai in the rear section staring into one of the cages.

My antennae—or whatever it was between my actress's ears—began to pulsate.

He could be in the store, I realized, for a number of reasons, and at least two of them might be most interesting.

When he came out, I was faced with a dilemma. If I kept following him, I wouldn't be able to go into the store. If I went into the store, I would lose him.

I went into the store. A young man with a bright red bow tie and baggy pants asked me if I needed help. I told him I was just looking.

I spent about five minutes staring at a gray parrot in a large cage with a price tag of $741. Would my cats like it? As a friend? As a meal?

Then I slowly meandered to the rear, where the beasties were boarded and sold.

"Clara," I screamed, not able to contain myself when I saw

the large white cat with the black-spotted rump and face in the cage. She regarded me coolly.

The young man in the red bow tie looked at me with severe disapproval for my outburst.

The trouble was, there were three Claras in three separate cages! It was an astonishing sight. I started to giggle crazily. Then I got hold of myself.

Why not? I thought. One was my Clara. The other two were the cats given to Risa and then taken.

I could see that Bukai had brought them some tidbits.

Only one of the Claras was eating the gift.

A sudden calm came over me as I basked in the safety of Clara and her friends. I was beginning to perceive a pattern. I was beginning to close the circle . . . to pull the strands closer to the center.

"Are you looking for a kitten?" the young man asked, smelling a purchase.

"Not right now," I said, and quickly walked out of the store.

19

It was ten A.M. the next day. I was having my second cup of coffee and treasuring the events and revelations of the previous day. Risa had decided that during her last few days with me she would make herself useful—so she was running up and down the stairs to the washing machines and dryers in the basement, carrying pillowcases full of supposedly dirty clothes, I had the feeling that she was wreaking havoc by throwing some things of mine into a machine that simply should not have been there. But her instincts and intent were so good and so refreshing that I didn't have the heart to intervene even to ask a question. Let her ruin a few things, I thought.

Then Basillio called. His voice was low, clinical.

"Grablewski is in the hospital, Swede, and I heard it's bad. He collapsed in that bar last night, or yesterday afternoon."

"What's the matter with him?"

"I don't know. Like I said, all I heard was that he collapsed and was taken to Beth Israel."

I was silent on the phone. The phone receiver seemed odd to me, as if it shouldn't be capable of transmitting sound. Inside of me there were all kinds of turmoil, but nothing came out. The thought that Joseph Grablewski was in pain was almost unbearable to me. It made me mute.

"Do you want to see him?" Basillio asked kindly when my silence persisted.

"Yes," I whispered.

"Wait there," Basillio said, bless him, and hung up the phone.

A half hour later Basillio and I stood at a reception desk in one of the small wings of Beth Israel's alcoholism ward. We circled each other nervously, waiting for a Dr. Wallace.

He arrived in ten minutes or so, a very tall, stooped man who looked about seventy-five. He had bulging eyes and glasses that were perched on his forehead.

"Who are you?" he demanded, unfriendly, impatient, skeptical.

"Friends of his. Can we see him?" I asked.

He shrugged mightily and moved off, gesturing with one hand that we should follow. We passed through an open door and then a locked door and came to a ward divided into small cubicles of two beds each.

Dr. Wallace stopped in front of one. He pointed. I stared at the figure on the bed. It looked like a dead man. Grablewski was lying on his back, his arms strangely folded, as if he had just emerged out of some kind of restraint. His body was absolutely pale . . . as if some fiend had drained his blood. I could see that he was breathing; his chest was moving. His eyes were half open but not focusing. He looked childlike on that bed. The sight of him made me weak. I grasped the end of the steel cot. Basillio reached out to steady me but didn't make contact.

"What happened to him?" I asked plaintively.

"Are you kidding me? I thought you were his friend," Dr. Wallace said, his voice stacked with contempt. His response confused me.

"If you're his friend," he continued, "you know he's an alcoholic, don't you? And you know he's been an alcoholic a long time."

There was silence. We were all standing, not speaking, and seeming at cross-purposes.

"Okay, ladies and gentlemen," Dr. Wallace said in a resigned, sardonic voice, "let me give you the lesson you crave. The gentleman you are looking at is suffering from a common condition called fasting alcoholic hypoglycemia. It is usually seen in malnourished alcoholics. It is characterized by conjugate deviation of the eyes, extensor rigidity of the extremities, unilateral or bilateral Babinski reflexes, convulsions, transient hemiparesis, trismus hypothermia. It is caused by a multifactorial inhibition of gluconeogenesis by ethanol—booze. Your friend was brought here in a comatose state and given glucose intravenously. He is coming around quite nicely."

Dr. Wallace, having finished his bewildering exposition, nodded and then left. He stopped once and called back: "By the way, only about eleven percent of untreated cases of this syndrome die. So don't worry too much about your friend."

There were other humans on other cots, but I felt totally alone with Joseph Grablewski.

I pulled a steel folding chair close to the cot and sat down. I was twelve inches from his face. It was sad . . . so indescribably sad. I was suffused with all kinds of bizarre guilt . . . as if somehow by *not* doing something I had put him there. *Not* become lovers? When? Years ago? Or now?

"Look, he's come to. He recognizes you," Basillio said. The patient's eyes were indeed flickering and he moved one of his arms down by his side. I noticed that there were tremors in his fingers and his tongue flicked in and out of the side of his mouth as if on a desperate search for water.

"He's trying to speak to you, Swede. Go closer to him, he's trying to say something."

Yes, I could see that. I could see that he wanted to speak to me. It made me ambivalent. I wanted to be close to him . . . I wanted to run away. His plight was threatening me. His alcoholism sickened me.

I touched him tentatively, on the hand, like he was a dying man and my gesture made me ashamed.

Then I pressed my lips to his head and whispered, "I'm glad you'll be okay."

He nodded feebly and twisted his head oddly.

"He wants to tell you something," Basillio said. "Put your ear by his mouth."

I did so and waited. I heard sounds but no words. Then, finally, he said something to me that I could retrieve. Then he seemed to collapse and lose consciousness.

We walked out of the ward and onto the street. We stood

there watching the traffic, watching the people enter and leave.

"What did he say to you?" Basillio asked.

"It was something odd. He doesn't know what he's saying."

"What?" Basillio was insistent.

"He said . . . no, he asked: Did Constantin bite you?"

Basillio laughed. "He was making fun of you. He remembered when you had asked him about those three Stanislavski disciples. Constantin was Stanislavski's first name."

"I'm aware of his first name, Tony, it's just that I don't think Joseph Grablewski was making some kind of joke."

"Then what does it mean?"

"He was trying to tell me something."

"Oh, come on, Swede, the man is in an alcoholic stupor."

I had to be careful. I didn't want to make a fool of myself in front of Basillio or anyone else when I discussed Joseph Grablewski. Even in a stupor the man upset me. He upset me . . . not his words. I had only a low-level buzz over "Did Constantin bite you?" Low-level but persistent, like an aching molar.

"If he wasn't making a joke, then who is Constantin?"

"Is there a vodka called Constantin?" I asked Basillio.

"I don't think so. At least I've never heard of that brand. Maybe Grablewski thinks he's Stanislavski."

"No, Tony, Grablewski knows he's Grablewski, that's his trouble."

"Well, look, Swede, I gotta get back to work. I'm sure your old friend will be okay. I'll be in touch."

"Thanks, Tony," I said, and watched him walk downtown quickly, heading toward one of his copy shops.

I didn't go anywhere. I just lounged in front of the hospital. Grablewski's stupid whispered comment was like a delayed-action fuse. When I'd first heard it, the words were meaningless. When I discussed it with Basillio, they began to nudge me. And now that I was alone, they were beginning to fester. What was he talking about? Did he mean Stanislavski? Bite me? Had I suffered some kind of attack or setback?

Maybe he was talking about another man called Constantin. Maybe he was talking about a place. Maybe he was talking about a bar called Constantin. Or maybe he didn't even know he was talking to me; maybe he thought he was talking to one of his drinking companions.

I could not leave that stupid phrase alone. Maybe it was the residue of unrequited love. I could not leave it alone. Watch it fester, Alice, I thought to myself. I walked to the corner and stared at the hospital. Poor man . . . locked in there . . . people sticking things into his arm . . . people restraining him when he got violent—and all so that he could crawl back to that booth on Forty-fourth Street and start all over again.

What was Constantin? Who was Constantin? Where was Constantin? What did the whispered words mean? Then, fifteen minutes after I left the hospital, I was headed uptown in a cab—my destination the same Lincoln Center Library of the Performing Arts that I had visited a short time ago with Basillio.

I knew exactly where to look now for memoirs and histories of the Moscow Art Theatre. But this time I wasn't looking

for references to Bukai, Chederov, and Mallinova. I was looking for a single reference to a single name—Constantin.

But all I could find were references to Constantin Stanislavski. No, I was sure it was another Constantin. I had the
odd feeling as I flipped through the indexes that Joseph Grablewski was somewhere in the massive library, laughing at me,
mocking me, guzzling his vodka.

And then, in a single beat-up book published in English
in 1948 by a Russian-émigré actor named Orlov, I found the
indexed reference: "Constantin, cat."

It was on page 131 of the very bitter memoir.

On that page Orlov recounted how Stanislavski was presented with a white cat named after him by his associates and
this cat became a company favorite, not the least because it
tended to bite.

I started to laugh right there in the library, so loudly and
with such abandon that one of the guards came over and asked
me if I could moderate my behavior.

It was impossible, so I had to run out of the library
and calm down by the Henry Moore statue. It was bizarre and
funny; imagine a line of white cats that began with a cat given
to Stanislavski—and now sixty years later at least one of its
progeny named Clara and two unknown siblings are hidden
in a boarding pet store on Hudson Street after having been
kidnapped by Bruce Chessler and then stolen back. And they
are brought goodies by an eighty-five-year-old émigré. But
why would Chessler have kidnapped the cats in the first place?

The whole thing was crazy, Grablewski was crazy. And for
all I knew, Bukai was crazy.

By the time I got home, I was totally exhausted. Risa had gone out and left me a note that she would be back in the late afternoon or early evening. I told Bushy and Pancho about the mysterious line of white cats . . . if indeed such a line existed.

When I had finally showered and eaten and napped, I realized that I ought to at least follow up Grablewski's clue. I pulled out the old programs from the Nikolai Group's travels that Bruce Chessler had so lunatically defaced with his obscenities and carefully went through them searching for something Chessler might have written about Constantin the cat or Clara the cat or any white cat—past, present, or future.

There was no such annotation. It was odd. If Chessler was so obsessed with the émigrés, he must have known that there existed some kind of émigré saying with a double entendre: "Constantin bite you?" There had to be such a saying, or else how could Joseph Grablewski know about it? And surely Chessler's grandmother must have known about it and said something to her grandson about Constantin, Stanislavski's cat.

Well, one couldn't force things. If it wasn't there, it wasn't there.

Going through those old programs made me very sad. All those performances done and gone and forgotten. All those people in all those plays in all capacities—gone.

I smiled as I saw the name of Maria Swoboda, my old teacher, so prominently displayed in the programs. And the pictures the émigrés had used! They were all so heroic! More like the photos of operatic tenors.

I began to feel very reverently toward them. I started to stack them by date.

In 1957 they had gone to Mexico City.

In 1958 to Ecuador.

In 1959 to Panama and Argentina.

In 1960 to Venezuela.

In 1961 to Nicaragua.

In 1962 to Brazil and Costa Rica.

In 1963 to El Salvador.

In 1964 to Chile.

In 1965 to Venezuela.

In 1966 to Peru.

In 1967 to Mexico City and Brazil.

After I had stacked them by date, I realized it was very strange that the Nikolai Group had never performed in Europe, only in South and Central America.

I suddenly became furious at myself for not having studied or even looked at the programs seriously before.

There were many other peculiar facts about the Nikolai Group that emerged after one studied the programs.

For example, in most of the years of their existence they made only one foreign trip each year—to one city in one country.

This was very strange. No other theatrical group I was ever attached to did that. Small groups have to perform many times in many places in the shortest period of time in order to recoup their expenses. The Nikolai Group seemed to give command performances as if they were the Bolshoi Ballet—

which they assuredly weren't. How could they have afforded to fly to Buenos Aires, for example, and play in one theater for three nights and then fly back? What was the point artistically, anyway, forget financially?

And there was something even stranger. In the years when they had visited two countries on the same trip, these countries were far apart. This also was unheard-of. European companies, for example, when they came to America to play New York and Boston and Washington, and perhaps Atlanta, always tried to schedule some performances in Montreal, because it was geographically feasible. They wouldn't schedule Kingston, Jamaica.

The itinerary of the Nikolai Group was in some way profoundly fake!

I was so excited at what I had discovered about the programs that I started to pirouette about the living room with joy, until I realized that I wouldn't even have picked up the programs again if the alcoholic Mr. Grablewski hadn't whispered a cryptic comment in my ear.

But the seven strands were indeed beginning to point toward a center. There were Constantin and his progeny—poor Clara. There was a surly diamond merchant. There was a theatrical group that seemed to have defied theatrical logic. There was a murdered young man obsessed by hatred. There were three ancient wealthy émigrés who met from time to time. There was an eccentric bohemian who had been a police informer before he was murdered. And the seventh strand was unrequited love—Chessler's for me, and mine, at one time in the past, for Grablewski. For the first time since that young man had appeared on my landing I could see dimly toward the center—where the strands were leading.

Oh, I had work to do—a lot of work—and some mice to catch. But I knew what I was going to do and I was quite sure where it was going to lead.

I picked up the programs and placed them gingerly on the table. They seemed much heavier now. They were laden with relevance. They were the journeys of a theatrical group whose itinerary was so eccentric that it was obvious their art was diluted in the service of some other agenda. That agenda was the center on which the strands converged. I drank a third of a snifter of very elegant brandy. Bushy purred.

20

"Who?"

"Me, John. Alice . . . Alice Nestleton."

There was a silence on the other end of the phone. Poor John Cerise. I was obviously one of the few people he didn't want to hear from.

"John, don't worry. I'm not going to get you beat up again."

He laughed.

"Are your wounds healed?" I asked. I realized I should be ashamed of myself for not calling him before, when he got home from the hospital.

"I'm fine," he said. "Just a bit stiff."

There was an awkward pause. Then he asked: "Did you ever find that white cat . . . Carla?"

"You mean Clara, John. Yes, she's alive and well and living in a pet shop."

"There's nothing like happy endings."

"Look, John, I need another favor from you," I said.

He laughed nervously.

"I want to borrow one of your cats . . . one of your Abyssinians."

"Borrow a cat? Why, Alice?"

"Well, it's really too complicated to explain, but it'll only be for a couple of days and I'll take good care of it."

"But I thought you told me your cats don't like visitors."

"Well, I won't keep the cat at my apartment—at a friend's."

"For how long, Alice?"

"A few days. It's just for some cat photographs for a friend of mine in advertising. He needs a beautiful Abyssinian and you have only beautiful Abyssinians." I was only half lying to him. I did intend to take a photograph, but it was not really for advertising purposes. Or, rather, it was for a different kind of offering.

"Well, Alice, how can I get the cat to you?"

"My friend has a car. We'll pick the cat up tomorrow morning . . . about ten . . . will ten be okay?"

"Good. That will be good. Ten o'clock is fine. I'll let you have Jack Be Quick," he said.

I hung up the phone. God bless you, John Cerise, I thought. He could always be trusted. Risa was on the sofa, playing an elaborate kind of hide-and-seek with Bushy. I smiled at both of them. I felt wonderful. Ever since I discovered that the Nikolai Group was not what it had appeared to be—that it must have had a very secret agenda—the pieces had been falling into place. I had been to the library many times, burying myself in back issues of newspapers and journals. I had a full-scale model of past, present, and future—but it had to be proved, and the cat from John Cerise was the first step.

I walked, almost danced, to the window and stared down onto the street.

Madame Swoboda would be proud of me now, I thought. For wasn't that the essence of Method acting? One does not walk out onto a stage and begin to act. One walks out and speaks words or does motions and they are totally authentic because they come from authentic recollections and understanding of oneself. One doesn't act—one is. One doesn't fret in the wings, because there is nothing to fret about.

"Why are you so happy?" I heard Risa ask.

"Oh," I said, "just middle-age mirth."

"And where do you go all the time lately? You're never here."

"Research," I replied, "research, inquiry, analysis, a little here, a little there."

She cocked her head like a cat. She didn't know what I was talking about.

"I think, Risa, that I'm very close to finding out why Bruce Chessler died," I explained.

She stopped asking questions. She pulled into herself. I had forgotten how she must have loved him; I had never believed her attempt to distance herself from him.

About an hour later she seemed to revive. She said: "I

think I'll move back to my apartment tomorrow. I don't want to interfere with your research, your analysis, your what-have-you,"

Her voice was contemptuous. I didn't rise to the bait. I didn't want to argue with Risa about anything. Now she was furious for some reason, standing in the center of the room, her hands clenched on her waist. What kind of odd transference had she made to me?

"Research, analysis . . . why do you say such stupid things? What does it have to do with Bruce's murder? He's dead . . . he's off the planet . . . out of the universe . . . gone . . . dissipated . . . vanished. How can *you* find out why Bruce died? You didn't even know him!"

She spat her words out to me as if I were the mother who had betrayed her. Yes, it was time for the girl to go.

∽

"Are you sure that cat is not going to jump around?" Basillio asked in a nervous voice. He kept staring through the rear-view mirror at the beautiful Abyssinian cat pressed against the backseat of the car, his back arched.

"Don't worry, Tony, he loves it there, he won't bother you at all."

I was turned completely around, staring at the cat we had just picked up at John Cerise's. His name, I remembered, was Jack Be Quick. It was a very good name for a cat. He had a ruddy-brown coat ticked with black, and green eyes. He was lithe, hard, muscular, and gave off those signals in movement that seemed to say: "Yes, I not only look like a miniature cougar, I can act like one if you don't watch out." Of course, it was just a joke. Abyssinians are very kindly pussycats—exotic, yes, but kind. And Jack Be Quick settled down very quickly, much to Tony's relief.

It wasn't until we were crossing the George Washington Bridge into Manhattan that Basillio said: "Swede, I really hope you know what you're doing this time."

"Are you frightened, Tony? It may well be the greatest performance of your life."

"Not frightened so much, Swede, as feeling stupid."

I patted his hand. "We all feel stupid sometimes, Tony," I said. "It can't be helped."

Basillio had been very difficult to convince this time. My plans were simple and straightforward. First I was going to create a bogus photograph of a white cat with black markings that looked very like Clara. And I was going to use the Abyssinian, Jack Be Quick, to accomplish that. Basillio said it could be done easily with color transparencies and all kinds of xerographic magic.

Then Basillio was going to take the photograph to Bukai and offer him the cat for ten thousand dollars. Bukai would throw him out. But then I knew a whole lot of interesting things were going to happen.

"And I think one of the reasons why I feel so stupid is that you refuse to tell me what you are doing," he complained.

I didn't reply. Why hadn't I confided in Basillio? I don't know. I usually did. But this crime seemed to be so elaborate, to consist of so many strands, to require the uncovering of so many details, that I simply had stopped using Basillio as an intellectual companion midway through. I really didn't know why. It dawned on me that his feelings must really be hurt—I had been ordering him around like he was a chauffeur . . . as if he worked for me. Maybe it had something to do with my meeting up once again with Joseph Grablewski. Yes, maybe that was it. I had heard that Grablewski had been discharged from the hospital. He was probably back in his Forty-fourth Street coffin once again, gazing down at his vodka.

When we finally pulled up in front of the copy shop, Jack Be Quick seemed to have developed a glaring affection for Basillio.

Once inside, Tony and an assistant got to work. I cannot really describe what happened. There were mounted Polaroid cameras . . . airbrushes . . . plastic overlays . . . strange whir-rings and screechings . . . dripping pieces of material that seemed to come from a hospital laboratory.

But within two hours Basillio presented to me an 8 ½-by-11 photograph, or copy of a photograph, that was in dazzling color—a brilliant portrait of Jack Be Quick. Only Jack had changed colors.

He was now white with black spots on face and rump.

Magic. It was sheer magic. My hand began to tremble as I held it.

I had the delicious temptation to take a cab immediately to that pet store on Hudson Street where Clara and her two friends were incarcerated and then show it to Clara . . . ask her opinion . . . ask her whether we had done a good job.

"Is that what you wanted?"

"Exactly," I replied.

"Well, they don't call Mother Courage the best full-service shop in downtown Manhattan for nothing," Basillio said. He winked at me. "Now what do we do?" he asked, staring at Jack Be Quick, who had leapt to the top of his desk and was staring longingly at his swivel chair.

"We proceed with the plan," I said.

"I was afraid you were going to say that."

It was just past two in the afternoon. Basillio and I stood across the street from Bukai's town house, making sure to be out of sight of the windows, more toward the Fifth Avenue end of the street.

Basillio was obviously nervous. It had been a long time since he'd played a difficult part.

"Okay, Swede," he said grimly, "let's go over this again. Step by step."

"Fine, Tony."

"Who am I?"

"No names. You're a guy who needs money. A lot of money fast. And you have what Bukai wants."

"You mean I have a white cat with black spots in my shop."

"Right."

"And I'll give it to him for ten thousand dollars."

"Right."

"And he has twenty-four hours to pay or forget it."

"Right."

"God, Swede, this is crazy. What kind of lunatic would pay ten thousand dollars for a white cat?"

"Just show him the photo, Tony. And tell the old man the cat is at Mother Courage. You'll deliver if he pays."

"Is he going to pay?"

"I don't think so, Tony. I'm banking that he won't."

"Then what's the point?"

"Are you ready, Tony?"

"Wait. What if I can't get in?"

"I told you. A young woman will answer the door. Tell her you want to see Bukai. Tell her Bruce Chessler sent you. You'll get in."

"I don't know why, Swede, but I find this very distasteful."

"I appreciate it, Tony."

He smiled. Then he drew his hand over his face as if he were changing masks, and what emerged was a snarling, ugly, yet strangely vulnerable thief . . . or gambler . . . or hustler.

"Look good?" he asked from the corner of his mouth.

"Right out of *The Threepenny Opera*," I assured him. Without another word he strode across the street to the doorway. I turned and started to walk toward the museum. It was there we would meet as soon as he finished his mission—by the small bar at the entrance of the museum cafeteria.

I didn't dawdle in the museum. I walked right to the appointed place and sat down on one of the divans and ordered a club soda with lime. The lunch crowd was gone but a group of German tourists were seated all around me.

Basillio arrived twenty-five minutes later. He knelt beside me as if he were imparting some kind of classified information.

"Okay, Swede. It was a piece of cake. I walked inside with the young woman. She pushed me into this room cluttered with books. Five minutes later this ancient Russian comes downstairs. I show him the photograph of Jack Be Quick turned white. I tell him I need ten thousand dollars fast. I'm in trouble, I tell him. The deal is simple, I tell him. Ten thousand right now in my hand. And I bring you the cat in a half hour. Then I figure I'm going too fast. So I modify the offer. Five thousand down and five thousand when I bring the cat."

He paused and then stood up.

"What happened, Tony?"

He knelt again. "The old man just stares at me like he's looking at some kind of ghost or lunatic. Then he tells me to get out. That's all. He tells me to get out. I leave him the card in case he changes his mind. And I'm gone."

I leaned back and closed my eyes. The game, as they say, had begun. And the first serve I had called correctly.

"Anything else for the moment?" Basillio asked sardonically.

"No," I said, "but could you give me the key to the shop? I want to go over tonight and make sure Jack Be Quick is fed."

"How long are you going to keep the beast in my shop?" he asked.

"Not long, Tony, not long."

"Have to go," he said, slapped me very gently on the cheek as a sign of comradeship, and was gone.

I had to move quickly now, I realized—quickly and carefully.

∽

Harry Hanks was seated at a desk that seemed to have been stolen from an insurance company—it was large and modern and the top was painted orange, which did not at all blend in with the green-and-white motif of the police precinct.

He was reading the *Daily News*, spread out on top of the desk as if he were hunting for coupons.

I stood in front of the desk for a long time before he even noticed me, and when he did, he didn't recognize me.

"May I sit down?" I asked, pointing to the empty chair next to the desk.

"What can I do for you, lady?"

I sat down and waited for him to fold up the paper and give me his undivided attention. He kept looking through the paper.

"Don't you remember me?"

"Not really," he said.

"We had a discussion in front of the Gramercy Park Hotel . . . about Bruce Chessler."

He grinned. He remembered. "Right, the lady who lost her student."

I didn't appreciate the sarcasm, but I really didn't have time to play games with him.

"Bruce Chessler was not murdered in a drug-related incident," I said to him.

He sat up suddenly, his eyes wide, folding the paper with disgust and shoving it across the desk.

"Say what, lady?"

"I said that Bruce Chessler was not murdered because of a drug deal gone bad, as you told me."

"Is that so?"

"Since the case has grown cold under your supervision," I reminded him, "I should think you'd be very happy at what I've told you."

"I am happy, lady. I am so happy that I can't even move. Because if I move I'll fall down on the floor and roll over and out the window and they'll scrape me up still laughing, still happy."

There was a long silence. I had realized he was going to be difficult—but not this difficult. I dug into my purse and came out with the *New York Times* article about me, which stated how I had been commended by the Nassau County Police Department for resolving the Starobin murder. He read the article and handed it back to me.

"What do you want me to say, lady?"

"Nothing. Just take what I'm telling you seriously."

"What are you telling me?"

"That Bruce Chessler was not murdered because of drugs."

"Okay, lady. If you say so."

"And," I added, "I am very close to being able to present the entire conspiracy to you."

"What conspiracy?"

"It's a long story. It's a criminal conspiracy." Should I tell him that Arkavy Reynolds and Bruce Chessler were murdered by the same gun? No! I decided against even bringing up Arkavy's name. That would entail discussing Detective Felix . . . it would bring in other jurisdictions . . . other complexities. Cops are afraid of bureaucratic complexities. They are afraid their noses will be bitten off.

Hanks swept the *Daily News* off his desk onto the floor with an angry flourish. "And you have proof of this so-called conspiracy? Of course you have, lady. Right? And you know the names of his killers? Right, lady? That's why you're here busting my hump, because you know all these things that we dumb cops don't know. Right?"

I waited until his anger abated. He was a difficult man to deal with. Very difficult.

"I am going to say something to you that is very strange."

"Everything you told me or didn't tell me so far, lady, has been strange."

"There is a cat in a copy store only a few minutes from here."

"Is that so?"

"And within the next few hours someone is going to try to steal that cat."

"The excitement mounts."

"And the person who tries to steal that cat is the person who murdered Bruce Chessler."

"So you're going to be hiding there with your video camera, is that it? And you're going to sell the tape to Channel

Seven news, and then you're going to write a book about the great criminal conspiracy . . . or was it the cat conspiracy?"

"You really dislike me, don't you, Detective?"

"You have it wrong, lady. I just don't like listening to fantasies."

I leaned over the desk and wrote the address on a small pad. He stared at what I had written.

"If you can spend the evening with me there, waiting, I will show you that they are not fantasies."

"Right, lady. After I get off work today, you want me to hold your hand for God knows how many hours in a copy shop, keeping our eyes on some cat."

"Yes, Detective Hanks. That is what I would like you to do."

"Well, lady, I have a better idea."

"What's that?"

He tore a sheet of paper off the same pad I had written on, wrote something on it, and pushed it at me.

"Now," he said, "I'm going to go home after work and take a shower and have a few drinks and then have some supper and then take a walk and maybe watch a ball game and then go to sleep. But if you're in that store staring at that cat and some killers come at you, well, you just tell them to hold on because you have to make a call—to me. That's my home number, lady."

The whole meeting had gone as wrong as it could go, from the very beginning. I realized it was to a large extent my fault. I shouldn't have expected Detective Harry Hanks to give me any help unless I gave him some very hard facts. I had dug up many of them, but it was too early to present them—

to anyone. Perhaps Hanks would think them relevant. For me, they were pointers. No, it went much deeper than that. Hanks thought me a dilettante . . . it didn't matter how many newspaper clippings I showed him about my crime-solving prowess. And I thought Hanks to be an arrogant fool.

I took the piece of paper, crumpled it, and dropped it into my purse like a piece of dirty candy given to me by a derelict whose feelings I didn't want to hurt.

"You see," I said, "as difficult as this may seem to you, Detective Hanks, we are both after the same thing."

"Which is?"

"The person or persons who murdered Bruce Chessler."

"Fine. Call me if you need help," he said, and I saw he was making a strong effort to get rid of his sarcasm and skepticism . . . to be professional . . . to be noncommittal— while at the same time distancing himself from a woman he obviously found hard to deal with. He kept his body turned away from me as if he were desperate for me to leave but didn't want to say so . . . didn't dare to say so.

I stood up and started walking away.

"Wait," I heard him say.

I didn't turn back toward him; I just stopped.

"I forgot your name," he said.

"Alice Nestleton," I replied.

"Look, Miss Nestleton, you know I want that kid's killer. Just as much as you do."

"I suppose so."

"So you give me something solid and I'll move on it."

"That's what I'm about to do," I replied.

21

I had moved Basillio's swivel chair to the long hallway between the office and the shop. It was quiet and dark. A single light burned over one of the large copying machines and it spread diminishing rays throughout the hallway.

Jack Be Quick was nibbling some chicken I had bought him on the way over.

From time to time he stared slyly at me.

"They're coming to get you, Jack," I said. "Three old Russians are coming to rescue you because they think you're white with black spots."

Jack didn't seem to mind at all.

I leaned forward and watched him. How beautiful his breed was; how suffused with a sense of wildness and mystery; yes, it was true—the Abyssinian reeked of Egyptian deserts.

Then I sat back. I was tired but determined. I didn't know which of the three old men would be sneaking through the door. Maybe it would be all three. I didn't care. It wasn't revelation I was there for—it was confirmation. It would be the last piece in the puzzle and I could present it to the world. The world? I was thinking like an actress again, not a criminal investigator. It was humorous. The world didn't care about Bruce Chessler. And the world didn't really care about the strange, tortuous journey of those Russian émigrés, now sequestered in their hard-earned homes, thinking God knows what thoughts, being obsessed by geriatric memories.

Time went slowly. Very slowly. Again and again I walked to the two doors through which someone had to walk. The front door to the store and the side door, leading from the office to the alley.

Which door would it be? What did it matter? How would the break-in happen? What did it matter?

At midnight I pulled the swivel chair back into the office and pushed it behind the desk. I sat down and swiveled in the darkness.

Jack Be Quick leapt up on the desk. His green eyes gleamed. He circled the desk and made a very deep purring sound, from his belly. Was he still hungry? Did he want water? No, both were available to him.

"Speak to me, Jack," I said to him.

He approached me warily.

"A penny for your thoughts, Jack."

He stretched, his legs and large paws elongated downward; his back arched. Is there anything more beautiful than a handsome cat stretching in the shadows?

My thoughts went to Grablewski and then to Bruce

Chessler. It was amazing how they always popped up together. And it was sad that my thoughts, when they focused on men, rarely dealt with past lovers . . . only with would-be lovers— men who were not . . . had never been . . . or could never be my lovers.

When I looked back up, Jack Be Quick had vanished from the desk. I could see his shadow against one of the walls.

I suddenly realized that I had nothing with me, no weapon in case of trouble. Nor did I have my bag or even a scarf. I had arrived at the Mother Courage Copying Shop like a Zen Buddhist monk, with only the clothes on my back. Why? I didn't really know. It was strange. Maybe I required simplicity in the face of a dense and grim conspiracy. Or maybe, since it had required a great deal of mental and physical effort to arrive at where I was in relation to the conspiracy—in relation to understanding how all the strands were proceeding toward an unfolding center—I had to be almost naked in my resolve.

The most horrible sound I have ever heard in my life suddenly cascaded through the store.

I didn't move. The sound seemed to splinter my bones . . . to make me shiver . . . to crush my will. I couldn't move.

Again and again . . . louder and louder . . .

It didn't stop. I closed my eyes. I scrunched down into the chair.

Glass. It sounded like glass shattering. Someone was smashing in the front window of the store.

I covered my ears. I got up. I pressed my hands tight

against my ears until they hurt. I ran into the hallway and then toward the front of the store. I didn't know what I was doing. I didn't know what was happening.

I let my hands drop from my ears. The sound began again . . . splintering, screeching, moaning, lunacy.

I could see something now.

Someone was smashing in the front window.

I started to scream.

The figure was inside now, through the window.

I looked around, desperate, searching for something to stop the intruder.

And then there was absolute silence. It was so quiet that I could hear the pads of Jack Be Quick's feet.

The intruder heard them also—the intruder was there for the white cat that did not exist.

Where was the light? I thought desperately. There must be a switch on the wall. Where *was* the light? I ran my hand along the wall like a crazed blind person. My hand touched something. I pushed up. The whole store was flooded with light.

In front of me, holding a steel pipe, stood a small thin black woman with a closely shaved head.

My God, it was the poet! It was the young woman from the bar! It was Elizabeth.

She stared at me. Exhausted. Frightened. Panting.

She dropped the iron bar that had splintered the window. It clattered to the floor. There were streaks of blood on her wrists.

"Why are you here?" she asked in a hoarse whisper, terrified.

"To make sure you don't get the white cat," I said.

I ran back and gathered Jack Be Quick in my arms and approached her, thrusting the large nonwhite Abyssinian close to her face.

"You see, there is no white cat here, none at all. We were just waiting for you."

Her eyes roamed over the walls and the windows and the machines, as if she were searching for a way out.

"Who sent you?" I asked.

She seemed to draw inside of herself.

"Was it Bukai . . . or Chederov . . . or Mallinova?"

She shook her head. "I don't know those names."

"Then who?"

"I don't know his name."

"He paid you?"

"No. He didn't pay. He paid for what happened in the bar. He paid me to point out Bruce. And then he threatened me. He said if I broke in here and got the white cat, he'd forget everything. If not, he'd tell the police that I was an accessory to murder."

"Why did you point him out?"

"I didn't know he would be murdered. I had no idea. I just wanted some extra money. Some spending money. You know—for books and things. Don't you believe me? I had no idea."

Her legs gave way. She sprawled on the floor. I remembered

our conversation in the bar, about that Indian philosopher—
Patanjali.

"How much did he pay you to point him out?"

"Five hundred dollars."

"And what else did he get for the money?"

"Nothing, I swear. Just that I would hold the booth in the bar so that Bruce would be there; so that he would not see the bar was too crowded and go elsewhere. That was all I had to do. Talk with Bruce in a booth until he came in."

"Who is he?"

"I told you, I don't know his name."

She started to weep. She kept raising her hands as if to explain, and then lowering them.

"Did you have a phone number?" I asked.

"Yes."

"Give it to me."

She shook her head. She was clearly frightened.

"Give it to me," I said, closing in on her.

She stared at me as if evaluating what kind of threat I represented, as if determining how far I was prepared to go. She understood she was in very deep hot water . . . either with the police or with the man who had hired her in the beginning.

Then she removed a crumpled paper from her pocket.

A phone number was penciled on one side.

I dialed the number. A recorded message came on. The voice said: "You have reached Sedaka and Sons, Diamond Merchants. If you are using a pushbutton phone, please press one for our accounting department . . . press two to schedule an appointment . . . press three if your call is personal. Thank you." The phone fell gently out of my hand and back on the receiver.

I smiled grimly. Everything was going just fine. Jack Be Quick walked regally over to the squatting, frightened poet and rubbed his back against her knee. She seemed to shrink further into herself.

22

I was sitting next to Detective Harry Hanks in his ugly un-marked police car, holding Jack Be Quick on my lap. We were double-parked across from the Café Vivaldi.

It had not been easy getting him there. The scene in the police precinct had been volatile.

"So what do you want me to do? Arrest the girl for break-ing your friend's plate-glass window? Okay. I'll do that. Or do you want me to arrest her for attempted kidnapping of a white cat that didn't turn out to be a white cat at all?" He was get-ting more and more irritated and he started accentuating his questions by poking his finger in the air. "Or do you want me to arrest her for accessory to murder? That's it, isn't it? That the same guy who paid her to steal the cat and to set up Bruce Chessler also murdered Bruce Chessler."

"Calm down, Detective."

"No, you calm down, lady. Because that little black girl never saw a person she could identify in the bar that night.

She was there when the shots were fired, but she didn't know who fired them. Were you ever in that bar, lady? Of course you were. Where the kid was sitting, you can't see your hand in front of your face. So you want me to arrest the black girl and the diamond merchant on the basis of phone calls? You must be kidding."

"I have a lot more," I told him.

"Where? In your pocketbook? In your shoes?"

"No, in a café not far from here."

And that was how, after a struggle, we ended up in the unmarked police car, staring across the street, against a strong sun, into a coffeehouse.

"These three old Russians . . . how do you know they're inside now? I can't see a thing."

"Oh, they're in there," I said. "The owner of the café told me. They have met for years on the last Thursday of each month."

"Listen, lady," he said, exasperated, "I don't want any more conflict with you. Just tell me what you want me to do and I'll do it. Then just promise to leave me alone."

"Go in with me, Detective, and protect me when I confront them," I said.

"From what you told me about their ages . . . are you sure they're assaultive?" he asked.

"We'll see, won't we?"

"Do we really need the cat?"

"Oh, yes, we really do," I replied.

We left the car double-parked. We shut the doors. The

three of us, including Jack Be Quick, walked through the door of the Café Vivaldi.

The three old men were sitting at the same table I had seen them sitting at before—that time I had followed Bukai to the pet store on Hudson Street where he had sequestered the white cats.

For a moment I was frightened . . . very frightened . . . not physically . . . and I clutched poor Jack Be Quick so tightly in my arms that he gave a long, low growl.

That was when the three turned toward me. I had never been this close to Chederov and Mallinova. Chederov had thick white hair that fell down over the most lined face I had ever seen. Mallinova had a painfully thin lantern face. They were all wearing cramped suits, as if they were the board of directors of some long-closed bank.

"May I join you, Mr. Bukai? We've already met, if you remember. And this is my friend Detective Harry Hanks." At the mention of the detective, they stared at each other. They said nothing. Detective Hanks pulled two chairs up to the large round table. We sat down. I still held Jack Be Quick.

There was a glass of double espresso in front of each of the old men. And toward the center of the table were two untouched pieces of Italian cheesecake.

No one spoke for what seemed the longest time. I could hear Bukai breathing heavily to my left.

It was I who must talk. But to whom? It was I who was going to indict them. But who was going to receive the indictment? It had to be the detective. I would talk to Harry Hanks.

I was about to do the kind of theater piece I had always despised: a one-woman monologue reciting facts. But there was no other option.

I began. Detective Hanks was the audience. I ignored the other three.

"We are sitting with three rich old men. They came to America penniless except for their reputations as dramatic art-ists, as professionals in the world's most prestigious theater company—the Moscow Art Theatre.

"Now they are very wealthy men. How did they get their money?

"Let me tell you. They formed a theater group in the 1950s—the Nikolai Group—and it survived for ten years.

"Each year the Group made a trip to South or Central America to perform.

"I have traced the itinerary of that group. It is very odd. One oddity is that they visited only countries or cities that were in the midst of either political or economic turmoil. Isn't that strange? One would think they would avoid those places. Most theatrical companies do. But not the Nikolai Group. Oh, no."

I hesitated and looked around the table. Mallinova was very pale. Bukai was grimacing and stirring his espresso with a tiny silver spoon.

"You see," I continued, "they weren't on tour for aesthetic reasons. They were smuggling in diamonds and smuggling out cash. For diamonds have traditionally been the repository of wealth for South Americans during wars and revolutions and inflation. In France and the Middle East, it is gold. But in South America it is diamonds."

Hanks arched his eyebrows. I slid across the table to him a piece of paper I had prepared; on one side was the Group's itinerary in South America . . . on the other side the visits were correlated with social, economic, or political turmoil. Hanks studied the sheet.

"It's a helluva coincidence," he noted. He pushed the paper toward the center of the table for any of the old men to study. None of them made a move toward the paper.

"But it's circumstantial as hell," he added.

I continued. I was beginning to grow into the heady role. I felt a sense of analytical power . . . that I was projecting it.

"We all know that Mr. Bukai is a partner in a diamond firm now run by a gentleman named Sedaka. His father, Daniel Sedaka, died in 1972. He died at home, among his family, content. But if you will retrieve from your files, Detective Hanks, a May 11, 1949, article in a now-defunct newspaper called the *Daily Mirror*, it describes how three individuals were indicted for the theft of a large shipment of diamonds consigned from Amsterdam to New York. One of those individuals was Daniel Sedaka. The diamonds vanished in Toronto. The senior Mr. Sedaka was tried but the jury refused to convict. Those diamonds were eventually sold on the black market in South America for huge sums of cash. And it was all clear profit."

Mallinova raised his hand for the waiter and gestured that he wanted water. I waited until the water was served.

"So," I continued, "the Nikolai Group eventually disbanded, with everyone happy—everyone rich. But then, alas, a crazy young man comes on the scene. He is the grandson of a colleague—Maria Swoboda. I'm talking about Bruce Chessler."

Mallinova drank his water. I could see his eyes staring through the top of his glass at Bukai.

"Now, Bruce Chessler was a very tormented young man. He lived a marginal existence . . . a typically pathetic out-of-work actor's life, surviving through small-time drug sales. One of his customers was a theater hanger-on named Arkavy Reynolds. One day, probably, Arkavy needed speed and had no money, so he gave Bruce Chessler some information instead. Dirty information . . . about some revered people. Arkavy thought Bruce would find their diamond-smuggling scheme amusing. How Arkavy got the information, we'll never know. But he was a very resourceful lunatic. Anyway, Bruce didn't find it amusing. Bruce loved the theater with a passion and he hated those who debased it. The hypocrisy of his grandmother's colleagues—these hallowed names from the Moscow Art Theatre—began to fester in him. Since they were thieves, he reasoned, he would steal something from them.

"Bruce Chessler didn't steal money from them. He stole something much more prized by the old Russians—their last link to the Stanislavski tradition of the Moscow Art Theatre. You see, Stanislavski had a white cat named Constantin, with black spots on its face and rump. And soon there were kittens and many such cats. And when the émigrés left Russia, they took their felines with them, and once in this country, they kept the line alive. If you want to see them, Detective Hanks, we can go to a pet store on Hudson Street, where they are now being boarded. There are three white cats with black spots in there. They belong to these old gentlemen here, and they were what Bruce Chessler stole.

"What a stupid childish act it was . . . stealing cats from old people. And then he just gave them away. He gave them away because he intuited that he had gone too far . . . that the three old men were afraid he was going to go to the police about the diamond smuggling of so many years ago. It never dawned on the old men that Bruce Chessler had absolutely no hard evidence and that the statute of limitations made any prosecution improbable. What they really wanted to protect above all were their reputations . . . their delusions that they were artists . . . that the great Moscow Art Theatre tradition rested nobly on their brows. So our three elderly friends had to make sure. They had to get rid of that irrational, vindictive young man. After all, he was threatening their immortality. They acted murderously. They frightened Sedaka Junior into killing Bruce Chessler and his bohemian information source, Arkavy Reynolds, and then stealing back the cats.

"You see, the Russians were not merely silent partners in the diamond firm. They owned the controlling interest. If Sedaka refused to comply with their wishes, they could have simply fired him. And Sedaka lived a very expensive lifestyle. He chose to murder rather than be poor. I'm sure, Detective Hanks, that if you put a little pressure on the diamond merchant, he will happily implicate his benefactors to cut his own sentence."

I leaned back, suddenly exhausted, talked out. My throat was beginning to tremble.

Detective Hanks was staring at me, obviously absorbed in my story.

I turned to Bukai. He, too, was staring at me. I smiled at him.

He picked up his espresso glass and flung the contents into my face. It happened so fast I couldn't evade the luke-warm coffee, which splattered over me.

Hanks stood up swiftly and started toward the old man. I raised my hand to stop him. He sat back down, reluctantly.

I wiped the coffee away, carefully, with Bukai's napkin, and then wiped Jack Be Quick's face, since he also had been splattered.

"Yes," I said, "these old men love their white cats so much they will go to great lengths to get them back if stolen. They were even going to take Jack Be Quick, whose photograph I had doctored to simulate a white cat with black spots. Why? Because they thought Bruce Chessler had stolen it from an-other émigré. They were the guardians of the white cats . . . as if that would redeem their prostitution. Stupid, sad old men, willing to do anything to die with some semblance of honor."

I stood up and placed Jack Be Quick on the center of the table.

"Now, there's a reason why I could use Jack Be Quick as a stand-in for one of the white cats. The white cats bear an uncanny physical resemblance to Abyssinians—which Jack Be Quick is. But they're not Abyssinians at all . . . they're just plain old Moscow Art Theatre wardrobe cats."

I pushed Jack Be Quick gently onto his back and began to stroke his stomach. He lay there happily.

"Look at him, Detective Hanks," I said.

"I'm looking. So what?"

"Can you see what makes Abyssinians different from other cats . . . why they look like cougars?"

"The paws . . . they're bigger."

"No, the pads, not the paws. They have larger pads on the feet."

"Okay, okay, so what?"

"Well, Detective, why don't you just take a peek into Jack Be Quick's front-left paw?"

"Why?"

"He has an important present for you."

He reached over, gently spread the pad, and said: "There's something in there."

"Right." I reached over and pulled out a small diamond-like stone.

"Is this the way they smuggled the diamonds? I know South American animal quarantine laws are a joke, but . . ."

I laughed. Tweaking the detective's nose was refreshing. But enough was enough.

"I have no idea how they smuggled the diamonds in and the cash out, Detective. Probably in their underwear. But in those years, before the drugged-out rock bands, traveling theatrical groups were never searched by customs agents in any country. It was a long-honored gentleman's agreement. In the 1950s, for example, a well-known British ballerina visited this country often with her troupe and her constant companion—

a bottle of Polish vodka . . . which was illegal to bring into the country at that time. No one bothered her. In those days, before the rock bands forced them to crack down, artists traveling on tour could bring into a given country whatever they wanted—and take out what they wanted. Provided they were discreet."

I dropped the fake stone, actually a pebble, into Bukai's empty espresso cup. Jack Be Quick walked over to inspect what he had been carrying.

The waiter dropped the bill onto the table. It was such an absurd ending to my performance that I started to laugh. Then I looked around. No one else was laughing. The faces of the three men had crumbled. Their bodies seemed to have been scraped of substance.

I turned away from them, toward the door to the café, and stared for a long time. I had the strangest feeling that Bruce Chessler was about to walk in. What a bizarre delusion. Did I require applause from his ghost? For what? For a fine performance? For unraveling the conspiracy? For making sure that the old men would probably die in a penitentiary somewhere rather than in their town houses? It was hard to understand.

23

"It's not often a beautiful woman buys me lunch in a restaurant where the house salad costs twenty-two fifty," Basillio said, staring at his sparsely laden plate with both horror and awe.

We were seated in one of those posh new restaurants on lower Broadway, south of Houston and north of Canal.

A week had gone by. I felt very good. I was still celebrating. Sedaka had blown the whistle on the three old men. Hanks said he'd get twenty years to life for the Chessler and Reynolds murders. As for the three old men, Hanks had no idea what they'd get. How does one sentence eighty-five-year-old men? I wasn't celebrating their coming pain; I was celebrating the truth, which was, in an odd sense, a vindication of Stanislavski and the Moscow Art Theatre. I don't know how, but it was. It was as if the Russian theatrical tradition had hired me and paid me with unspoken affection.

"What I still don't understand, Swede, is how you tied

together the fact that there was something strange about the Nikolai Group's tours and the fact they only went to countries where diamonds would be very much in demand because of turmoil."

"Well, look Tony, I've been around the theater too long not to recognize that those tours were somehow fakes. Theater companies can't do it that way. The Group had to be going to each specific country for a reason, and that reason had to be lucrative. What little underfunded company can fly down to Rio for two days with their whole cast and baggage and then turn around and fly back? No way. So I took the month, year, and place of each trip and checked it against the *New York Times Index* for those dates. Each visit was the same—the Nikolai Group seemed to be courting danger. They went only to places that were in turmoil one way or another. They had to be bringing something in or bringing something out. Then I remembered that Bukai's original connection with the diamond firm had been with the father, not the son. So I started researching old man Sedaka . . ."

"And the rest is history," Basillio added, grinning.

"The white cats are still a problem," I said, suddenly noticing one of the strangest little rolls I have ever seen nestled in the wicker bread tray. I extracted it and studied it as a cat would.

"Where are they?"

"Oh, they're still in the pet store. But the pet-store owner won't release them unless Bukai signs a consent order. And the old man won't sign anything. He wants them to stay there. He still believes other white cats exist and are being threatened."

"What about the fake white cat?"

"You mean Jack Be Quick? He's back with his owner."

"I still don't understand why they tried to steal him."

"Bukai and his friends obviously lost count of the progeny of Constantin. They don't know which émigrés own which cats. That's why he went for Jack Be Quick. He didn't know if it really was a descendant of Constantin's. It sure looked like one. Better sure than sorry."

"Only in the theater," he mused, finally giving up on the salad and staring at the remarkable dessert wagon that hovered in the distance.

I realized that I was still holding the strange roll, so I dropped it back into the basket.

"Eat it, Swede. It's good for you. It'll fatten you up."

"I like bread in the morning only."

"You always were weird, Swede," he said. I thanked him profusely for his compliment. We sat there for another half hour or so, eating tarts and drinking delicious coffee. Then he went back to work and I started home.

On Fourth Avenue, just before Fourteenth Street, I passed a flower store and saw an expensive bouquet of yellow flowers. I bought it and kept walking.

When I reached Twenty-third Street I stopped. I was perplexed. Why was I going home? The cats were fed. There was nothing more to do. Why had I bought the flowers? For *him*?

I stepped into the gutter and hailed a cab, which took me to Forty-fourth Street. Had I really bought the flowers for Joseph Grablewski in celebration that he was out of the alkie ward in the hospital? But he had been out awhile.

I walked gingerly into the bar. I was excited, like a girl on a date.

He was there, in the same booth. I started to walk toward him, self-conscious, like at an audition. My vulnerability angered me. God, I was past forty. I had never even slept with that drunkard.

I slipped into the booth across from him and laid the flowers on the table. A glass of what looked like cola was in front of him.

"Another attempt at seduction?" he asked weakly, staring at the flowers.

He looked pale and thin and his hair was cut shorter. He kept his hands palm-down on the table. They were shaking slightly.

"How do you feel?"

"Wonderful."

"Where's your vodka?"

"Don't you know? I'm now a recovering alcoholic."

"What's in the glass?"

"Root beer."

"I want to thank you for your help . . . for the information you gave me."

"What help?" he asked.

"About Lev Bukai's diamond connections."

"Were you one of the people who visited me in the hospital?"

"Yes."

Since he hadn't even seemed to remember anything about Lev Bukai, I left it alone.

"Why?"

"Why what?"

"Why did you visit me in the hospital?"

"To bring you flowers," I said, smiling and pointing to them.

"I don't like flowers . . . in hospitals . . . in bars . . . onstage."

I pulled the flowers close to me.

"What do we do? What do we do? Sleep together or not?" He recited the questions in a singsong manner and then began to laugh.

"You must forgive me," he finally said. "Sobriety brings out my lack of control. But it won't last long. I've never been able to achieve sobriety for more than three days running."

"Maybe this time."

"That's what my students always say."

I was perplexed. What students was he talking about?

"Do you teach now?"

"When sober. Didn't you know? Don't you know that for the past ten years the great Joseph Grablewski has been earning vodka money by teaching psychotic students how to really act . . . how to bring heaven, hell, Marx, and De Sade into their genitalia."

"No, I had no idea you were an acting coach."

"Coach? My God! Not a coach. Never a coach. Master, guru, savior, shrink—but not ever a coach."

He drank some of the root beer, very slowly, as if it could kill him.

"Everybody's heard of crazy Joseph Grablewski's classes."

"I haven't. Who studies with you? Maybe I know some of them."

"Psychopaths study with me," he yelled, "and those who are heartbroken and those who despise what there is, and those who are broken by the stage, and those who . . . Not you, lady, never a beautiful lady like you."

He had misjudged me again. He had made me into the enemy again.

"I don't make them feel good. I don't prepare them for stupid plays. I make them into performance artists. I make them grapple with the world. Sometimes it even kills them."

"You're talking stupid now, Joseph. Calm down."

"Am I talking stupid? Am I really? What do you know? A student of mine was murdered a few weeks ago. What an actor he might have become under my tutelage! His assignment was simple: I told him to fall desperately in love with a woman . . . to pine for her . . . to write her love letters . . . to engage her . . . to go to the very limits of romantic fakery . . ."

I put my hands over my ears. I suddenly understood what I was hearing. But I could not deal with the horror of what I was comprehending. I wanted to be dumb, to be senseless.

Grablewski was still talking. I could see his lips moving wildly.

I ran out, spilling the flowers onto the floor. Bruce Chessler had loved me as an assignment! As a classroom exercise projected out onto the world! I walked ten, fifteen, twenty blocks, quickly. Then I stopped, exhausted. And right there, on the street, I began to laugh. Had ever an actress been so elegantly hoisted on her own petard?

24

Thanksgiving came and went. Christmas came and went. In January the diamond merchant Sedaka was sentenced to twenty-five years to life for the murder of Bruce Chessler. The charges against him for the murder of Arkavy Reynolds were dropped. The three old émigrés were sentenced to eight to fifteen years each for conspiracy to murder. All charges relating to diamond smuggling and theft were dropped. Mallinova died from a heart attack two weeks after the sentencing. Chederov suffered a stroke and was hospitalized. Only Bukai, of the three, went to jail.

I don't like to see people sent to the penitentiary, but I really had no sympathy for the Russians and Sedaka. They were murderers. In fact, I was on a sort of permanent high because it had been my efforts that solved the case. As for Joseph Grablewski's revelation that the young man's love for me was an acting-class exercise—well, I felt a bit stupid, but then I realized that it was probably my swallowing the tale of "doomed love" that had started my investigations. So my foolishness had paid off.

Everything was going well with me. There was a good possibility that I would land the part of an old crazy woman in a very strange and very beautiful play written by a Chilean woman, which was to be staged in the spring at Princeton University by a new drama society. I loved playing old crazy women with thick corrosive makeup dripping all over. It was a harmless perversion. As for cat-sitting, it was always there when I needed it.

My own cats were doing quite well, although Pancho had developed a mange-type rash on his back that required me to rub some evil-smelling substance on it a few times a week. This meant I had to catch Pancho. Which in turn meant that I was becoming physically fit, because to catch Pancho when he knew he was about to get anointed was more than difficult. I had to plot strategies . . . to lie in wait for him and then pounce. Once I grabbed him, he would fix his betrayed eyes on me until the deed was done. Poor Pancho, he never really trusted me.

In fact, I was so "up," I decided to buy a toaster oven. It was just when I was percolating in the last phase of that decision that Basillio called and asked me to meet him for a drink.

The moment I saw him at the bar on Second Avenue just north of St. Marks Place, I knew he had something important to tell me; a plum of some kind. He was drumming a tune on the bar and bouncing up and down.

He patted the stool next to him. I sat.

"Now," he said grandly, "before I begin telling you my news, I have to ask you a personal question."

"How personal?" I asked, ordering a glass of club soda with a twist.

"Trust me, Swede, trust me. What I want to know is: have you gotten over Joseph Grablewski?"

I exploded. "What are you talking about? Nothing happened between him and me. Nothing. It was just a kind of nostalgia for me. You were the one who sent me to him. Remember? Yes, I was happy to see him again, and acted like a little girl. But nothing happened. Nothing could happen. He's a walking tragedy. I haven't seen him in months. It was another one of my temporary aberrations."

"Good. I was afraid that if I gave you some terrific news about him, it might send you into a tailspin. You did love him once, Swede."

I sipped the club soda. He was insulting me, in a way. He was saying I would begrudge Joseph Grablewski some kind of happiness. He was saying I was a vindictive spurned woman.

All I said was: "Tony, you're very close to getting some club soda on your head."

He laughed, kissed me on the head, and pulled a newspaper clipping out of his pocket. Dramatically, with flourishes, he spread it out in front of me.

It was an advertisement from the theater section of the *Village Voice*:

ANNOUNCING THE
WORLD PREMIERE OF . . .
Why Not?
By the famous Russian Symbolist Poet

A. A. Blok
Produced and directed by
Joseph Grablewski

The long-lost play by the most respected artist of revolutionary Russia is finally brought to the stage, in English, directed by one of the legends of the American theater.

The advertisement then went on to announce that the
first previews would be the week of February 19 at the Cherry
Lane Theatre. Then it listed the cast and some other credits.

I sat back, astonished. It was truly wonderful. Almost
wondrous. The man seemed to have risen from the dead. I
remembered the last time I'd seen him, in the bar, when he
had said his usual limit for sobriety was three days.

I turned to Basillio. I was crying. I said to him: "Believe
me, Tony, I am extremely happy for him."

He nodded in assent. I could see that he too was engaged
with the sheer heroism or luck or whatever it was that had
prompted the reemergence of Joseph Grablewski.

But all he said was: "I never knew he wrote a play."

"Who?"

"Blok. I read all his poems as a kid. Remember 'The
Twelve'?"

I had heard of that long revolutionary poem, but I had
never read it.

"I think Blok died in 1921." Basillio kept talking about
Blok, slowly at first, and then escalating into one of his crazed
drama lectures about the problems of putting poets on in the
theater . . . about how you needed plain speech.

I wasn't listening. I wanted to do something. I wanted to celebrate. I wanted to give Joseph Grablewski something . . . a poem . . . a flower. I wanted to let him know that everyone who ever listened to him in the old days, everyone who ever heard him talk about theater, was grateful.

"Remember what he looked like when we visited him in the hospital?" Basillio suddenly asked.

Then it dawned on me what I must give him. I had in my possession what he really would appreciate—the love letters his pupil had penned to me as an exercise. Yes, Bruce Chessler's letters.

"Have to go, have to go," I called out as I started out of the bar.

"Wait, Swede, wait . . . where the hell are you going?"

But I was gone. I was walking back to my apartment, fast. I was like a twelve-year-old kid who had finally found the right gift for her teacher.

Sixty seconds after I flew through the front door of my apartment, scaring poor Bushy half to death, my enthusiasm dampened.

I couldn't find the letters where I thought I had left them.

I couldn't find them in the cartons. I couldn't find them in the closets . . . or the files . . . or the cabinets . . . or the valises. They were nowhere . . . gone . . . vanished.

My balloon was deflated. But where were they?

Risa! It had to be Risa! She probably took them with her when she left.

How sad! It was probably her pathetic way of getting back at me. She probably also thought that Chessler's love for me was legitimate—not a classroom exercise. She didn't know it was all a fake.

It was stupid . . . sad . . . I wanted the letters back . . . I wanted to give them to Joseph. I started searching for Risa's phone number, remembering that I had written it down on a piece of paper after she had put it on my wrist with a Magic Marker. I found it and dialed. A voice answered. It wasn't Risa. The voice said there was no such person as Risa living there and never had been.

I hung up the phone. Could Risa have given me the wrong number by mistake? Unlikely. Could I have transcribed the wrong number from my wrist to the pad? Never. If there is one iron law of life, it is this: actors and actresses never make mistakes in phone numbers. They can't! Phone numbers are crucial. Directors, producers, agents, jobs, hairdressers. I have done a lot of wrong things in my life but I never dialed a number that I had transcribed wrong. My head is like a desktop computer when it comes to phone numbers.

Maybe Risa was not in fact Risa. Then who was she? And where did she live? The astonishing fact was that I had never even found out the girl's last name when she was staying in my apartment.

If she was, however, not who she said she was—then what really was her relationship to Bruce Chessler?

And if she was, in fact, Bruce Chessler's lover, then she had to know that the love letters were fake—an acting assignment. Lovers in the theater discuss acting classes.

Therefore, if she knew the love letters were fake, why would she want to steal them from my apartment?

Was there something in the letters I had missed? Some kind of code? To what end? Coding what?

I dressed warmly and walked to the New School, where I had taught the summer before. There was something there I had to see and had neglected to pick up. It was the bunch of short essays I had asked my students to write on that first day of class. The subject matter was "Theater," and all I wanted from them was a kind of ad hoc free association to that word.

The New School had sent me several postcard reminders to pick up the papers and other pieces of property I had left behind after the summer term was over—a small umbrella and a few books.

I found them in a massive file hidden behind boxes in the old faculty lounge, categorized under N—for Nestleton.

I leafed through the papers quickly. Few were more than one page in length. It had turned out to be an idiotic exercise, but what did that matter? I wasn't interested in literary enlightenment or psychological truths.

I found Bruce Chessler's one-page effort.

What I had suspected or feared turned out to be absolutely true.

The paper I was holding in my hand and the love letters that Risa had stolen from my closet were not written by the same person.

Had Risa written the letters for Bruce? If so, so what? Lots of girlfriends help their boyfriends out in acting classes.

It didn't make sense, her stealing the letters, when she had written them.

I walked out of the New School, dropping the entire file

in the garbage. It was freezing cold outside, but I walked slowly . . . very slowly. What else about little Risa was fake? Maybe her red punk hair? What about the murderous attack that drove her from her apartment to mine? Was that a lie? Why not? Was the point of that to be able to steal the love letters?

I started walking downtown, toward the Cherry Lane Theatre, where Joseph Grablewski would be rehearsing.

Across the street from the theater was a building awning that shielded an outside alcove from the wind. I nestled in the alcove, keeping my eyes glued to the stage door. The cold meant nothing to me. This new thread, Risa, was fascinating.

It began to grow dark. The rehearsal was over. Couples and solitary individuals began to exit, their shoulders bent against the wind as they walked off.

I felt like I was in an old Katharine Hepburn movie, waiting in the darkness outside a Broadway theater . . . a kind of *Stage Door* adventure . . . Stage Door Alice Nestleton. I felt an intellectual apprehension that was so palpable it seemed to smell, like my brain was churning, smoking . . . an absurd image.

Then Joseph walked out. He was dressed for a summer day. His only tribute to winter was a beat-up scarf wrapped like a European talisman around his neck.

He leaned against the theater, waiting.

I knew what he was waiting for. He was staring across the street, but he didn't see me. Why would he notice? I was not on his mind.

Time passed. We were frozen in our places. Was it a half hour? An hour? I didn't know.

A young woman appeared on the uptown corner. She started to walk slowly toward the theater.

As she got closer, she began to walk fast, then run.

She flung herself into Joseph's waiting arms. They embraced wildly. Their passion for each other seemed to radiate and make me weak. She began to kiss him, crazily, holding his head between her hands.

I stared at the old alcoholic and the young woman I knew as Risa.

I knew then that even though the murderers of Bruce Chessler were safely in prison or dead, there was another scenario that could explain the murder.

It was a very possible scenario.

It was very clear to me.

Risa had listened as Bruce spewed out his hatred for the émigrés . . . for their hypocrisy . . . for their diamond smuggling.

She helped him steal the white cats as a vindictive lark . . . as a bizarre way to pay them back for their betrayal of the Moscow Art Theatre.

She wrote the love letters he needed for his acting-class assignment with Joseph Grablewski.

Then something unforseen happened.

She fell in love with Joseph Grablewski.

She wrote blackmail letters to Bukai and his associates, threatening them with disclosure of their diamond smuggling.

The émigrés believed it was Bruce Chessler who was blackmailing Bukai.

At first they paid up, not knowing who was collecting the payoff.

But then the demands became too steep. So they murdered Chessler, never knowing that Risa was the blackmailer.

And what were Risa's demands?

Money, of course, money. They had plenty.

But something else, also—some of the many valuable scripts the émigrés had managed to smuggle out of Russia when they fled. Among them A. A. Blok's *Why Not?*

Which scenario was correct? I didn't know.

Risa and Grablewski started to walk. Their arms were locked almost desperately. I watched them until they vanished from sight.

Suddenly I was cold. I started home. As I walked, I began to think about Clara. I hoped she was in a good home—a home with a samovar.

Read on for a sneak peek of the
next book in the
Alice Nestleton Mystery series,

A CAT IN WOLF'S
CLOTHING

Available in November 2012 as an e-book from Intermix.

And look out for *A Cat by Any Other Name, A Cat in the Wings,* and *A Cat with a Fiddle,* books four through six in the series, also available as e-books in November and December from Intermix.

Why was the woman whispering?

I had been in the Salzmans' apartment for about twenty minutes when I finally realized that Mrs. Salzman had whispered to me from the moment I entered. And that I had whispered back. The entire conversation was being conducted in whispers.

I was there to be interviewed for a cat-sitting job. Mrs. Salzman needed someone to visit her lonely feline three mornings a week while she was seeking medical treatment in a neighboring state. In other words, she would be sleeping elsewhere and her cat had to be reassured. The nature of the medical treatment was never mentioned, nor were the whereabouts of Mr. Salzman, if, indeed, he existed at all.

The cat's name was Abelard.

When the cat's name was revealed to me, I had a sudden insight that Mrs. Salzman was quite mad . . . that her cat had been surgically altered and the poor woman was caught in a delusion that her cat had been altered for love of Heloise. She was acting out a medieval castration romance. But the thought vanished as quickly as it had emerged; it was only one of my dramaturgical fantasies—an occupational hazard for actresses.

Mrs. Salzman kept whispering to me what a lovely cat he was.

The problem was, where was he?

I couldn't see him.

"He's very frightened of people," Mrs. Salzman said, which was the first rational reason she had presented for this whispering.

Mrs. Salzman lived in a very confused apartment on East Thirty-seventh Street in Manhattan. The furniture, and there was a lot of it, lined the walls like a military procession. Abelard could be under any one of the pieces.

If I couldn't see Abelard, maybe I could hear him. Maybe I could hear his movements. Maybe that was another reason she kept whispering . . . so as to be aware of Abelard's movements.

"I am so happy to be able to deliver Abelard to a real professional cat-sitter," Mrs. Salzman whispered.

I burst out laughing, very loudly. I couldn't help myself. Mrs. Salzman drew back, shocked, her hand involuntarily smoothing her hair. She was an impeccably dressed woman except for garish green leather shoes.

It was impossible to explain to her why her remark had collapsed me into laughter. But only two hours before I had entered Mrs. Salzman's Murray Hill apartment, I had been reading a short squib about myself in the neighborhood newspaper *Our Town*. The anonymous "People" columnist had mentioned me as a neighborhood resident and noted that: "The stately, long-haired, still-beautiful Alice Nestleton is one of our finest little-known actresses . . . little known because of her penchant for obscure roles in obscure off-off-off Broadway plays."

The anonymous columnist then went on to add: "Alice Nestleton has long been a cult heroine to theater buffs."

The comment was absurd. Where were these "buffs"? In the supermarket on Third Avenue? I never met them.

Anyway, the whole point about that ludicrous description of me in the newspaper was that it *didn't* make me laugh. But it laid the groundwork. And when Mrs. Salzman characterized me two hours later as a "real professional cat-sitter," the cumulative effect made me laugh out loud, heartily, raucously.

Mrs. Salzman quickly forgave my outburst and took me on a brief tour of her convoluted apartment. She pointed out the location of the cat food and the watering can for the plants and the lists of emergency numbers and several other key locations and objects.

There was still no sign of Abelard.

"What kind of cat is Abelard?" I asked.

"A lovely cat," replied Mrs. Salzman, thinking I was asking about his disposition rather than his breed.

"What color is Abelard?" I persisted.

She paused, cocked her head, and smiled. "Mixed."

"Mixed what?" My question came out a bit testy.

She ignored that question and led me into one of the hallways. "There are your three envelopes," she said. They lay on a small elegantly carved French cherrywood table.

"One for each day you'll be cat-sitting next week," Mrs. Salzman explained. She picked up one of the envelopes and opened it—I could see there was a single hundred-dollar bill inside.

My God! Three envelopes! Three hundred-dollar bills! For three visits of about forty-five minutes each to a cat I hadn't even seen yet and might never see! Was this woman mad? It was a truly exorbitant rate of pay. Unless of course . . . unless there were problems associated with Abelard that she hadn't disclosed.

I was about to ask for a modest reduction in pay when Mrs. Salzman suddenly and dramatically put her finger against her lips, urging silence.

Had she heard Abelard? Was the mysterious cat about to emerge from the shadows?

We waited. Mrs. Salzman closed her eyes and seemed to go into an anticipatory trance. What a strange woman she was: gray hair; thin, serious face; tall, with a stoop at the shoulders; the very slightest hint of an Austrian accent clinging to her whispers; an abstracted manner, as if she were very far away.

We waited. And we waited. And we waited. Where the hell was Abelard?

"Maybe we should call him," I suggested gently.

Mrs. Salzman opened her eyes in horror. I had obviously said the wrong thing.

"He does not like to be called," she said in a compassionate voice, as if, even though I was a professional cat-sitter, I was suffering some kind of mild learning disorder.

"What *does* Abelard like?" I retorted a bit sarcastically.

The sarcasm passed blithely over Mrs. Salzman's head. "He likes flowers and fruit and fresh turkey and music and birds . . ." She stopped suddenly in the middle of her hysterical list, a bit self-conscious. She smiled and led me to the door, telling me that Abelard wanted more than an employee—he wanted a friend.

I walked home quickly, thinking about *my* cats, Bushy and Pancho.

Granted, they were a bit peculiar. Bushy, the Maine coon, was no doubt one of the drollest beasts ever created. And Pancho, my stray rescued from the ASPCA, well, he was borderline psychotic—spending most all day and all night fleeing from imaginary enemies.

But at least my cats were visible! Not like Abelard. And my cats obviously had a grudging affection for me.

I climbed the stairs quickly. Thinking about Bushy and Pancho always made me miss them fiercely—even though I had been away from the apartment for less than two hours.

"Alice! You're finally home!"

I stopped suddenly and peered up the badly lit landing toward the voice.

It was Mrs. Oshrin, my neighbor, the retired schoolteacher.

She was standing at the top of the landing. On either side of her was a very dangerous-looking man.

Kidnappers? Rapists? Junkies? Neighborhood derelicts?

I panicked. I turned sharply on the stairs and started to run back down to seek help.

"Alice!" I heard her call out. "Wait! There's nothing wrong!"

I turned back, confused, still frightened.

"They're police officers, Alice! They want to see you—not me!"

I waited, tentative.

"It's all very hush-hush," Mrs. Oshrin pleaded, as if that was an explanation. There was something about the way she used that very old-fashioned phrase—"hush-hush"—that sent an anticipatory tingle along my spine. But it wasn't fear.

About the Author

Lydia Adamson is a pseudonym for a noted mystery writer and cat lover in New York City.